Alfred T. Story

The Life of John Linnell

Volume 2

Alfred T. Story

The Life of John Linnell
Volume 2

ISBN/EAN: 9783337332488

Printed in Europe, USA, Canada, Australia, Japan

Cover: Foto ©Andreas Hilbeck / pixelio.de

More available books at **www.hansebooks.com**

THE

LIFE OF JOHN LINNELL

BY
ALFRED T. STORY

IN TWO VOLUMES
VOL. II.

LONDON
RICHARD BENTLEY AND SON
Publishers in Ordinary to Her Majesty the Queen
1892

CONTENTS OF VOL. II.

—◦○◦—

CHAPTER VI.

CHAPTER VII.

CHAPTER VIII.

CHAPTER IX.

CHAPTER X.

CHAPTER XI.

CHAPTER XII.

CHAPTER XIII.

CHAPTER XIV.

CHAPTER XV.

CHAPTER XVI.

ILLUSTRATIONS TO VOL. II.

LIFE OF JOHN LINNELL

CHAPTER I.

Love of the Old Masters—Copies made of their Works—'The Four Ages'—Hook—David Roberts—French Ultramarine.

BEFORE leaving this period, it is necessary to dwell a little more upon Linnell's love of the Old Masters and the many copies he made of their works. His admiration for them was so great that he never felt it a toil to sit down and make an exact reproduction of a picture he liked. Even in the prime of life, when his hands were the fullest of business, he would spare the time to indulge himself in this way. On several occasions he had commissions to make copies of certain pictures, as in the case of the two Titians for Captain Digby Murray, already mentioned. But as a rule he painted them for the pleasure of doing so, without any thought of selling; albeit, as a matter of fact, many of them were purchased by connoisseurs. Thus he made a copy (in 1822) of Rembrandt's 'Abraham putting away Hagar,' which was sold to Captain Murray. About

the same time he copied a landscape by Titian —
'The Coming Storm'—now in the royal collection
at Buckingham Palace, but then in the possession of
Mr. R. R. Reinigale. This fine copy still hangs,
where it hung during the artist's lifetime, in the
library of his house at Redhill.

Mention has been made of his highly-finished
miniature copy on ivory in water-colour of the magnificent Raphael—'The Virgin and Infant Saviour'
—the property of Earl Cowper; also of the landscapes by Raphael and Titian, the property of Mr.
Samuel Woodburn, which he copied in 1833 and
1837 respectively.

Between 1828 and 1834 he executed a series of
highly-finished water-colour drawings of pictures in
the National Gallery for Mr. Pye (the line engraver)
to engrave from. They were, 'Christ appearing to
Peter,' by Annibale Carracci ; 'Silenus,' by the
same artist ; 'Susannah and the Elders,' by Ludo-
vico Carracci ; 'The Coronation of St. Nicholas,'
by Paolo Veronese ; the portrait of Lord Heathfield,
by Sir Joshua Reynolds, and 'The Crucifixion,' by
Rembrandt. In 1839 he made an oil copy, the
same size as the original, of Lord Francis Egerton's
Titian, 'The Four Ages.'

This picture was at that time in the School of
Painting at the Royal Academy, and Linnell made
his copy there in company with the students. John
Hook, the Royal Academician, who was then a
student, was copying 'The Four Ages' at the same
time, but wanting to proceed more expeditiously

than he could do alone, he got someone to help him, which caused Mulready to tell the latter that he ought to write over the picture, ' This was copied by Hook and I.'

Amongst the last works of the kind that Linnell executed was (in 1843) a highly-finished oil copy, the same size as the original, of a ' Holy Family,' by Sebastiano del Piombo (the property of Mr. W. Cunningham), which was bought in 1846 by W. W. Pendarves, Esq., M.P., for 150 guineas ; also (in 1844) a copy of a picture of ' Christ in the Garden of Gethsemane,' attributed then to Raphael, which Mr. Cunningham had just then acquired from Italy, but which has since been assigned to the Florentine School by the authorities at the National Gallery, where it has now found a home. Linnell's copy is still in the possession of the family.

Although these are the chief copies of Old Masters that our artist made, they by no means exhaust the list, which includes examples by Backhuysen, Gaspar Poussin, Domenichino, Vandervelde, etc.

Linnell has again and again in his writings explained the keen appreciation he had of the qualities of form and colouring exemplified in the Old Masters ; and it may be that his constant practical study of their works in this way kept fresh, and possibly even intensified, his own perception, especially in regard to colour, which was recognised as a rare gift by his fellow-artists.

Mr. Horsley, R.A., relates an incident touching

Linnell's fine sense of colour which is worth repeating. At a dinner given by Mr. George Young, at
which many Academicians, besides others, were present, amongst them being Mr. Horsley himself,
Leslie, Creswick, Hart, Webster, and Roberts, the
latter was expatiating on the character and virtues of
the new colour, French or artificial ultramarine, and
seemed hardly able to find words strong enough to
express how valuable an acquisition he considered
its production to be to artists. He explained in his
broad Scotch that it had been subjected to all the
different tests for colours, and that it had come out
triumphantly, and was therefore entitled to take its
place as a substitute for real ultramarine, lapis
lazuli, etc., which were so expensive, whereas it
could be had for sixpence a tube.

When Roberts had finished his enthusiastic eulogy,
Linnell, who was seated next to him, said: ' Mr.
Roberts, in your description of the numerous tests to
which this colour has been subjected, there is one
which you have omitted to mention.'

' Ah, indeed !' said Roberts, turning round and
looking down at his neighbour ; ' one test that I
have omitted ? And pray what may that be ?'

' It won't bear looking at.' replied Linnell very
quietly and deliberately.

That the other artists thought he had struck the
real defect of the new colour was evidenced by the
fact that his answer was greeted with a great out-
burst of laughter and applause, which grievously
discomposed Mr. Roberts.

CHAPTER II.

THUS Linnell patiently laboured on until about 1845,
when a surprising change came over the scene,
when, in short, there arrived a tardy recognition of
his powers. He was now fifty-four years of age—
an old man as some would be at his years. But
Linnell seemed to have learned the secret of perennial youth. Since his breakdown in the twenties he
had wonderfully recovered his constitutional vigour,
thanks to a naturally tough frame, and perhaps, also,
in some measure to that careful regimen which he
had established in his household, and from which he
never afterwards departed.

As we have seen, a certain amount of fame had
arisen out of the exhibition of the ' St. John preaching in the Wilderness' at the British Institution in
1839. Perhaps this recognition of his ability may
have acted as a stimulus to his still latent powers,
and done much to call forth a fresh efflorescence of

talent.   Certain it is that he began to paint with renewed vigour about this time—that is, roughly speaking, about his fiftieth year.

There is nothing more remarkable in the history of great men than this fact regarding John Linnell. Nor was it in art alone that he manifested this renewed vigour.   It penetrated and revivified his whole intellectual and moral being, and made the man of fifty begin as it were a fresh youth.   It was a fresh intellectual youth, at all events, for it was at this period that he resumed, with increased zest, the thread of his studies in Greek and Hebrew, which he had commenced with such assiduity and delight under Mr. Thomas Palmer, but had been obliged to lay aside on account of the growing demands of his family.   He had never ceased, however, his study of the Scriptures ; but this had been confined chiefly to the English version, and to such exegetical works as were then procurable.   But now, at a time of life when most men are beginning to think that, not simply their days of learning, but their days for work also, are well-nigh done, this man took down his school-books and recommenced his studies with all the ardour, and more than the ordinary energy, of a young man.

He may have been stimulated to do this through the influence of a new order of minds with which he about this time came in contact.   As already stated, he in 1843 became acquainted with the body known as the Plymouth Brethren, a sect which has distinguished itself by its careful study of the original

texts of the Scriptures, and has produced several
men of exceptional learning in this department of
research.   With these people he associated in religious communion, and occasionally attended their
meetings in London for ' breaking bread,' etc.

He had strong sympathy with the Brethren in
their principles and in their practice, where he considered these in agreement with Scripture precept
and example.   He was in accord with them in that
they had no paid preachers or ministers, and gave
no titles ; that they recognised the equality in standing and privilege of all believers, all the brethren
having liberty of speaking, etc., in their assemblies ;
and that they professed to receive one another in
fellowship at ' the Lord's table ' simply on the ground
of having faith in Christ.   He recognised that they
had clear spiritual perceptions of many truths as
revealed in the New Testament, having learned
these by sincere, careful, and critical study of the
texts, and by believing in the simple and literal
meaning of the Scripture words.   Thus they believed that they acquired light as to prophetical
truth, especially the truth of the pre-millennial personal advent of Christ, etc.

It is essential to give these details, as showing
Linnell's turn of thought in these matters.   But
after awhile he found that he could no longer
yield the Brethren that sympathy which he had at
first given.   He thought that, through lack of the
humility that is proper and becoming to Christians,
and the unity that arises from real brotherly love,

a sectarian and intolerant spirit had sprung up among them, certain of them presuming to judge and censure others, and to usurp authority over them, which caused separation and exclusions from communion one of another.

Thus in January, 1846, at their headquarters in Plymouth, the body became divided into two opposing parties. The division, and the consequent intolerant action, spread to the different gatherings in London, some of the leading men connected therewith assuming what Linnell considered priestly prerogatives. This was one of the things against which he had always warred, and so in 1848 he and his family discontinued assembling with the Brethren, losing sympathy with them, and being unable any longer to co-operate with them in what they considered their unscriptural action.

This intercourse with the Plymouth Brethren was more of the nature of an incident in Linnell's life than a matter which affected either his principles or his habits. He took no active part in their public meetings, and hardly ever spoke in them, preferring the position of listener and learner, and simple partaker in the Christian fellowship of the body. As regards all they wrote and said, he tested and judged them strictly and impartially by the text of Scripture, as he had always done with regard to the productions of everybody else. He was ever ready to receive help in the understanding of the inspired text from anyone, and thankfully availed himself of every such afforded help ; but to the man himself who might be instrumental in giving such help he allowed no authority.

As already said, his acquaintance with this body probably stimulated his Biblical studies at that time, but had no further effect. He was always grateful to the Brethren for the books they had produced, which afforded much assistance in the study of the Greek and Hebrew texts, such as ' The Englishman's Greek Concordance of the New Testament,' and ' The Englishman's Hebrew Concordance of the Old Testament.'

Returning thus to his early studies, he devoted himself to the texts of the Old and New Testaments with all the zeal and patience that he brought to bear upon whatever he undertook, and he mastered their spirit so thoroughly that he was enabled to throw light upon more than one disputed passage. The results of these studies on certain points he afterwards published in several pamphlets. Of these, however, it will be necessary to speak in a subsequent chapter. It is sufficient here to refer to the fact as a sign of the renewed vigour of his intellect.

After losing sympathy with the Plymouth Brethren, Linnell never again joined any body of professing Christians, being satisfied to worship in his own way, and in accordance with what he believed to be the direction of Scripture. He never at any time of his life adopted what is called ' family worship' in any shape, considering it too formal and unreal a thing, and, moreover, a hindrance to

business and work.   Accordingly, all worship, prayer,
etc., on the part of himself and his family was of a
private nature, as directed in Matthew vi. 6.

He had the greatest objection to anything like
formalism, considering that it was the death of the
spirit.   In this respect, Dissenter though he was,
he objected quite as much to the extemporary
prayers of the non-episcopal bodies as to those of
the Established Church, considering them inspired
by vanity more than by spiritual fervour.   For the
same reason he was opposed to anything like a
regular ministry.   Such, he held, always resulted in
what was virtually a priesthood, or, in other words,
in a domineering attitude in regard to spiritual
matters towards those over whom they were placed.
His contest was against what he was wont to
describe briefly as the ‘ one-man system.’   He did
not consider it healthful for any one man to be the
final judge of what was true or right in regard to
doctrine or practice.   Every man so placed as the
arbiter on points of truth must, he held, from the
very nature of man, end by becoming a pope and
usurper.   Hence his life-long protest against all
systems which allowed of such a state of things.

His dislike, and at the same time his criticism, of
this system is set forth in the following vigorous
lines :

> ‘As Christian perhaps you’d get on faster
> If you had not a hired pastor ;
> He gives you words, ’tis true, as sweet as honey,
> And in exchange he gets your ready money ;
> And if he gets not that, he gets the power,
> Sweeter to many than the richest dower.

He's always uppermost, pre-eminence he seeks,
Therefore he always teaches, preaches, speaks ;
And so the one-man system is established sure,
And, through the lack of faith, will for a time endure.'

As was Linnell's attitude towards ecclesiastical systems, so it was to some extent towards medicine. His intolerance of all arbitrary domination, together with his strong sense of individual responsibility in forming a right judgment on all subjects, led him to hold decisive opinions in this respect also. He would never put himself 'into the hands' of any medical man, nor would he take medicines without knowing what he was swallowing, and something about the drugs they contained.* For this reason

* On one occasion when his grandson, More Palmer, the son of Samuel Palmer, had been ill, and Mrs. Palmer wrote a letter to Mr. Linnell, telling him of her son's recovery, he sent the following impromptu :

'Anny, thou doest well
To praise thy Dr. Bell,
If he will tell
    What medicines he gave ;
But if he won't disclose,
And finger puts to 's nose,
    Then he's a knave.

'You'll say that he has cured your son,
Sure as a gun ;
Which certainly he may have done
    By mere negation,
Preventing calomel and jalap
From giving his inside a wallop
    Of violent purgation.

'The Allopath might easily have killed—
Rash, unwise, and most unskilled
 In Nature's course, which often
    Leads into health from death's dark door,
Making our hearts with gratitude to soften
    For so much given, with prospect still of More.'

he always required his physician's prescriptions to be written so that he could himself understand them. He held that the chief use of a doctor was to instruct the patient as to the nature of his complaint, and how he had incurred it, so that he might avoid similar error in the future.

In regard to his own health, he had a theory which probably served him in good stead of a great deal of physic. He held that Nature is all the while endeavouring to keep a person well, or to get him well if ill, and that the best medicine is patiently to aid her efforts. In this respect, also, as in many others, he appears to have taken a hint from Mulready, who once when ill, being asked what he had taken, replied, ' The best of all medicines—nothing.'

In 1835 Linnell sent to the British Institution a small panel (9 by 15 inches) entitled. ' Windsor Forest,' which was purchased by Mr. Vernon for 30 guineas (and of which an engraving appeared in the *Art Journal* for 1851). It afterwards went, with that gentleman's collection, into the National Gallery, where for a time it was almost the only specimen of a work by a living artist.

Ten years later (1845) another of Linnell's landscapes found its way into Mr. Vernon's collection, and with it subsequently to the National Gallery. The picture in question was ' The Windmill,' a beautiful little composition (17 by 21 inches) with cows in water, and a delightful breezy sky. It was sold to Mr. Vernon from the British Institution for 50 guineas. This picture also was engraved for the *Art Journal.* A replica of it, painted in 1848, sold for 150 guineas.

These and some few other landscape and figure subjects were disposed of at small prices, but as a rule they came back from the exhibitions to hang upon the artist's own walls and accumulate in his studio. At length an important factor in Linnell's career came upon the scene in the person of Mr. Ralph Thomas, barrister-at-law, and, in a private way, picture-dealer. Thomas was something of a character, being what is usually called a self-made man. He had originally pursued some humble calling, but, being dissatisfied with it, he devoted himself to study, and became successively book-seller, auctioneer, and barrister. He was, however, above all a shrewd business, money-making man.

Linnell and Thomas met for the first time on October 30, 1845, when, as the former records in his journal, he had occasion to call and see the lawyer at his office in Chancery Lane. The same day Mr. Thomas went to Porchester Terrace to see Linnell's pictures, and he appears to have been so struck with them that he at once opened negotiations to do business. He proposed to sell to the artist a house he owned on the Terrace, Hammersmith, valued at £480, taking pictures in exchange for it. By November 10 terms had been agreed upon, and in due course the house—No. 3, Hammersmith Terrace—passed into Linnell's possession,*

* The house in question was one in which Linnell as a boy used to visit Sir Benjamin West.

and ten of his pictures, together with some sketches, into Thomas's.

This was the beginning of a number of business transactions between the two that proved mutually advantageous. On March 4, 1846, Thomas made Linnell an offer of £1,000 for fifteen (afterwards increased to seventeen) pictures, which was accepted. The pictures, some of which required retouching, were all delivered, and the money received, by May 8. About the same time Linnell worked upon an unfinished picture by William James Muller, who had died a year previously at Bristol, for his new patron. The picture was the artist's ' View of the Ruins of Pinara, Asia Minor.' Linnell completed it from Muller's original water-colour sketch, and received 50 guineas in payment for his work.

Among the pictures which thus came into Mr. Thomas's possession were several notable ones. ' The Meal in the Wood : Woodcutters in Windsor Forest ' (30 by 43 inches), a sketchy replica of a previous ' Woodcutters ' painted in 1816, was sold at Christie's in 1848 for 200 guineas, and was subsequently bought by Mr. Birch, of Birmingham, for 300 guineas. It shows a clearing in the forest strewn with the trunks of trees. In the foreground are a number of figures, some of them seated, eating, others at work ; in the distance is a wooded glade.

' The Cow-yard ' (a small panel), already mentioned as one of Mr. Sheepshanks' gift to the nation (purchased by him for £78 15s.), is, perhaps, the gem of that collection, the drawing of the cows being exceptionally fine.

' Noon,' another of Thomas's purchases, has already been mentioned.

The barrister art-connoisseur and dealer was thus the means of bringing grist to the artist's mill, and, at the same time, of helping to make his works known. As a set-off to the benefit thus conferred, Linnell was enabled to do Thomas a good turn by procuring the coif, a coveted distinction, for him. His journal contains the entry :

'*January* 12.—Went to Lord Lyndhurst to ask him to give Mr. Ralph Thomas the coif, but could not see him.'

This is followed by another entry, on February 24, to the effect that, at the request of Mr. Thomas, he wrote a letter to Chief Justice Tindal, enclosing one from Mr. Thomas, applying for the coif for him. The application proved successful, and thus to some extent Thomas owed his serjeantship to Linnell.

Thomas proved to be the forerunner of a host of dealers, who now began to compete with each other for the artist's work, and continued to do so for many years to come—almost, indeed, to the day of his death. Mr. Gibbons, of Regent's Park, a private collector, was the first to follow Mr. Thomas with purchases to any extent. In September, 1846, he bought Linnell's portraits of William Mulready, R.A., and William Collins, R.A. In November he bought also the portrait of Samuel Rogers, and the painter's copy of Mr. Harman's Vandervelde. He

also purchased at this time a small landscape—
'The Gateshead Windmill' (exhibited at the Royal
Academy in 1847); and in the following January
(1847) he acquired the picture then in hand, and
exhibited in that year's Academy, entitled 'Mid-
day,' giving for it 100 guineas.

There is a story connected with Mr. Gibbons'
early purchases which must not be left untold.   Mr.
Webster, R.A., was always Linnell's good friend,
and a great and sincere admirer of his art.   It was
to him at this time a matter of as great regret as
astonishment that the artist's pictures continued to
crowd his walls, whilst those of inferior men found
a ready market; and it is to his credit that he did
what he could to make them known and appreciated.

On one occasion when he was executing a commission for Mr. Gibbons, he asked that gentleman if
he knew John Linnell; and upon his saying he did
not, proposed that they should walk round to his
place and call upon him.   Mr. Gibbons was agree-
able, and they went; but though Linnell's walls
were covered with pictures, the art-patron saw
nothing that took his fancy, and they left without
his purchasing a single thing.   Webster was annoyed, and told Gibbons that he was surprised that
he had not bought anything.   The latter replied
that he had seen nothing that he cared for.

After parting with Gibbons, Webster returned to
Linnell's, and expressed his regret that his friend
had selected nothing.   Linnell replied that it was
very kind of him to try to get a purchaser for some

of his works, and thanked him for his good-will.
Webster, however, was not satisfied, and said he
would like to buy something himself. He had, he
said, just then a little money, and he would like to
have a bit of his work, if there was anything he
would sell at a price within his reach. He finally
chose a small picture, 9 by 15 inches, entitled 'The
Woodcutters' Repast,' and asked him what he
would take for it. Linnell said he would sell it
to him for 40 guineas. Webster agreed, and the
picture was duly paid for and carried home, where
it was hung in a central position, surrounded by
some of Webster's own canvases.

A few days later Mr. Gibbons again called to see
how his commission was progressing, and his eye at
once fell upon ' The Woodcutters' Repast.'

' What is that ?' he exclaimed. ' Is it yours ?'

' No ; of course it isn't,' said Webster. ' I can't
paint half as well as that ; I wish I could. It is
one of Linnell's — one of those you could see
nothing in.'

Gibbons now admired the picture so much that he
wanted to buy it ; but Webster said he would not
sell it—he would keep it as long as he lived, which,
in fact, he did.

Gibbons, however, was so taken with the little
picture that he asked his friend to take him to see
Linnell's works again. Webster accordingly went
round with him, and the result was that he at once
bought several pictures, and afterwards became one
of the artist's best customers at that time.

Two months later (March, 1847) a still more important patron made his appearance. This was Mr. Joseph Gillott, the well-known pen-manufacturer of Birmingham, who gave a number of commissions for pictures, and also purchased (for £1,000) a famous picture then in progress, 'The Eve of the Deluge.'

This was the first picture for which Linnell obtained a large price. He thought he had excelled himself in it, and, in order to pique curiosity, he kept it covered with a drapery when he was not working upon it. Over it he wrote the words 'Aspetta tu vedrai'* (Wait, and you shall see).

Mr. Gibbons was one of the very few who were permitted to look at it. He admired it greatly, and was disposed to become a purchaser. Linnell asked him to name a price, but he would not. Mr. Gillott called and saw it a few days afterwards, and asked the painter what he would take for it. Linnell asked him to make an offer.

'But I might offer more than you want for it,' Mr. Gillott replied.

'I will write the amount I wish for it on a piece of paper,' the artist answered; 'and if you offer more, you shall have it at my price.'

Gillott offered £1,000, and the artist then showed him the paper on which he had written his price: it was £1,000.

'The Eve of the Deluge' was exhibited in the

---

* These were the words put up outside the Vatican by Pius IX. in 1847, when all the world were looking to him for the institution of reforms.

Royal Academy in 1848, and is one of Linnell's greatest pictures. In size it is one of the largest he painted, being 59 by 88 inches. On a rocky eminence to the right is seen the ark, with animals and birds flocking into it. In the foreground is a group of seven figures. Another figure, followed by two greyhounds, approaches from the left ; while beyond a rocky gorge in the foreground is seen a distant view. It is evening, and the stormy sky is lit up by the setting sun.

This picture may be said to have set the final stamp and seal to Linnell's growing fame. It quite took the public by surprise, 'from the sublimity and daring with which the painter invested his subject.' Even Turner, who was not a man to give rash judgments on pictures, remarked to Gillott, who took him to see it in the Academy, that it was no common work.

But, notwithstanding the intrinsic merits of the picture, the effect it produced was greatly aided by an altogether fortuitous circumstance. William Westall, A.R.A., the water-colour painter, happened also to exhibit the same year a canvas representing ' The Commencement of the Deluge.' It was known that Westall had been working on his picture for some time, and great expectations were entertained of it. Though undoubtedly a fine work, it appeared flat and colourless in comparison with Linnell's glowing canvas ; and being both on the line, and in near juxtaposition the one to the other, the effect was unfortunate for the Associate.

'The Eve of the Deluge' was purchased at Mr. Gillott's sale in 1872 by Mr. W. Agnew, and subsequently became the property of Mr. Angus Holden, M.P., of Bradford.

About the same time (1847) was painted 'The Last Gleam before the Storm' (canvas, 35 by 50 inches), which, with its grand clouds and gloomy landscape, constitutes another of the artist's master-pieces of composition and colour. The 'Last Gleam' was exhibited in the British Gallery in 1848, and, like the former, was purchased by Mr. Gillott, the price being £250. Twenty-four years later it was sold at his sale at Christie's for £2,500. As a result of this sale—which, of course, did not in the least benefit the painter—a curious thing happened : Linnell had his income-tax doubled.

In the same year (1848) was painted for the same munificent patron 'The Return of Ulysses,' on a canvas 48½ by 72 inches. It was exhibited in the Royal Academy in the following year, and sub-sequently in the Manchester Art Treasures Exhibi-tion. The picture represents an incident taken from the 'Odyssey,' and bears the quotation, from Chap-man's translation of the 'Odyssey':

> 'And first brought forth Ulysses : bed, and all
> That richly furnisht it ; he still in thrall
> Of all-subduing sleepe. Upon the sand
> They set him softly downe ; and then, the strand
> They strewed with all the goods he had, bestowed
> By the renowned Phæacians.'

In the foreground Odysseus is being carried ashore by four men, followed by other figures ;

while the rocky shore of Ithaca and the sea are seen stretching away in the distance.

Although what is called a 'self-made man,' Mr. Gillott had very fine perceptions in art, and seldom made a wrong judgment ; and it is to his credit that he was among the first to give Linnell large prices. It need hardly be said that he was a 'character' in his way—not to say an oddity.   When he came to town he used to put up at Furnival's Inn, where he had a suite of rooms, and where he was wont to feast his friends in the most sumptuous manner. Linnell eschewed his dinners, but on one or two occasions took tea with him, and used to recount with amusement how the queer little pen-manu-facturer would empty out the pot, and make fresh tea for every cup they drank, saying that they could not drink it stale.

Gillott continued to give Linnell commissions, and to buy largely of him for several years. Among others who commenced dealing with him about the same time as Gillott was Mr. Weathered, who, in September, 1847, made the first of a series of pur-chases which extended over twelve years.

Thus began that full tide of success which kept the artist's brush busily employed for the rest of his life.

CHAPTER III.

Making Oil-Copal Varnish—Death of William Collins, R.A.—Wilkie
Collins—His Estimate of Linnell—John Everett Millais—His
First Love.

REFERENCE has previously been made to the circumstance of John Glover, the landscape-painter, having
made Linnell acquainted with the superior qualities
of oil-copal as a medium for oil-painting. In the
early part of his career our artist, as well as Mulready, had been in the habit of using only boiled
linseed-oil, diluted with turpentine, and many beautiful works by both artists exist in excellent condition
which were painted with this medium, though they
have not the brilliancy and transparency of their
later works in copal. For some time Linnell used
the ordinary oil-copal sold by the artists' colourmen,
but finding it not entirely to his satisfaction, he
finally took the matter in hand and resolved to
make his own varnish. This was about the time
(1847) when he began to devote himself entirely to
landscape-painting, and he was determined to have
everything of the very best quality to work with.
He accordingly studied the making of varnishes

very thoroughly, consulting the best books on the subject from Cennino Cennini downwards, and then arranged with a varnish-maker to produce some under his supervision.

The necessary apparatus (consisting of two iron furnaces) was erected at the end of the garden, and early one summer morning, before people generally were astir, the varnish-maker set to work, and, under the direction of the artist, made a large quantity of copal varnish, the best materials procurable—picked gum copal, old linseed-oil, and zinc dryer—only being used. The oil employed, however, proving doubtful as to quality, Linnell took the means to obtain some that was above suspicion, and about a month later another lot of varnish was made. On this occasion both copal and amber varnish were produced.

Mulready was greatly interested in the success of these operations, and was present on the latter occasion.

On two subsequent occasions, namely, in the September of the same year, and again in 1848, there were further experiments in varnish-making. On the first occasion it was made with raw oil, on the second with two oils. These concluded his varnish-making operations, having now secured a sufficient quantity of the best quality to more than last his lifetime.

Creswick afterwards followed Linnell's example, and employed the same firm to make him some varnish, but he did not succeed so well.

In the same way, feeling that one of the secrets of

success in painting is to work with the very best pigments, Linnell ground some of his own most important colours, and spared neither trouble nor expense in procuring the best materials.

It is, perhaps, natural to find that these and other labours which Linnell conducted in order to obtain articles he needed of the highest possible quality led at one time or another to the circulation of humorous skits at his expense, and in some cases to actual misrepresentation, as when it was said that he carried on the manufacture of canvas under his roof.

At a later period it was also spread about that he even made his own shoes. Some of these reports were possibly meant to injure ; but they never hurt the subject of them, and few could enjoy the humorous side of such tales better than he.

In 1847 Linnell's old friend, William Collins, died, and he was some little time afterwards asked to assist Wilkie Collins in the compilation of a life of his father. Incidentally the matter is referred to in the following letter, addressed to Mrs. Linnell, which, unfortunately, has no date :

' My dear Mrs. Linnell,

' My brother and I are very anxious to take advantage of your kind invitation to us to pay you a visit at Porchester Terrace some evening. I now write to know whether to-morrow or Friday evening will be convenient to you. We are disengaged on either day.

' I shall hope to find Mr. Linnell at home, as I hear he has some hints to give me respecting the early parts of my father's life, which will, I am sure, be of very great use to me in the biography I am now writing.

' Do not trouble yourself to write. A verbal answer by the bearer, either for to-morrow or Friday evening, will be quite sufficient.

' Truly yours,
' W. WILKIE COLLINS.'

' *Tuesday evening.*'

The brother referred to, of course, was Charles Collins, who, following in his father's footsteps, became an artist. Linnell gave Wilkie Collins all the aid he could in respect to the biography, and the author was recognisant to the extent of referring to him in its pages as being so capable an artist as to be able to arrange a row of blacking-bottles in such a way that they would look picturesque.

Several other letters from Wilkie Collins are included in Linnell's correspondence. One of them, evidently of a somewhat earlier date than the foregoing, is interesting as having reference to his studies in art, to which he at first thought of turning his attention. It is as follows :

' MY DEAR SIR,

' You were kind enough to say that you would give us some advice about the treatment of our oil-sketches, when we had them ready for your inspection. If you can conveniently call on us, either Monday or Tuesday next, at any time before three o'clock, we shall be happy to show them to you.

' Faithfully yours,

' W. WILKIE COLLINS.'

Amongst other correspondence belonging to this period is a letter from Mr. (afterwards Sir) John Everett Millais.   He writes from 83, Gower Street, Bedford Square, saying that he wants to find 'a small deep river with willows overhanging the banks,' and asking if there is such a thing at Under-River, ' a place I fancy you are familiar with,' he adds.   Linnell does not appear to have kept a copy of his reply ; but on the fly-leaf of the letter he has jotted down the following stanza in pencil :

' No river deep, though small,
With willows overhung,
Whose tender branches fall
In graceful forms along,'—

at Under-River, he no doubt meant, but whether he was able to direct Mr. Millais to some other place for what he wanted we have no means of knowing.

It is worthy of note that Linnell had the greatest admiration for Millais' art, but more especially for that of his earlier period.   Later he thought he had fallen off somewhat, and on one occasion, when they met, he exclaimed, ' Ah, Mr. Millais, you have left your first love—you have left your first love !'

CHAPTER IV.

Settlement in Surrey—Tunbridge Wells—Balcombe—First Visit to
Redhill—Purchase of Redstone Wood Estate—House Building
—Further Purchase of Land—Mr. Holman Hunt—Encouragement of the Pre-Raphaelite Brotherhood—' I like Good Ale ; I
like Good Wine '—Anecdote of Gambart the Dealer.

WE now come to John Linnell's last change of
residence, and the most important of all. For
upwards of twenty years he had lived at Bayswater,
and during the earlier of those years he was kept
so busy with portrait-painting and engraving, as
well as with his landscape work, that he had little
leisure for visits to the country, which were in
consequence few and brief. For many years he
seldom went away from home, unless it were on
business, and then he returned as quickly as possible.
His early sketches in Wales, in Windsor Forest,
the Isle of Wight, and elsewhere, supplied him with
abundant material for his pictures ; besides which
he still had the country, so to speak, at his door.

When he first built himself a house in Porchester
Terrace he was surrounded by fields. He had on!y
to go a few steps to be in the midst of rural sights
and scenes, while Hampstead could still be reached

by open field-paths. In 1830 he made a chalk study at the north end of Porchester Terrace of a bank with sheep, etc., and from this sketch he painted the picture entitled 'Morning,' which was exhibited at the British Institution in 1832. In 1834, again, he made oil studies from nature at a brook near Wale's Tea-Gardens, Bayswater, from one of which he painted his picture of 'The Hollow Tree' (or 'The Nest'), exhibited at the Royal Academy in 1836.

But gradually, as the demand for his landscapes increased, and, concurrently, as the education of his sons and daughters took up less of his time, he found more leisure for trips into the country, and indulged himself to the utmost of his ability. Moreover, as Bayswater was now becoming more and more built up, he found these visits needful, not only for himself, but for his sons, three of whom were now Royal Academy students (having been admitted in 1840), and were no longer satisfied, as formerly, to make studies of the scraps of 'nature' left in the neighbourhood of their home, and in Kensington Gardens.

Accordingly, he went in 1840 with his three sons to Sevenoaks, and having procured them a lodging in the town, he returned to London. This was their first excursion into the country, and they made studies in Knoll Park, at Little Under-River, and at 'Rook's Hill.' A few days afterwards our artist took Mrs. Linnell and family to Under-River, where they remained until the end of September, he staying with them from Saturday till Monday, and making excursions with his wife and children about the locality.

In July of the following year he accompanied Mrs. Linnell and family to Thatcham, where they remained until October. As before, Linnell went down from Saturday till Monday, visiting, and generally making studies at, Cold Ash Common, Beacon Hill, Kingsclere, Newbury, and Donnington. Thatcham was visited again in like manner in the following year. During the next four years no excursions to the country were made, both the artist and his sons being too fully employed at home painting and engraving to be able to spare the time.

In 1847 Linnell repeated his visit to Little Under-River, and in July took lodgings in the village for his family. These relaxations from labour became more and more enjoyable to him, and in order to make the most of them he used to hire a covered van and make excursions to places in the neighbourhood. In this way he visited Brasted Chart, Westerham, and Sundridge (where there are some fine pine-trees), also Tunbridge and Tunbridge Wells, Erridge's Rocks, Penn's Rocks, etc., and made studies at Under-River and at Wimlet Hill (or Rook's Hill).

Returning to London after a few days, he sketched out a design in chalk and crayons for the subject of the ' Disobedient Prophet killed by the Lion ' (introducing the Sundridge pines). Then, visiting Under-River for a day or two at a time, he made more studies in chalk and crayons, and driving to Sundridge with his son James, who assisted him, he proceeded with and completed his study of the pine-trees.

In 1848 Linnell settled his family for the summer at Balcombe, just over the Sussex border, running down himself for a day or two at a time whenever he could, but chiefly at the end of the week. In October he spent several weeks together making studies from nature in this charming neighbour-hood. These sketches are amongst the finest he ever did, and a number of them were exhibited, along with his other works, at the Old Masters Exhibition in 1883.

There being nothing now to tie him to London, Linnell resolved to gratify his love for the country to the full. Bayswater was now built up on all sides, leaving very little of the ' Nature ' a landscape-painter requires, and hence for some time he had felt a growing need for change. In May, 1849, therefore, he went with his son James to Eden-bridge to look out for a suitable locality in which to settle within easy reach of London. At Red-hill Junction there was a delay, and they took the opportunity to walk up the hill to Redstone Wood. Linnell had previously noticed a wooded knoll on the left of the line from London to Brighton, and had remarked that it seemed just the place for an artist's cottage.

A nearer view of the spot enhanced his satisfac-tion with it, and to his surprise he found that it was for sale. Well wooded, overlooking a magnificent stretch of country, and in the midst of a thoroughly agricultural district, it seemed the very place for the home of a landscape-painter, and so convinced was Linnell of the fact, that, after making the necessary inquiries and investigations, he resolved to buy it.

His solicitor told him the price asked by the vendor was excessive. Linnell's reply was : ' Never mind, the land will prove a good investment ; it will give me foregrounds—indeed, most of the materials I need for my pictures.'

It was a small estate, consisting of about eleven acres, and belonged to a Mr. Allsop, of the Stock Exchange, a well-known follower of Robert Owen, the Socialist, to whom he afterwards introduced Linnell, who, it may be mentioned, had but a poor opinion of his ' intellects.'

Linnell's first visit to Redstone Wood occurred towards the end of May. By June 20 he had agreed upon the purchase, and on July 19 he had sold out Bank of England stock to pay for it.

In the meantime he had taken lodgings at Redhill for Mrs. Linnell and family, and the summer and autumn were spent in excursions about the neighbourhood, the artist himself spending as much time in the country as he could spare from his work in London. Superintending the building of his house, which he at once set about erecting, necessitated the taking of lodgings at Redhill again in the summer of 1850.

It had at first been his intention to build only a small cottage for use in the summer months, purposing still to reside the greater part of the year in his house at Bayswater. He soon changed his mind, however, in this respect, and employed an architect to draw up designs for a substantial house such as would meet all the requirements of his

REDSTONE WOOD.
(From a sketch by John Linnell, jun.)

family, which now numbered four sons and five daughters, the two youngest ones, Thomas and Phœbe, being twins.

The original plan of the structure was his own, and the execution of the design might have been his, too, considering its many defects. But it is roomy, convenient in spite of faults, and on the lower floor well lighted. As regards light, when building his house at Bayswater, Linnell had been prevented from making his windows as large as he would have liked because of the window-tax ; but now that that objectionable impost was done away with, he resolved to have all the light he wanted. Hence all the principal windows at Redstone were made of the largest size, and in the chief rooms they were in such a position as at one season of the year or another to afford glimpses of the sunset.

The house occupied the better part of two years in building, and it was not until July, 1851, that the family finally removed into it. The house in Bayswater was then let, and henceforth to the end of his days Linnell lived and worked at Redhill.

Some four or five years after acquiring the Redstone estate, Linnell added to it by the purchase of thirty-one acres from Lord Somers. The addition consisted of three arable fields and some woodland adjoining Redstone. From one of the fields, which was planted with barley, Linnell painted a ' Harvest' picture, seeing which the farmer who rented the land remarked that he supposed that the artist would get more out of the field than he should, meaning that the painting would probably fetch more than his year's crop.

Subsequently Linnell added still further to his landed property by the purchase of the Chart Lodge estate, consisting of thirty-two acres, which, being in Chancery, was sold at the Auction Mart in 1862, his little demesne now consisting in all of about eighty acres. A large portion of it was woodland, and this he kept almost intact, hardly ever felling a tree, or even so much as lopping a branch.

In all this Linnell had an artist's eye to the enjoyment of his surroundings; and on every side of him, as he went about his grounds, were presented to his sight views such as few landscape-painters could enjoy from their own domain.

Situated as his house was on the slope of the hill, he had, on the one hand, a charming bit of woodland; on the other, a wide-stretching vale, with the blue hills in the distance. Upon these and the sunset he looked from his library window; and it was his delight, when the weather permitted it, to sit in the open, facing the west, and watch the magnificent panorama that gradually unfolded itself to his eye, as the sun, coming down from his noonday elevation, sloped through the lingering afternoon, shedding gold upon the fields and woods, and finally disappearing with deepening and ever-varied splendours.

On the summit of the hill, whence naturally there is a still broader view, extending to Leith Hill on the one hand and to Cookham Hill on the other, he would often sit throughout the summer afternoon, possibly with a sketch-book before him, making note of a bit of sky, a sunlight effect upon the near woods, a distant hill-slope, or what not; or it might be allowing his wonderful memory to be impressed like a photographic plate with facts of sky and cloud and weather, to remain there until the time came for them to become instinct with life and reality upon his canvas.

It is of importance to note this, because Linnell never painted topography, but aspects of Nature. The distinction may not be easily intelligible to the matter-of-fact mind, although to spiritually artistic natures the truth will be at once apparent. In the one case, the painter, if unendowed with the imaginative gift, seizes upon and records dry, hard details ; in the other, he is seized upon by the phenomena, and tells to the best of his ability what they convey to him.

A writer recently, in a somewhat dithyrambic strain, gave a glowing description of the impressions produced upon him by a day's sojourn in the domain chosen as his home by this most idiosyncratic of English artists.

'From morning till night,' he writes, 'the panorama changes, and from the slopes and summit of the hill upon which the colony* nestles the whole is visible, from the golden sunrise, gradually clearing the mists of the valley, through the broadening day, to the down-closing of the star-spangled lid of night. In every direction there is a more or less remote horizon, here with beautiful outlines and an ever-changing phantasmagoria of colour, yonder with shadow mingled with the light to the verge of

---

* There were at this time three houses upon the estate, that which John Linnell, senior, built for himself, and those which he had built for his sons James and William.

gloom and mystery. One does not wonder that the
place was a continual inspiration to one who has left
an indelible name in the annals of English art. At
every turn there is a picture ; wherever the eye
lights, whether on earth or sky, there is beauty to
entrance the mind, and to enthral the heart, too, if
it have any tenderness for the Divine. And on
every hand there is life ; on the ground at our feet
a life innumerable as the blades of grass, and so
varied and wonderful that the mind never ceases to
see freshness and newness in it ; in the over-arching
space above a life grand and majestic, as of the
ceaseless procession of armies, or of all created
things moving to another ark ; and at night the
shapes of the processioning creatures are picked out
with stars. . . .

‘ The thick wood that clothes the hill-slope is full
of charming “bits,” to use the language of artists
—bits that, paint they never so deftly, will possibly
elude their brush. Here the bright light trickling
through the undergrowth, and falling like glittering
diamonds upon the leafy floor, there falling with a
splash of golden colour upon a lichen-covered trunk.
Above the wood, where the hill-brow bares itself to
all the winds, the eye wanders over far fields to
distant and more distant hills. Meadows and corn-
fields, with woodlands, hedgerows, farms with their
hay and corn stacks, fill the intervening space with
endless diversity of colour. Yonder is a brown,
heath - like space, and near it a piece of water
glistening like burnished steel ; over it there is a

shimmer of heat, though the wind comes from the east ; beyond, hills in mist. The diapason of colour runs up from the glowing yellow of a field of char-lock to deeper and deeper shades of purple ; and over all is the vast transparency of blue.

'It is enough to make one break his palette and throw away his brushes in despair. But the artist who first settled down here, John Linnell, set him-self to paint the whole, and succeeded to a marvel in transferring to his canvas the varied beauty of the landscape.'*

Here it was, then, that, from the summer of 1851 till the end of his days, Linnell continued to dwell in quietude and repose, living, as Mr. Holman Hunt, who visited him shortly after he had settled in his new abode, puts it, like a patriarch, with his grown-up family about him, painting the pictures which were a wonder and delight to all who saw them, and in his leisure time devoting himself to those studies which had become dearer and of more serious import to him than the labour by which he earned his bread.

'This,' he observed to an artist who visited him somewhat later—'this is the serious labour of my life.' Then, pointing to a landscape on the easel, he added, 'That is but my recreation.'

His eldest son, who, having remained unmarried, always lived with him, describes him as being ever filled with fresh delight by the varied and never-ending beauties of nature about him. Spring,

* *Tinsley's Magazine*, October, 1890.

summer, autumn, and winter—it was always the
same.   In the infinite panorama that moved to the
music of his heart he found an unfailing interest,
and was in consequence never dull or lonely.   He
never tired of it ; he never grew weary of his work.
If his hand flagged, he turned to his books for rest ;
from his books he turned again to his easel.   He
rose early, and was out and about directing the men
who were at work in the grounds ; and if there
happened to be any building or alterations or repairs
going on, he would be constantly about, directing
and superintending, and allowing nothing to go
wrong for want of the master's eye.

This he continued to do to the last, never
relinquishing his authority, or trusting wholly to
others.   It was part of his principle.   A household,
he considered, should be controlled and directed like
an army.   There might be counsel with subordinates,
but no divided authority.   Hence he would call
himself οἰκοδεσπότης, 'the master of a house or family,'
and such in reality he was.   In this respect it is
characteristic of him that, whilst ever holding the
command, he did not govern by command so much
as by injunction.   He held that in this he was
following the Biblical example, inasmuch as the
commandments do not command, but rather enjoin,
the original Hebrew saying, not 'Thou shalt not
kill,' 'Thou shalt not steal,' etc., but 'Do not kill,'
'Do not steal,' thus showing how rigorously he
applied the lessons derived from his Scriptural
studies.

Although a generous host to those who were con-
genial to him, he did not care to have too many
guests at a time.   He liked best to have those about
him who had ideas and could express them, and
especially those who had a love for nature and an
eye for beauties of landscape such as he could offer
them.

Those who visited the artist invariably went away
wonderfully impressed with much that was peculiar,
and some brusqueness, perhaps, but also with an
originality, a vigour, and oftentimes a brilliance of
thought, very rarely to be met with united in one
person.

Mr. Holman Hunt, who, as I have said, visited
Linnell about this time, has favoured me with a few
notes of his recollections of this visit, and I cannot
do better than give them in his own words.   Linnell
had from the first recognised the high aims and the
undoubted abilities of the gifted young men who
banded themselves together as the Pre-Raphaelite
Brotherhood, and who, determined to do doughty
deeds for the cause of art, only succeeded for long
years in raising a dust of obloquy and scorn.   But,
not content merely to be satisfied himself of the
rightness of their endeavours, he must needs seek
them out and give them his God-speed to help them
on.   This is the light in which one of the brotherhood regarded his encouragement :

' About his generous recognition of our school
when it was new, and had enemies innumerable and
savage among the elder of the profession, I can

never speak with too much admiration. His very position at the time (having won, after a hard struggle, recognition and patronage from the art world, and without any aid, and therefore in opposition to the Academy) was an encouragement to us to continue our fight with hope as long as possible. And his seeking us out on one varnishing morning, and giving us a cordial invitation to come and spend a Sunday with him at Redhill, was a proof that independent judgment in a generous mind would champion us.

'At this visit he was most hospitable and cordial. The house was new; the fare was simple, but most liberal, and the host was reigning in patriarchal state. After the mid-day dinner, taken in a large hall with the door open to the breezy hills, some choice wine was brought up from the cellar, and over this he assured us of his admiration of particular works which we had done, and of his confidence in the course we were pursuing. In the afternoon he took us out for a walk on his little domain, then clustered with trees, which only here and there had an opening.'

In regard to Linnell's 'choice wine,' it is worthy of remark that as soon as he could afford it he kept a good cellar. His motto was, ' Moderation in all things, but the best of everything.' He was very careful in choosing his wine. He would go down to the docks himself and make his selection, and when he had obtained the order for it, he would fetch the cask himself, and never lose sight of it until it was safely deposited in his cellar. No man was ever more careful to see that a thing was done well by doing it himself; and his energy in the prosecution of an object never flagged until it was accomplished. Nor did anyone, perhaps, ever more enjoy the fruits of his labours. Having got his wine, he made the most of it. In one of his poetical fragments he says :

'I like good ale, I like good wine,
  But I don't care a jot for brandy,
Not even when with water mixed
  And sweet as sugar-candy.

'I like a glass of good home-brewed,
  Or a glass of port or sherry ;
But what I like best, with all the rest,
  Is a friend to make me merry.'

Those hearing him recite Tom Taylor's 'St. Swithin's Day,' which he greatly admired, might have deemed him a devoted son of Bacchus, and perhaps less sincerely religious than he really was. But, despite some apparent contradictions in his character, there was a striking congruity throughout, and in regard to this, as in other respects, Linnell was ever prepared to justify his point of view. His attitude in this regard is aptly shown in the following lines, in which the vine and the divine are equally celebrated :

'The purple grape, in sunshine blushing,
  Yields its sweets alone by crushing ;
When most trodden under foot,
Then flows its blood in liquid fruit,
Which the wise will store away,
To cheer their hearts another day.

'So the truth when most oppressed
Sheds its benefits the best ;
Its glories shine, 'tis proved divine,
And those who treasure it are blessed.'

After Linnell's removal to Redhill, and he began
to produce more and more brilliant landscapes, the
demand for his works greatly increased.   He could
hardly paint pictures quickly enough, and frequently
they were bought and paid for while still in their
initial stage.   The dealers found a ready market for
all they could get, and for a time the demand seemed
never satisfied.   To this, perhaps, is largely attri-
butable the circumstance that, while so many of his
contemporaries are represented in our public galleries, and especially Turner and Constable, only
eleven specimens of Linnell's works are to be found
divided between the National Gallery and the South
Kensington Museum, and these for the most part
are of minor importance.

In 1851, soon after his settlement at Redhill, Mr.
Oxenham, the dealer of Oxford Street, appeared
upon the scene, and, as will presently be seen, made
a number of purchases.   Then, about a year later,
Mr. E. Gambart sought Linnell out (for in no case
did the artist ever go after a dealer), and for two or
three years became a large buyer, giving good
prices.

Linnell used to relate an amusing anecdote of
Gambart.   He gave Mr. Holman Hunt a commission, when he went to the Holy Land, for a large
picture similar to his ' Light of the World.'   Mr.
Hunt painted for him ' The Scapegoat,' which, when

delivered to the worthy dealer, so greatly disappointed him that he refused to accept it. Visiting Linnell about the time, Gambart complained of his treatment by Hunt, and said :

'I wanted a nice religious bicture, and he bainted me a great goat !'

The dealer had reason afterwards to regret his refusal of the picture, as the artist obtained a larger price for it than he had agreed to give.

Shortly after Gambart, Messrs. Hooper and Wass, amongst others, became extensive purchasers of Linnell's works, and their commissions continued for several years.

CHAPTER V.

Love of Nature—'Advice from the Country'—'Summer'—'The
World of Beauty'—Blake's Influence on Linnell—Parks—'The
Woodcutters'—'The Hawthorn-Tree'—'Up Rays.'

In speaking of Linnell's art, one would fail to give
its true character if one did not point out the depth
and sincerity of his love of nature. In that his
noble landscape art had its root; to that rich soil it
owed all its wonderful efflorescence in the latter half
of his life. Nothing more striking is to be met with
in the lives of men of genius. Born a Londoner,
and brought up almost within stone's-throw of Drury
Lane and the Seven Dials, he yet developed a love
of nature and a power of realizing it in art that was
on a par with the highest expression of the great
poetical painters of the past.

It was manifested and had its early fostering in
those rambles, now along the Thames at Millbank
—at that time charmingly rural—now higher up
stream by Richmond, Teddington, and Hampton
Court, sometimes with Mulready, sometimes with
William Hunt, not unfrequently alone. The growing delight impelled him to take those long and

often solitary walks of which record has been made, at one time through Kent, at another in the Isle of Wight, or in Wales. And everywhere he felt the spirit of Nature as a something mysterious and divine, as a brooding and indwelling presence, some of whose deeper moods might from time to time be surprised and transferred to canvas in all their burning fervour of colour and entrancing witchery of form.

In a hundred pictures we have the record of his poetic perceptions ; in hundreds of studies from nature he has shown us how he obtained his mastery. But from these we do not learn the whole story : for that we must go to his writings. He tells us that 'in going to draw nature you must bear in mind what you see depends upon what you take with you.' It is not by simply going and copying what we behold with the external organ of sight that we can attain to his excellency of transcription ; we must take with us that devoted love which is as the 'open sesame' that unlocks and reveals all secrets. In other words, it is necessary to bring to the study of Nature a cultivated mind and a heart attuned to her rhythmic utterances.

Constable has said : 'No arrogant mind was ever permitted to see Nature in all her beauty.' Linnell has given expression to the same truth in several of his poetical pieces, as, for instance, in the following, which he entitles 'Advice from the Country.' It was written, as were all his verses, after his removal to Redhill :

' Live in the country if you can,
If you're a thoughtful, sober man,
If you love to look upon Nature's face,
Where the sky is clear, and a heavenly grace
Shines out in all the eye can see,
Urging a secret bended knee,
In thanks and praise for the wondrous things
Which every season round us brings.

' Live in the country if you can,
If you love the mind of God to scan
In the only book through every age,
The only key to Nature's page,
And where the choicest treasure lies
Far from the sight of carnal eyes ;
But where, if born of God above,
You'll read the mystery of his love.

' Live in the country if you can,
Cease from toil and cease from man,
If fashion has not chained you down
To a ceremonious life in town.

' But if you to the country come,
Parting from city's busy hum,
Be sure you leave it all behind,
And bring a lowly, docile mind,
If peace you wish and hope to find ;
For your reward will ever be,
Just as in the sweet country,
Where you may learn, if you do not know,
That you reap according to what you sow.'

The same reverent spirit in which he approached
nature is expressed in the following lines, which at
the same time show his fervent piety :

' Not in tree or mountain,
Not in cloud or sky,
Not in brook or fountain,
Or what human eye
Can apprehend or art can amplify,
Is God's own presence to the soul made nigh,
Unless his love, through his Spirit given,
Be poured into the heart.

> Then God is seen in all his works,
>   The all and every part,
> In mountain, tree, and śky,
>   In sun, and moon, and stars,
>   In all far off or nigh.
> And his love is seen in all,
>   As never seen before ;
> He is nigh in the lightning-flash,
>   And close in the thunder's roar ;
> But nearest of all his love is felt
>   In the rain when it down doth pour.'

Such was his attitude towards that world of beauty to the study of which he gave so unswerving a devotion ; and both in his life and his work he acted upon his perception in the most humble and obedient spirit. Whatever of brusqueness or suspicion there was in his manner towards men was mellowed into gentleness and trust in the presence of Nature, and of the Creator whose hand brought it into existence. In that presence his whole being became, as it were, transfused with a feeling of reverent humility.

By long discipline he seems to have attuned his mind into almost perfect harmony with Nature's varied moods. How intimately the poetic worked with the artistic sense in this respect is shown by the following fragment, entitled ' Summer ' :

' The summer is past like a grand melody with its chorus, and the great Master's hand has upon Nature's harp wrought wondrous music of ever-varied sweetness and energy—gentle sultry calm, with choruses of thunder ; and now the note is changed into the plaintive minor key, awakening

quiet sadness in the mind, with some forebodings
of coming winter's blast.   It seems as if there was
a lull after the struggle of the elements, after the
efforts of the earth's fruition, and the gathering in
of her bounteous produce, but for which man would
be extinct.   No one hath seen God, yet we see him
every hour in his acts.'

This attitude towards nature and the Divine spirit
which dwells within and works through it was
not attained at once, but gradually, partly through
his own observation, partly also through the study
of the Old Masters.   Later his whole being became
kindled, as it were, into a higher and more intense
life through the study of the inspired writings, and
his attitude towards the beauties of creation was
much the same as that of the prophets and poets
of the Hebrew Scriptures.   The very strength of
his emotions frequently communicate to his verses
—often rough in form and hampered by his lack of
lyric art—something of the fervour of true poetic
insight.   The following little poem, which is, perhaps, one of his best as regards form and feeling, is
doubly interesting because of a certain reminiscence
of Blake that it carries with it.   The first three
stanzas especially remind one of some of his ' Songs
of Innocence ' :

'THE WORLD OF BEAUTY.

' What a beautiful world ! only look
    At the fields and the trees and the flowers,
And the clouds how they show in the brook,
    On the hills how they're breaking in showers !

' Oh, look at those beautiful sheep,
  As they feed on the side of the hill ;
How happy they seem as they ramble the steep,
  Wandering whither they will !

And where they've climbed the height,
  And where the sky looks so blue,
How they look like angels of light,
  They sparkle so out to our view !

Then why not so happy as they,
  When I beyond them am so blessed ?
'Tis the thought of how fleeting the hours of the day,
And how soon all this beauty must come to decay,
  That makes my heart sink in my breast.

' But only one moment that pang of the heart,
  Which the frailty of nature revealed ;
There's a firm ground of hope when from this world I part,
  There's a better which now is concealed.'

I have previously referred to Blake's influence
on Linnell. In nothing does it appear more
marked than in the enlarged perception and deeper
poetic insight which it gradually brought about.
When the latter's life is studied intimately in his
works and his writings the inspiring cause may be
seen. At first he was not, perhaps, ripe enough to
benefit to the full from the mystical poet-artist's
influence, and it had by no means produced its
complete effect when all that was earthly of Blake
was laid in the unmarked grave in Bunhill Fields ;
but gradually and insensibly the work went on until
he united to his other powers some of the latter's
contemplative spirit, and he became a great poetic
interpreter of nature.

At first Blake's influence on Linnell was shown
in his impatience of forms and ceremonies, and in

his reliance on the spirit alone. With this came a broader perception and a deeper and more spiritual philosophy. That he never attained to that visionary altitude which characterized the former is due, perhaps, not so much to a more circumscribed imagination or less spiritual perception, but to a keener love of nature and a greater and possibly saner unity with it.

A man may become so wrapped up in his contemplation of nature as to be thereby unfitted to look at things in any but the one aspect. Such to some extent was the case with Linnell in the latter half of his life. Thus he came to be impatient of man's interference. Nature, and nature only, was his desire. In his own words, he would have nothing touched, or, if it must be, then as little as possible. He wanted nature's own expression, free and unsophisticated: in that he found delight. and inspiration; in that lies the charm of so many of his landscapes.

Hence it arose that he came to dislike the formality and restraint of parks, and the studied picturesque in landscape-gardening.

'Of all places in the country,' he says in one of his occasional writings, 'parks are to me the most desolate. There seems to be a dearth of intelligence and sympathy with Nature, or rather with the design of the Creator, whose thoughts or intentions are not perceived because men seek to bend Nature to express their sense of their own importance, their riches and powers; and they put Nature as far as they can into a kind of livery, as they do their servants, degrading both with what pretends to be ornament. The landscape is reduced to a toy-shop sentiment on a large scale ; everything is denuded of those accompaniments which give the true expression of grandeur or beauty to the scene.

'It is true the trees are left to grow unrestrained, looking like aristocratic "swells," isolated from all undergrowth ; and, with the ground shaved under them, they look like large toy-trees placed upon a green board. It is not until one gets upon a common, near a forest, or into farm lands, that one begins to breathe again, and feel out of the influence of man's despotism. Man stamps his own thought and character upon everything he meddles with, and, unhappily in most cases, he obliterates the work of God and substitutes his own.'

In some of his poetic pieces Linnell manifests a rare perception of nature's methods, and not unfrequently hits upon a happy, though perhaps quaint, form of expression, as in the following, entitled 'Summer':

'And must the summer die
    Before you come to see
The fervid beauty that doth lie
    In every flower and tree,
Asking your admiration with a modesty
That to the beauty addeth intensity ?

' For your pleasure it is there,
    And therefore so enticing looks,
Aided by balmy fragrant air
    And sounds of happy birds in leafy nooks.

'The nightingale is yet a guest, sweet bird,
   Who like a cheerful guest, unasked, unflattered, sings ;
The cuckoo, seldom seen, may yet be heard,
   Measuring the woodlands as he flies on level wings.

'Soon will the ripened bending grass,
   Emblem of man, who alike to earth is bound,
Feel the mower's scythe through its heart to pass,
   And in its fall shed from its slaughter-ground,
   Like a martyr'd saint, a perfume all around.'

Thus Linnell became after his settlement at Redhill a simple child of Nature, and all his pictures
painted after that time, especially those of his best
period, strike one as being as intimately in accord
with, and as truthfully interpretative of, Nature as the
reedy notes of the shepherd feeding his flocks.   By
living continuously in her midst, with but few dis-
tractions from her contemplation, and those chiefly
of a character to increase his devotion, he became,
as it were, her confidant, knew her moods as a
devout lover would, and was intimate with all her
operations.   Thus, though he may strike us sometimes as being prosy, and not unfrequently prolix,
yet there are times when he approaches the rapture
of the poet and seer, especially when he touches
religious themes.   Then we are permitted to see
the reason of the close sympathy between him and
Blake.   These moods, however, are not the rule.
His art is based on a more median plane.   It
delights in the pastoral, and revels in the homely
rather than the idyllic life.   Howbeit, there is never
anything common or gross in it, while the fine
thread of poetry running through it saves it from

the reproach of being mere transcription. A number
of pictures might be named, painted at this time, the
like of which for poetic perception and sympathetic
rendering of English landscape are rarely to be
met with. Amongst them may be mentioned 'The
Woodcutters (21 by 28 inches), showing an open
space in the midst of Windsor Forest, such as Pope
described in the lines :

> ' There, interspersed in lawns and opening glades,
> The trees arise that shun each other's shade.'

This landscape, painted in 1855, fully justifies
Ruskin in his 'Modern Painters,' where he says :
'The forest scenes of John Linnell are peculiarly
elaborate, and in many points most skilful.'* It
is rich in colour, and admirably though, like all
his works, simply composed. Another characteristic
picture belonging to this period (1853) is 'The Hawthorn-Tree' (39 by 54 inches), showing, in the foreground, large trees meeting overhead, with figures
beneath listening to a shepherd-boy playing on a
pipe ; sheep, a thickly-wooded slope in the middle
distance, and a distant landscape to the right, fill up
the canvas. All is harmony and proportion ; and,

---

* It is worthy of note that Mr. Ruskin, considering apparently that
he had done but scant justice to so great and so original a genius as
Linnell, makes reference to him in the addenda to vol. ii. of 'Modern
Painters,' speaking of his close study, pursued through many laborious
years, characterized by an observance of Nature, scrupulously and
minutely painted, directed by the deepest sincerity, and aided by a
power of drawing almost too refined for landscape subjects, and only
to be understood by reference to his engravings after Michael Angelo.

as is usual in Linnell's landscapes, the view, wandering from the focus of interest in the foreground, is lost in cloudland, for the forms of which he had almost a sculptor's eye and hand.

The same or similar qualities are seen in 'On Summer Eve by Haunted Stream,' showing a tender sunset sky over a distant hilly landscape;

WINDSOR FOREST.
(From a water-colour drawing made in 1815.)

in 'The Road through the Wood;' in the 'Wheat Harvest' of 1854 (36 by 57 inches); in 'The Dusty Road' (1855); in 'Sheep reposing,' representing a boy watching some sheep lying under the shade of a wooded knoll; in 'Sunny Scenes' (catalogued as 'The White Cloud' in the 'Old Masters' of 1883), in which we have one of

Linnell's finest effects of aërial movement and transparency of cloud-forms ; and, not to mention any
more, in the ' Harvest Dinner,' shown at the International Exhibition of 1862, and sold at Christie's
in 1879 for 1,690 guineas.

The last-named picture was bought by Messrs.
Thomas Agnew and Son, and was one of the first,
if not actually the first, of a series of purchases and
commissions extending through a period of ten
years.   During this time Mr. William Agnew's
relations with the artist were of a very intimate
nature ; they were based on sincere mutual respect,
and were broken off through what can only be
characterized as an unfortunate misunderstanding.

During a part of the same period Mr. Arthur
Tooth, amongst others, was a customer for a number
of pictures.   One of his purchases was a picture
named ' Up Rays,' which exhibits a small arc of the
sun above a cloud low on the horizon, with vivid
rays of light shooting upwards.   A companion to
it is entitled ' Down Rays.'   When he bought the
first-named picture, Mr. Tooth asked the artist to do
some retouching on it, and, wishing specially to have
it by a certain day, he undertook to send Linnell a
salmon if he did not disappoint him.   The artist
promised that he should have it in time.   On the
morning of the day appointed for the picture to be
delivered to him, Mr. Tooth telegraphed to Redhill,
requesting that it might be sent on without fail   In
reply he received a telegram desiring him to ' send

the salmon first.' The fish was duly forwarded,
and in acknowledgment Linnell sent the following
lines :

'That which rhymes to gammon
Has just arrived thro' mammon,
Relating to an art sale,
And thereby hangs a tail.'

CHAPTER VI.

Views on Art—Dialogue between the Painter and his Friend—Morality
in Art—Murillo—Rubens—Rembrandt—Raphael—The Dutch
School—The Italian School—Taste and Morals—Qualifications
of an Art-teacher—Figure-drawing.

INCIDENTALLY here and there in the preceding
pages we have obtained hints and glimpses of
Linnell's views on art in general, while, at the same
time, we have been enabled to gather what his
opinions were in regard to particular artists and
their work. We have seen, too, what his own aims
were, and to what extent he realized them. Those
views are probably not such as would be endorsed
by the generality of artists, but in art, as in other
matters, Linnell brought so much thought, knowledge, and experience to bear upon his subject, that
not only are his ideas worthy of respect, but, even
if sometimes erroneous, they cannot be otherwise
than helpful.

Fortunately we are enabled to give his views in a
very clear and telling form from his own writings.
In the years 1853-54 he contributed a couple of
' Dialogues upon Art ' to the little periodical before

mentioned, entitled *The Bouquet.* It was published
at first for private circulation only, and probably
never had many readers. *The Bouquet* was edited
by ' Bluebell ' and ' Mignonette,' and all the contribu-
tors had floral quill-names. Linnell's was ' Larkspur,' and under this pseudonym he contributed
dialogues to Nos. 25 and 33, in which he sets forth
in detail some of his views.

The first dialogue is between the Painter and
his Friend. The latter begins by affirming that
art is nothing, after all, but the imitation of Nature.
' Whoever comes closest to that,' he says, ' is the
greatest artist, I suppose. Is he not ? The stories
of Zeuxis and Parhasius show this, I think, where
it is related how one deceived the birds and the
other Zeuxis himself.'

The Painter replies : ' The best story is that of
Zeuxis when he deceived the birds and failed to
deceive them at the same time.'

' How do you mean ?' asks the Friend.

' Why, don't you remember the story of his painting a boy holding a basket of grapes, and that the
grapes were so like nature that the birds came and
pecked at them, in spite of the figure of the boy,
which would have frightened them away had it
been as well painted as the grapes, and that the
painter justly considered his work a failure upon
the whole on this account ?'

' Good ! I remember now ' (replies the Friend),
' and it reminds me of Fuseli's criticism upon Northcott's picture of Baalam and the Ass. " Master

Norcott," said Fuseli, " has painted de ass like
an angel, but he has painted de angel like an
ass." '

The Painter replies that it is certainly easier to
paint inferior objects so as to satisfy most people,
than to paint tolerably the expression of elevated
thought ; but, strictly speaking, he says Northcott
could not have done as Fuseli said, for if he had
possessed the power of painting the brute with
angelic skill, he would not have handled the angel
so brutally.

This leads the artist to controvert the common
notion that the most deceptive imitation of Nature
is the greatest triumph of art, and to develop his
own theory of art. Such stories, he considers, are
degrading to art, as the vilest imitations sometimes
deceive the eye. Such imitation of the mere ' skin
of nature,' he avers, is but the handwriting of art,
though rather a difficult one to learn ; and even
that cannot be found in any great perfection, un-
combined with higher art—qualities resulting from
a perception of the more spiritual and deeper-seated
attributes of Nature. For if those most beautiful
qualities escape the observation of anyone, he cannot be a good imitator of even Nature's mere surface
qualities. He may satisfy some who see no further
than himself, and, like the false prophet, may deceive
many ; but those who can perceive the spiritual
qualities of Nature will be disappointed, and feel
that the chief end of art is not attained or even
aimed at.

Thus, while he grants that the only way to be original and to produce the best works is to study nature, and that all the finest principles are founded upon nature, he yet holds that something else is needed. In short, the artist must add something to the product, and that something must be himself.

This is undoubtedly what he means by those ' spiritual qualities of Nature ' which are to be studied and imitated. Such, however, he perceives, is not what is commonly thought of when the imitation of nature is said to be everything in art. All that is then meant is that the picture should look real, and if it deceives the eye, as in the Zeuxis stories, it is thought perfection.

Linnell held that a picture may be as like nature as possible to the minds of some people, and may deceive the eye, and yet be worthless compared with others not possessing, or even aiming at, that eye-deceiving quality, but having an emphasis of imitation upon those qualities of nature which give us ideas of sublimity and beauty ; and those are the higher or more refined principles of art which regard the perceptions of those qualities of nature, and teach how the ideas of beauty and sublimity may be best excited in the mind by a work of art. These principles themselves lie in the deeper aspects of nature ; that is to say, they are found in it, as Shakespeare so well expresses in the lines :

'Nature is made better by no mean,
But Nature makes that mean '—

a perception on the part of the poet as profound as it is aptly put.

Linnell's view, therefore, was that the great end of art is to develop the perceptions of beauty and sublimity, not to make us stare with wonder how one thing can be so like another ; for the feeling of mere wonder is the result of ignorance, while the perception of beauty and sublimity is the result of knowledge—is knowledge, in short, for it is reading something unintelligible to others.

Our astonishment may be excited without admiration or any pleasant feeling whatever, the work which excites it may be disgusting ; but such art is not to be praised or cultivated, for that would be to make art a Gorgon's head. The skill of imitation is wasted unless the representation teaches some moral or spiritual truth.

The business of the artist should be to create spiritual perceptions ; and all the powers of imitation, the skill in design, and the facility in colouring and expression, should be used to this end. The artist has, indeed, to do with the senses ; but his object should be to reach the heart, the inner man, through that medium. What is called ideal art, poetic, imaginative, or high art, results not only from a vivid perception of those qualities of nature which most affect the mind with emotions of moral sympathy, and the sense of sublimity and beauty, but also from a perception of the means by which the effect is produced.

The effect is traced to its cause not only in its

broad result, but in all the details in the machinery. Not only must there be a dissection of the plan, but a reading of the design—in other words, a perception of what every variety and shade of emotion depends upon. Then, superadded to this, there must be the power of reproducing these qualities in a work of art, divested of all that is calculated to hinder those impressions, and heightened by an increased emphasis upon some things, together with an enlarged and more perfect combination upon nature's own principles than is commonly found to exist in nature itself. A true genius for art can only coexist with an intelligence and a moral perception capable of receiving and producing in others such impressions as these.

Such are, in a brief and succinct form, Linnell's views in reference to art. As to those among the Old Masters whose works attest their fidelity to these principles, Linnell placed first and foremost, as we have already seen, the great artists of the Roman, Florentine, and Venetian schools; whilst he holds that Murillo in his religious art exemplifies all that is to be most avoided.

In the second dialogue in *The Bouquet* we are given the artist's reasons for condemning the Spanish painter's art. I cannot do better than give his views in his own words.

'I met a gentleman,' the dialogue begins, 'who had just come from the British Gallery, where the two large Murillos which had lately arrived from Marshal Soult's collection were hanging. One of the pictures was "The Prodigal Son," the other the "Three Angels appearing to Abraham." My friend asked me if I had seen the pictures, and finding I had, he inquired rather eagerly :

' " Well, how do you like them ?"

' " Not at all," said I ; " I cannot bear them."

' " Oh," said he, " I am delighted to hear you say so ; for, to tell you the truth, I felt disgusted with .the pictures, but was afraid to say so, because the praise was so general, and the price said to have been given for them so large," ' etc.

In reply to the query why he dislikes these Murillos so much, the artist says :

' I can give you some idea by telling you what a friend of mine said to me when we were looking at the two pictures together at the British Gallery :

' " I say," said he, whispering, " what do you think of those three angels ? Don't you think if they were to make their appearance in Belgrave Square that the new police would be after them pretty soon ?"

' " To be sure," said I ; " and they would be taken up on suspicion, and locked up for want of bail."

' " I see what you mean, and I remember the expressions are anything but elevated. However, you must allow the design and colouring to be splendid."

' " Indeed I cannot ; nor do I think that fine design and fine colour are found in original works combined with such expression and character."

' " What ! Doubt that fine design and colour can be found united with vulgar forms ? Look at Rem-

brandt and Rubens: all speak of these masters as
great in design and colouring. Why, nearly all the
lecturers on art wind up their discourses with the
praise of Rubens for these qualities."

' " Rembrandt certainly was a colourist, and composed finely ; and though his figures are not fine
specimens of form as to limb, the action is natural
and unaffected, often beautiful, and always original,
the expressions also generally true and sincere ; but
above all, he displays such a profound sentiment
and depth of feeling in everything by his extra-
ordinary treatment of the light and shade, that he
stands alone as a wonderful example of what may
be done, in spite of certain defects, by working out
with confidence and diligence original perceptions
by an original method. Rubens I think very inferior to Rembrandt in all these qualities. He was
natural, but very coarse, and in some respects corrupt ; and there is no veil like Rembrandt's twilight
thrown over his defects. His vulgarity stands out
with a brazen front in broad sunlight, and is the
more offensive. But though Rubens is not without
affectation in his allegorical and religious subjects,
and exhibits in the latter some of that hypocrisy so
common in the second-rate painters of sacred history,
yet he is not so hypocritical as Murillo."

' " Hypocritical ?"

' " Yes ; and Raphael has been justly praised for
the opposite. His cartoons alone are sufficient to
establish this. Look at the action and expression of
every figure, how both correspond most sincerely !

Do you remember the figure which steps forward
to present the sacrifice to Paul at Lystra, and the
calm dignity of the Messiah giving the charge to
Peter to feed His sheep? Why, if you can remember these enough to compare them with the dancing-
master attitudes of the figures in the Murillo before
us, and especially the figure of the youthful Christ in
the centre, I think you will agree with me that the
whole is more like a scene in a ballet than anything
else; and as to the colour, I think it is as inferior to
the colouring of the Roman, Florentine, and Venetian schools as the design, the drawing, and the
expression." '

In regard to these criticisms on Murillo, Linnell
used to repeat a saying of Mulready's respecting a
' Holy Family' of the Spaniard in the National
Gallery. Referring to the air of fashionableness and
conventionality about it, Mulready once said, 'You
can't help thinking that it is Master Christ with his
mamma and his papa.' But while he condemned
Murillo's religious pictures for their false sentiment,
Linnell had much genuine admiration for his secular
subjects, such as his ' Beggar Boy,' finding them
full of truthfulness and sincerity.

In his antipathy to Rubens' grossness, the artist
was undoubtedly betrayed into doing an injustice to
the great Flemish painter, overlooking, amongst
other noble qualities, his pre-eminence in composition.

But even while recognising this error of judgment-
we are enabled all the more distinctly to perceive

and appreciate Linnell's point of view in regard to
art.   He has only one criterion whereby to test the
truth of things.   As in his daily conduct, so in his
views of art : he finds the Scriptures the only safe
guide.   ' I cannot find the true principles of fine art,'
he says, ' anywhere but in the inspired writings ; and
in my opinion it is only by the knowledge of what is
therein taught that true taste can be acquired ; for
as the most minute things exist, and are sustained
by the same laws which uphold the universe, so the
Divine laws of universal truth must base and sustain
our least perceptions if we expect to build up an
edifice of truth in our minds.'

He therefore holds, with Ruskin, that all corruption of art proceeds from moral corruption, and that
one of the very worst of moral corruptions is hypocrisy.   ' Christ said with great emphasis to his
disciples, " Beware of the leaven of the Pharisees,
which is hypocrisy ;" and I believe it is the deadliest
of poisons wherever it is found.'

We may see in his judgments on the Old Masters
what was Linnell's aim in his later art, in the works
that proceeded from his brush when he could devote
himself freely to the form of art he loved best.   In
his earlier days he had been much influenced by the
Dutch and Flemish schools, and not a few of his
pictures then produced show many of the excellencies
of the Teniers, Ruysdaels, Hobbemas, Paul Potters,
etc.   It was only when, later, he came to know more
about the Italian masters, and perceived how greatly
superior they were in conception and expression,

that his views broadened and his art ripened, till it became like nothing else in the English school—a style *sui generis.*

It was not then so easy to study the Old Masters as now. Specimens of their work had not at that time been reproduced by photography, and such copies as were to be seen were scarce, and often bad. Hence he took every opportunity that was afforded him of procuring copies of Raphael, Titian, Michael Angelo, etc.

Thus he strengthened his belief that fine design and fine colouring invariably go together. ' Fine design and fine colour,' he said, 'can only proceed from a well-disciplined and superior mind, where perceptions—of every excellent quality—are more likely to exist from the same cause.'

This he held to be the reason of the wonderful universality of genius displayed by the first-rate painters. Giulio Romano, Andrea del Sarto, and, above all, Da Vinci, he considered, support his view that fine colour and fine design are found together only in the works of the best masters, because they are imagined or conceived together, being one perception of the poetic vision.

' Did you ever see,' he asks in the second dialogue, 'the copy by Da Vinci's favourite pupil, Marco Oggione, of the " Last Supper," which the Royal Academy possesses, in which the design, expression, colour and light and shade, all work out one profound sentiment of the sublimest pathos ?'

He goes on to say that 'the holy sincerity of

expression in those figures is enough, in my opinion, to make one sick of Murillo and Rubens for ever,' and holds that whoever perceives and delights in the highest qualities of the best works of the Roman and Florentine schools, will be too much disgusted with what he meets with generally in Rubens, and nearly always in Murillo, to care much about either of them.

'It appears to me that, if anyone does not see what those masters are deficient in, they are pleased only as children, by something affecting merely the visual organs ; or they have a depraved taste, which may soon be detected in things of more importance than pictures, and that is a serious matter ; for there is a woe to those who call evil good, and good evil, in all matters more or less according to the nature of the subject.'

'That which is not good is not delicious to a well-governed and wise appetite,' says Linnell, quoting Milton ; and while he holds that the difference of temperament and organization gives a different bias towards different kinds of beauty, and such differences are legitimate if connected with knowledge and discipline, yet no one should love what is corrupt and debasing.

In short, in John Linnell's opinion, the question of taste is a moral one. It is also a religious question ; for to him there is no distinction to be made with safety.

'It seems to me that he whose morality is not essentially religious, or whose religion is not essen tially moral, has little of either morality or religion. Taste, therefore, though depending on organization for its bias to one kind of beauty more than another, is kept pure and good by the moral sense.'

Similar views in regard to the connection between morals and art were expressed by our artist in a letter which he wrote about this time in answer to a landscape-painter who was a candidate for the position of drawing-master to the City of London School, and who applied to him for a testimonial. It has an additional value, because it gives very precisely his views as to the requirements of a teacher of drawing. The letter, which is dated 1852, is as follows :

'DEAR SIR,

'I have great pleasure in being able to express my admiration of the works which I have seen of yours in the Exhibition ; but as the testimony you seek relates entirely to your qualification as a teacher, of which I know nothing, I really think my opinion of your general artistic power as a landscape-painter ought not to weigh much in the matter. For my notions of a good drawing-master are that he should draw the human figure accurately, divested of all peculiarity of manner or style in the process ; be able to show clearly how such drawing of the figure is the only true basis of artistic power ; make science the means of developing a perception of beauty, and to prove that perception to be the great end of art ; be able to show that taste in art

is intimately connected with moral feeling, and that
no one can innocently admire a corrupt style : to do
all which you may be fully competent, and if so, I
hope you may succeed in your application ; for he
who has most of that sort of ability is, in my
opinion, best calculated for the office.'

His views in regard to figure-drawing are empha-
sized in the following aphoristic lines written about
this time :

> ' There is a race of scribblers in art,
> Who cannot well delineate one feature,
> Muddling and dabbling on through thick and thin,
> Not knowing when to leave or how begin.
> For want of discipline in figure-drawing,
> Their work is feeble, or presumptuous pawing ;
> Handling it can't be called, for from a hand
> Should come some handiwork that well would stand
> The test of knowledge, by sound practice got,
> And workmanlike, without a smear or blot.'

CHAPTER VII.

Biblical Criticism—Early Studies—Desire for Tranquillity—Hebrew
and Greek Studies—Diatheekee—Abraham's Covenant—'The
Lord's Day'—Views in regard to Sunday—Burnt-offerings.

REFERENCE has already been made to the circumstance that Linnell was early attracted to Biblical
studies through his surroundings as a religious man,
but chiefly by the example of his future father-in-
law, Mr. Thomas Palmer. He does not appear to
have carried his studies very far, however, at that
time, and they were probably soon relinquished—
albeit, the taste he had manifested from boyhood
for reading, and for book-learning in general, was
hereby greatly increased.

His Biblical studies were not taken up or resumed
in any definite and continuous way until 1843, when,
in company with his sons, he set to work in earnest
to study the original texts of the Scriptures. He
had now more time for literary pursuits, and returned
to his early love with great zeal. What he had
learned as a young man at Mr. Palmer's house in
Swallow Street—not much, perhaps, in amount—
served him in good stead, and proved to be a

useful basis to work upon. He at a later period
put it on record that the foundation of the critical
knowledge of the Bible which he afterwards attained
was laid in those early days, adding that his subsequent attainments, small as they were in amount,
he esteemed as the greatest of his acquisitions.

So great became his desire to widen and deepen
the extent of his knowledge about the time that he
reached the fiftieth year of his age, that he was led
by it to forego many amusements and recreations in
order that he might give the more time to reading
and study. Indeed, it now became his first thought
how he could best promote tranquillity and peace of
mind, and thus cut off many possible sources of
interruption. The adoption of this principle of
action, together with a daily recourse to literature,
and especially to the Scriptures, as the source of all
truth and the anchorage of all hope, spared him no
end of trouble and annoyance, and caused him in
advanced age to write :

' I cannot recount all the benefits I have derived
from pursuing this method. It has been my
guiding-star, my compass, my sail, and my rudder.'

He was greatly aided in his Biblical studies—and,
indeed, was to some extent stimulated thereto—by
the publication of several works, which served as
helps to the study of the Old and the New Testaments, and the languages in which they were
written. One of those works was Liddell and
Scott's Greek-English Lexicon (the first edition of
which was published in 1843). Other works from

which he derived great aid were 'The Englishman's
Greek Concordance to the New Testament,' Daw-
son's 'Analytical Lexicon to the New Testament,' Lee's Hebrew Grammar, Gesenius's Hebrew
Lexicon, and 'The Englishman's Hebrew Concordance to the Old Testament.'

He also obtained facsimile reprints of the uncial-
letter texts of the Greek New Testament Scriptures,
likewise many of the best critical works on the
texts. In short, he spared no pains, and counted
no cost, in his desire to arrive at the true meaning
of the Sacred Writings.

It cannot be said that he became a thorough
master of Greek and Hebrew ; but he acquired a
sufficient acquaintance with them to be able to
compare the English version with the originals, and
to draw his conclusions as to their true meaning
and form of expression.

His researches in this field resulted in the publication of several pamphlets on Biblical subjects, all of
which are characterized by careful research and considerable critical acumen.

His first work, which was published by Trübner
in 1856, when, therefore, he was in his sixty-fourth
year, is a comprehensive argument against the mis-
naming of the Scriptures the Old and the New
Testaments, instead of, as he contends they should
be called, 'The Old and New Covenants.' It is
entitled 'Diatheekee,' the word which, in the
Septuagint Greek Version of the Old Testament,
is the translation of the Hebrew word בְּרִית (*breeth*).

In the Old Testament this word is rendered *covenant ;* but in the New Testament portion of the Authorized Version the Greek word (*diathēkē*) the equivalent of *breeth* is in some instances given as *testament,* following the Old Latin Version, which, however, in every case has *testamentum,* whereas the English Version has *testament* in thirteen places, and *covenant* in twenty places. Hence it is that we get our word ' Testament.'

Linnell's contention was that if the word ' testament ' ever in Old Latin signified ' pact ' or ' covenant,' it now has such signification no longer, and so misleads. The main object of his pamphlet, therefore, was to prove that the word ' covenant ' should be used throughout the New Testament as the translation of the Greek word *diatheekee* in the original ; and he supports his view with great cogency and force.

Since the issue of this little pamphlet a new and independent version of the Scriptures has been made by Wellbeloved and others (published by Longmans in 1862), which, in every instance where the word ' testament ' occurs in other translations, substitutes the more correct term ' covenant.'

The ancient form or ceremony of making a covenant, or, literally, ' cutting a breeth,' was pic-torially represented by the artist in a painting executed in 1853, a varied replica of which is still in the possession of the Linnell family. Accord-ing to the ancient rite, a sacrificed victim was cut or divided into two portions, and the covenanting

parties (who bound themselves thereby) passed
between the divided pieces. Thus the covenant,
or promise, was confirmed or ratified. This ceremony is described in Jer. xxxiv., and an illustration
of it is given in Gen. xv. Here we see how
'Jehovah made a covenant with Abram.' As
directed, Abram divided the victims into two portions, and set them opposite each other, and while
in a deep sleep, in the darkness after sunset, 'a
smoking furnace and a lamp of fire' (representing
the Divine presence) passed between the pieces of
the slain animals.

In his tract Linnell quotes as follows from Gen. xv. :
'Take to me an heifer of three years old . . . and
a turtledove, and a young pigeon. And he took to
him all these and divided them in the midst, and
laid each piece one over against another.'

He explains that the last clause, literally translated, would read, 'gave each piece to meet or
answer to its fellow,' *i.e.*, opposite—to correspond
—leaving a space between the corresponding pieces,
for the party covenanting to walk through, as
described in Jer. xxxiv. 18 : "And I will give the
men that have transgressed my covenant, which
have not performed the words of the covenant which
they had made before me, when they cut the calf in
twain, and passed between the parts thereof." '

Then follows the sublime narrative of the peculiar
deep sleep, or trance, which fell upon Abram, in
which he learns the long-to-be-endured affliction of
his posterity, and their ultimate possession of the

land ; also his own peaceful departure. And to
confirm and witness, or ratify, the appointment of
these things, God gives Abram the vision of the
smoking furnace and lamp of fire passing between
these divisions of the animals.

This is the scene represented by Linnell in his
painting. A majestic form, or suggested Divine
presence, is dimly seen passing between the two
halves of the offering while the patriarch sleeps.
It is a very fine composition, and grandly suggestive. Later he made a small oil sketch of it, in
which the mysterious presence of Jehovah is represented by a flame of brilliant whiteness, the effect
being to give an added mystery and sublimity to the
subject.

The pamphlet concludes with an examination of
the passage in Heb. ix. 15-18, in the light of the
conclusions he has arrived at. In the words of the
text referred to, the ratification of the ' new covenant '
is spoken of. Here, by a more literal rendering of
the original, and by consistently translating *diathcekee*
by ' covenant,' the true sense of that word is main-
tained, and the argument of the writer has its full
and proper force and meaning.

In ' The Speaker's Commentary ' (published in
1881) the principle of translation and interpretation
of the passage in question (Heb. ix. 15-18) which
Linnell contended for in his essay is adopted. The
rendering given of the clause in question is as
follows :

' By reason of this, he is the mediator of the

THE COVENANT WITH ABRAHAM.

(*From an oil-painting by J. Linnell, 1853.*)

new covenant, that a death having taken place for the redemption of the transgressions that were under the first covenant, they which are called may receive the promise of the eternal inheritance. For where a covenant is, there must needs be alleged the death of him that made the covenant. For a covenant is steadfast that is made over the dead : whereas it hath no force when he that made the covenant liveth. For which cause neither was the first (covenant) dedicated (or inaugurated) without blood,' etc.

Another of our artist's striking works in the field of Biblical criticism is his treatise, published in 1859, entitled 'The Lord's Day the Day of the Lord.' As we have seen, Linnell was strongly opposed to Sabbatarianism, and in this little work he gives us his reasons for not believing in the common doctrine of a Sunday Sabbath. The phrase 'The Lord's day' occurs, he tells us, only once in the whole Bible (Rev. i. 10), and he explains his reasons for believing that it is another form of 'the day of the Lord.' '"The Lord's day" and "the day of the Lord,"' he says, 'are nothing more than two different modes of expressing the genitive case of the same noun.' And he supplies a number of quotations to show that this 'day of the Lord' meant an extended period, 'a thousand years being as one day, and a day as a thousand years, with the Lord'; in short, that it refers to the time and to the events which form the subject-matter of the prophecy contained in the Apocalypse.

Linnell gives his own translation of the words in
Revelation upon which so much is based, and holds
it to be a correct rendering, and one that conveys
the true signification of the words of the original,
viz. : ' I became by the Spirit in the day of the
Lord, or day of Jehovah.' He adduces many instances in proof of the correctness of his rendering,
and in support of his view that the phrase ' Lord's
day' (in Revelation) is not a designation of the
first day of the week he quotes Milton in his
' Christian Doctrine ' : ' Whether the festival of the
Lord's day (an expression which occurs only once
in Scripture, Rev. i. 10) was weekly or annual,
cannot be pronounced with certainty, inasmuch as
there is not (as in the case of the Lord's Supper)
any account of its institution, or command for its
celebration, to be found in Scripture. If it was the
day of His resurrection, why, we may ask, should
this be considered as the Lord's day in any higher
sense than that of His birth, or death, or ascension ?
Why should it be held in higher consideration than
the day of the descent of the Holy Spirit ? And
why should the celebration of the one occur weekly,
whereas the commemoration of the others is not
necessarily even annual, but remains at the discretion
of each believer ?'

And again : ' Those, therefore, who, on the
authority of an expression occurring only once in
Scripture, keep holy a Sabbath day, for the con-
secration of which no Divine command can be
alleged, ought to consider the dangerous tendency

of such an example, and the consequences with which it is likely to be followed in the interpretation of Scripture.'

Men will venerate something, is Linnell's conclusion ; but, in proportion to their ignorance of the true God, they have always worshipped the created more than the Creator, and among the many superstitions arising from that ' ignorance,' the observance of days seems to have been one which has been highly esteemed from the remotest times. ' Howbeit,' he continues, quoting from Paul to the Galatians, 'that when ye knew not God, ye did service unto them which by nature are no gods. But now, after ye have known God, or rather are known of God, how turn ye again to the weak and beggarly elements, whereto ye desire again to be in bondage ? You observe *days*, and months, and times (*seasons*), and years (*anniversaries*). I am afraid of you, lest I have bestowed labour in vain upon you.'

As we have before seen, when John Linnell arrived at a conclusion on a given subject, he was never afraid to follow it to its logical consequences ; and so, in regard to this question of the Sabbath, having satisfied himself that there is no warrant in Scripture for the observance of what is called the Lord's day, he ceased to regard it as in any special sense holy. Hence he ' regarded every day alike,' and, touching himself personally, he did just the same on Sunday as on other days, working at his painting, and attending to other matters without making any difference. At the same time he did not interfere with the liberty of other people, but left everyone to act as he chose.

Subsequently his daughter Mary translated, with his approval, a work from the French of Louis Victor Mellet, entitled 'Sunday and the Sabbath' (Trübner and Co.), the argument of which is that the Sabbatic rest is simply a Judaical ordinance peculiar to the first covenant, belonging to the whole mass of legal ceremonies, and that there is no day of rest ordained of God for the Christian. This, in brief, was Linnell's belief, and he acted upon it unflinchingly to the day of his death.

His labours in Biblical criticism include still another work. It is entitled 'Burnt-offering not in the Hebrew Bible,' and was published in 1864 by E. Allen, Edgware Road. In this little work of twenty-six pages a revised version is given of the first four chapters of Leviticus. The chief point argued is that the sacrifice described by Moses (in Lev. i. 2, 3) is to be rendered, if we would strictly adhere to the sense of the words of the original, not a 'burnt-offering,' but an 'ascension-sacrifice'; and that the offering was not *burnt*, but *fumed* upon the altar.

Thus the Hebrew text of Lev. i. 2, 3, 9 he renders: 'Speak to the sons of Israel, and say to them, If any man among you bring a gift to Jehovah, ye shall from the cattle of the herd, and from the flock, bring your gifts. If his gift be an ascension-*sacrifice*,* he shall bring from the herd a

---

* Heb. *Gohlah*, that which ascends. 'This word, which is uniformly rendered *burnt-offering* or *burnt-sacrifice*, is from the verb *Gahlah*,

perfect male to the door of the tent of appointment ;
he shall bring it for acceptance before Jehovah.
And he shall put his hand upon the head of the
ascension-*sacrifice*, and it shall be accepted to pro-
pitiate for him. And he shall kill the bull before
Jehovah. . . . And the priests, Aaron's sons, shall
arrange the pieces, the head, and the fat upon the
wood, which is upon the fire, which is upon the
altar . . . and the priest shall fume (*kahtar*) the
whole on the altar, an ascension by fire of an odour
of fragrance to Jehovah it is.'

The Hebrew word *kahtar*, Linnell explains, signi-
fies '*to fume, to raise an odour by heat.*' ·'In the
original of the Book of Leviticus, everything is said
to be fumed until, in the fourth chapter, the sin-
sacrifice is, with wonderful emphasis, ordered to be
burned (*sahraph*) outside the camp. The use of
this word *sahraph*, the proper word for *burn*, for
the first time in connection with the sin-sacrifice, has
a poetic force entirely lost in the Authorized Version,
where everything is said to have been burned previously, which in the original is said to have been
fumed.'

'With what sublime moral emphasis,' exclaims the
writer, 'is the hatefulness of sin expressed by all the
previous sacrifices being fumed only for an odour of
fragrance to Jehovah, incense forming an essential

"to ascend," as Josh. viii. 20, "the smoke of the city *ascended up*";
Prov. xxv. 4, "who hath *ascended* up into heaven." . . *Gohlah* is seen
to have the same radical signification as the verb in Ezek. xl. 26, 31,
34, "There were seven steps *to go up to it.*"'

part of such sacrifices ; and then the *whole bull* for
the *sin-sacrifice* taken outside the camp, and burnt
in a fire with wood : " where the refuse is poured
out *shall he be burned.*"   The two ideas are totally
opposite ; one is the expression of peace, the other
of execration.'

The sacred text, Linnell affirms, does not place
foremost the action of the fire by which the ascension of the soothing odour to Jehovah was caused,
'but the ascension itself,' and 'calls the sacrifice an
ascension by fire of an odour of fragrance to
Jehovah.'   All, he goes on to say in conclusion,
was intended 'to express gratitude, acceptance,
atonement, and pacification ; whereas burning of
the sin-sacrifice was the expression of hatred and
execration against sin.'   Everything was done to
express some important idea, but to confuse those
ideas, as the Authorized Version unavoidably does by
its inaccurate renderings, is a great loss to those who
can only read that version while seeking for exact
knowledge of Divine things.'

It will be confessed that all that the author
advances on this interesting point of criticism, as
on others with which he deals in his various works,
is highly suggestive, and exhibits in a striking light
the original and penetrative genius of the man, one
of whose leading traits appears to have been a
burning passion for the truth.

CHAPTER VIII.

The Painter-poet—Poetry and Art—Beauty of Redhill—Begins to write Poetry — Humour — 'Winter' — 'Spring' — 'The Soul's Struggle '—' The Poet '—' Gradation '—' The Turk,' etc.

It is one of the surprising facts in John Linnell's life that his removal to Redhill should have awakened in him a poetic vein which had not hitherto manifested itself, except in connection with his art. Of the various poetical pieces he wrote, all were composed subsequently to 1851. He had always been a great lover of poetry, and it was one of his doctrines that an artist should constantly reinvigorate his mind by excursions into great domains of thought if desired to avoid the deterioration of his art. He held that the best technical work becomes merely mannered and conventional unless constantly vivified by renewed inspiration and deeper and wider perception. In this respect he had found the reading of the poets of great advantage. Their ideas stirred thought in him ; their inspiration kindled his imagination and kept the poetic perception fresh and clear. But it was only after his settlement at Redhill, and therefore when he was close upon sixty years of age, that the poetic faculty found expression in verse. It seems to have been the direct outcome of his residence amid the beautiful surroundings of his new home. His greater leisure also doubtless had something to do with it ; for now, exempt as he was from the toils of portrait-painting, he could devote more time to reading, and give greater latitude to thought.

One of his earliest poetical compositions was an impromptu, written in a note to his daughter, Mrs. Palmer, a few months after his settlement at Redstone (November, 1851). In the missive in question he writes :

' I only wish you were here. I saw a sunrise this morning that was worth a winter's sojourn in a desert to behold. It was on that slope to the south, where we are planting an orchard.'

He gives a pen-and-ink sketch of the view as he saw it from this southern slope, subscribing it : ' 7 a.m., looking S.-E.' Then follow the verses.

> ' Come with me to the southern slope
>   And enjoy the rising sun ;
> Though the north is chill,
> On this side the hill
>   The cold has scarce begun.

> ' 'Tis late in the year I know full well,
> And reminded I am by that sounding knell
> Of the falling leaf which the tale does tell,
> That we who on this earth do dwell
> Must fall like the leaf that just now fell.

> ' But when I look at the pushing buds,
> Adorning each branch with shining studs,
> I feel the hope of future joy,
> Of pleasures pure without alloy.

' So come with me to the southern slope,
And enjoy a scene so full of hope,
And here you shall feel the autumn sun,
  Though his rising is late
And his course soon run.

' The trees are decked in gayest attire,
And in evening sunshine seem on fire,
Though scantily clad like a lady full drest,
  They show their bare arms
In their richest vest.'

Some of his verses appeared in *The Bouquet*, signed with his floral pen-name, ' Larkspur.' In sending his first verses to the editress, he wrote :

' Redhill,
  '*June*, 1853.

' DEAR THISTLE,

' I send you my feeble effort as a contribution to *The Bouquet*, trusting that you will put it into the fire, or into the *B.*, as you please. If you think either of the attempts worth insertion, I shall make the same request to you that a working man made to the editor of a newspaper, to whom he sent a letter, viz., "to mend the spelling for me, and put in the stops."

' Yours truly,
  ' LARKSPUR.'

The following verses, addressed ' To the Young Ladies, Projectors of *The Bouquet*,' appeared with the letter :

' Children, whose aspirations pure
  Are told in such delightful measures,
  Giving me far greater pleasures
Than from sense I can procure,—

'Will you grant a boon to me,
    To let me join your youthful band?
    Though I am old, my heart and hand
Are ever with simplicity.

'The difference is not great between
    Us children of the dust ;
I in my second childhood am,
    And you are in your first.

'Such sweet fraternity does childhood make,
'Tis wisdom, highest wisdom to partake
Of the similitude, and thus to bear
That image which alone can heavenly glory share.

'Oh, let us seek with fervour to possess
All those rare qualities, that spiritual dress,
Taught us by all that God doth richly place
In childhood's precious image, full of heavenly grace.

'The guileless spirit that is childhood's own,
    In lovely children found, with love that fain
Would have all happy and, without a moan,
    Would be the slave of all to save but one from pain.

'And if we such became—we ought, we know—
Then should we still for ever younger grow,
Nor care to find this thread of life outspun :
Once children of our God, our life is but begun.'

The humble fruits of the artist's poetic vein
may be broadly classed under the three heads of
Humorous, Descriptive, and Religious. That he
was possessed of a strong sense of humour will
have been perceived ere this. The wonder is that
it did not show itself to a greater degree in his art.
It is the more surprising because in one or two
minor things that he executed the humour is
distinct and of a very refined quality. This is
notably the case as regards four drawings that he
did for a little book of 'Nursery Rhymes,' by Felix
Sommerby (Mr., afterwards Sir, Henry Cole, the

originator of the South Kensington Museum), which contained illustrations, among others, by Mr. Redgrave and Mr. Horsley, the Academicians. Linnell's sketches are unquestionably the most humorous in the book, and call to mind some of the best hands at this sort of illustration.

The following, entitled ' An Imitation of H. W. Longfellow, by a Short-fellow,' is a parody of lines seventy to eighty in the first part of ' Evangeline,' and is based on an incident which occurred at Redstone :

' By a roadside that leadeth to somewhere, in England so famous for learning,

Standeth a labourer's cottage, that once had ten steps to its porch-door ;

But now will those steps be in vain sought, by any who once stumbled up them,

For all have been taken away, and flowers are there blooming fragrant ;

Pity that such desire of change did ever come into the hearts of

The dwellers in that pleasant cot, whose children might yet have been with them.

List, ye admirers of routine, how dangerous a little of that is ;

Ye who think that minds can be dealt with as if they were clockwork.

From this cottage went every morning two urchins sent forth by their parents,

With satchel and books rather dog's-eared, and, what they liked better, their dinner.

To the school of the parish priest they went, their lessons to say like a parrot.

In the evening home they came, without being any the wiser.

Cleaner were they on a Sunday morn, with best coat and hat on ;

As down the hill they toddled to church, the bell going ding-don̥,

Marring the holy quiet with sounds like butchers' rough music,

When round a house with cleavers and bones they scatter dismay on its inmates.

More pleasant in woodlands the nightingale's voice, or far-sounding cuckoo,

With blackbirds and thrushes that throng thereabouts in the spring-
time,
Though mostly in showery weather, foretold by the braying of
donkeys.
A sullen demureness sat on the face of each of these urchins,
For they were oppressed with learning by rote and vain repetitions,
Always on one note of their voice, and that rather alto,
To say they believed what they didn't, and thus to tell stories.
To the question, " What is your name ?" they oft had to answer,
And " What did godfathers and mothers do for you when christened,"
And so on, and so on, repeating without variations,
Which made these poor ignorant urchins such creatures of habit,
They only could go in routine, in a track they'd been used to,
And thus they became one day so completely bewildered,
As home they returned from school, and found not the ten steps,
Because in the morning soon after they left their own dwelling
Those steps were removed and a roundabout way to the door made,
Which bothered them so that they could not believe they at home
were ;
But further went looking for ten steps, from habit, like question and
answer ;
And so wandered on until no one can tell where they are or about
them ;
But every day, just at school-time, their voices are heard in the
distance
Repeating their names and who gave them, and why they were
christened, when seeing
By reason of their being babies, they nothing could know of the
matter,
But godfathers promised all for them, how they should renounce
when they grew up
The devil and all pomps and vain things, and so through the whole
Catechism ;
And then they say, " Let us go home now ; we know the way up by
the ten steps."
And small feet are heard to pass close by the spot where the steps
stood aforetime,
But never those urchins were seen more, those children of rigmarole
custom.'

The next piece, entitled ' On seeing Turner's
Picture of Ulysses deriding Polypheme,' is in a
different vein :

‘ When Ulysses had put out old Polypheme's eye,
Who had eaten so many of his men, and him, too, very nigh,
    He left him sprawling,
    Roaring and bawling,
Which roused his friends who lived hard by.
    And as they saw him lie,
    They asked him what 'twas all about,
    He made such a confounded rout :
        Says he, " It's all my eye."

‘ Ulysses then gave Pol the slip,
And hied him to his ship,
    And on the prow he stood,
    In his hand the burning wood,
And though he was so wise, and was not very young,
Like many other folks he could not hold his tongue.

‘ And to revenge him for his losses by the giant's cruel maw,
He, in addition to his black-eye, gave him some of his jaw.
    So standing on his vessel's prow,
        He lustily did cry out,
    " You bloodthirsty villain, here am I,
        And there you go with your eye out." ’

Some specimens have already been given in which
the artist's love of Nature finds fitting expression.
The following, entitled ‘ Winter ’ and ‘ Spring,’ may
be added thereto :

‘WINTER.

‘ Is it only when the fields are green,
    And the flowers begin to show,
That the beauty of this earth is seen ?
        Oh no !

‘ Is it only when the ploughman ploughs,
    And the sower begins to sow,
And the maid in the meadow milks her cows ?
        Oh no !

‘ Is the beauty only then perceived
When the forest trees are fully leaved,
Or the ripened corn is reaped and sheaved ?
        Oh no ! Oh no !

' For beautiful as fields so green,
   Or flowers in spring, when first they're seen,
   When ploughman ploughs and sower sows,
   And maiden in meadow milks her cows,
   And trees full-leaved, and corn just sheaved,
   Is the sun on the hills 'mid the winter chills
   Shining upon the snow.'

'SPRING.

' The north-east wind has ceased,
   The bitter freezing sky relents ;
   Clouds from the west, a lovely band, arise,
   And showers fall sweetly o'er the awakened earth,
   Roused from its frosty winter's dreary sleep.
   Its snowy covering softer than fleece of lambs,
   Which soon shall gambol on its grassy floor,
   In Nature's wardrobe now is laid.
   Balmy winds breathe soft, and sunny gleams,
   With shadows of the quickly-passing clouds,
   Reveal the distant woods and hills,
   And every graceful turn of the far-winding stream.
   Nature is at her toilette,
   And soon will show herself decked out so fair, .
   That all her favourite children will with rapture gaze,
   When she comes smiling in her robe of May,
   With flowers bespangled and with odours sweet,
   Her feathered choristers attending in her train,
   Chanting the praises of her mighty sire.'

The chief characteristic of the poetry which I
have designated religious, and some specimens of
which I give, is that it is bristling with thought,
and with the kind of thought peculiar to Linnell's
religious views. Perhaps ' The Soul's Struggle '
is too theological to suit the tastes of most readers,
but no one can deny to it great vigour, and not
unfrequently rare felicity of expression.   The same
objection will not apply to ' The Poet ' and
' Gradation,' both of which give utterance to a

deep thought, aptly and beautifully expressed. Of
'The Turk' nothing need be said, save that it gives
a measure of the man's character from another point
of view.

'THE SOUL'S STRUGGLE.

'Shall siren melodies seduce our hearts
And serpent fascinations steal our sympathies,
When superstition in poetic garb salutes,
Chanting her bribes and threats to lure us to her sway?
What if the measure chimes, and in the verse are woven
Words of love, and purity, and truth—
Unholily united to the poisonous false,
Like beauteous innocence betrayed by force and craft—
To wed deformity and vice?
Shall we, because she sings of angels, saints, and heaven,
Be led unwarily by her to hell?
Oh, how can they escape that condemnation,
Who, like the Pharisees of old, offspring of vipers,
Always resist the Holy Spirit, and make void
The Word of God by their inventions?
How can any, fallen in their pit, be saved,
If not snatched like brands from the consuming fire
Of lust and passion fierce, most craftily concealed
Behind a seeming sweet serenity?
No sultry stillness, prelude to earth's throes,
To hurricanes and storms,
More certainly portends the evils we should flee,
Than that same mimicry of peace and holiness,
Which ever is with aspect of devotion seen,
Pretending to communion with the God of truth,
Whose word it sets at naught, to whom it gives the lie.

'Is it not prophesied in Holy Writ,
And by the Spirit there expressly said,
That in the latter times some from the faith will turn,
Apostatizing, led by seducing spirits, and by demons taught
In all hypocrisy and lies, with conscience seared,
Prohibiting to marry, and forbidding meats which God created
That the faithful, who the truth well know,
May take the same with thanks?
And are not these the times foretold, even this present age,
When convents rise, prisons for the weaker sex seduced,

With monasteries and other fortresses of crime ;
Where the seducers sit, and where in secret they concoct
Their evil charms, distil their poisons, forge their fetters
Both for body and for mind,
Their instruments for torture and for death ;
Where they prohibit marriage—ordinance of God—
And abstinence from meats command ;
And even deny all access to the bread of life—
That heavenly manna sent by God—
Even his precious Word,
Able through faith to save the soul :
This they keep back, and in its place
Force all entangled in their snares
To fill themselves with a most poisonous counterfeit
Of what the soul most needs to satisfy and guide
Its yearnings after immortality.
How great, then, is that wickedness that starves the soul—
Withholding that which to man's life
More needful is than bread !
For it is written, " Not on bread alone shall man exist,
But upon every word proceeding from the mouth of God."
Well may the crafty foe that word withhold,
Seeing it is the weapon he most fears—
Chief of that perfect panoply of heaven
Provided for the soldier of the risen Christ—
Armour complete, that both detects the foe
And shields from his assaults.
Secure in this against the devil's wiles he stands,
His loins girt round with precious truth ;
And on his breast the righteousness of God,
His feet shod firmly with the tidings of that peace
Which everything surpasses for the good of man ;
The shield of faith quenching all fiery darts,
Salvation for a helmet, and the Spirit's sword
The Word of God, with living energy replete,
And sharp to pierce to the dividing of both soul and spirit,
Even to the marrow of all being.
Truly not fleshly are those weapons rare,
But powerful through God to level with the dust
The strongest holds and citadels of evil,
With everything that riseth up against
The knowledge of His glorious truth.

' Nor is the struggle against flesh and blood,
But against chiefs, authorities, and worldly powers

Of that dread darkness now o'er all the earth
That spiritual wickedness usurping heavenly places—
This, the direful mystery of evil,
Already working with the energy of Satan
In seeming miracles and lying wonders,
In all unrighteousness deceiving those
Who perish rather than accept the truth that saves.
But thanks to God—whose thoughts and ways
Are as the heavens to earth, higher than thoughts of man—
His promise has been given, that as the rain
Descending from the heavens returneth not
Until the earth, satiate with refreshing streams,
Breaks forth in praise,
Speaking from the abundance of its heart in buds and fruits—
Giving, as if with joy and gratitude,
Seed to the sower, and to the eater bread—
Even so the Word proceeding from his mouth
Shall not return unfruitful or devoid of good,
But must accomplish all those purposes of grace
Whereto he sent it forth.'

'THE POET.

' Poet, thou canst not find
  Rest for thy troubled mind,
  Nor for thy dearest longings for eternal fame
  A settled ground of hope, or even a name,
  To last beyond the present age,
  By looking on that page
  Which thou call'st Nature.   No, not there :
  Not all those beauties, though so rich and fair,
  Will e'er reveal to thee that longed-for goal,
  Which in the yearnings of thy soul
  Thou fondly didst expect to know and see,
  And thereby reach thy aim and glory win to thee.
  No ; it is written, " As the fading flower,
  So is man's glory ;" but for one short hour,
  And, like the grass that withers in the field,
  No lasting good will man's exertions yield,
  If but on Nature based, or works of man.
  Only in that beyond all Nature's scan,
  In God's own written Word, the key to Nature's page,
  Can e'er be found the life beyond the age ;
  There, only there, can ever be discerned
  That gift of grace which never can be earned,

That life which all those ardent longings meant,
And to which all thy deepest thoughts intent
Do tend, didst thou but know and feel
What to thy peace belongs, and what the seal
Of that inheritance which those shall share
Who Christ confess on earth, and dare
Despise the Cross,
When earth and heaven—all shall pass away,
And Christ shall reign and all their worship pay.

'GRADATION.

' Not every stormy wind that blows
　　Blows always at its worst,
Nor every ocean wave that flows
　　With equal rage doth burst ;
But stays, as if to gather force,
　　Renew exhausted power,
Relaxing in its onward course,
　　Till, at its own right hour,
In renovated impulses of strength,
It works its mission to its fullest length.
Claim not, then, of man that he should do
Always like well in every effort new,
For he may not expect, whene'er he will,
His utmost to display of might or skill.

' In all the storms that rave
　　Upon the ocean vast,
There's an emphatic wave,
　　A climax of the blast.
Through Nature's wrath,
　　Through Nature's sadness,
There's a method in its madness ;
And as in gentler moods there's music still
From graduated force, by the Creator's will,
All Nature to th' observance of this law doth call,
And we must e'en obey the heavenly rule or fall.'

'MAN'S DEPENDENCE.

' Is there in man aught good or great ?
　　Then God has placed it there,
To his own glory ultimate,
　　But now for man to share.

'Remember, thou, that not in vain
    Thy efforts will be made
To win, by patient toil and pain,
    The crown that ne'er will fade.'

'TO BE PUT UP IN ALL PLACES OF WORSHIP.

'Let no one sing who in his heart
    No melody doth make,
Nor name the name of Jesus Lord,
    Unless he doth forsake
All evil ways, all idols vain,
    Hypocrisy and pride,
Renouncing all unrighteous gain,
    For sake of Christ who died.'

'THE TURK.*

'The work of peace is done,
    After the piece of work
Which we have had, through snow and sun,
    All for the sake of the Turk.

'O Turk! O Turk! you deserve our care,
    For after all has been said
Of your being infidel, I will declare
    That you by most truth are led.

'More than most states who have the name
    Of Christian falsely given,
Worshipping idols to their shame,
    And lying before high heaven.

'Thou Turk, together with the Jew,
    Hast kept that one great truth,
That "God is one" to open view,
    And taught it to thy youth.

'By Turk and Jew to the Christian world
The name of infidel may back be hurled.

'For they have sold that precious truth,
    Through lust of power and gain,
And every holy precept broke
    Their idols to maintain.'

* Written at the close of the Crimean War.

I have deemed it necessary to give these poetical pieces, in order the more fully to carry out the aim with which I started, namely, to show the man exactly as he was. That some of them are not poetry in the true sense, no one will deny ; but they none the less mirror the artist's soul, and that is the foremost object of this Life.

CHAPTER IX.

Character—Early Habits—Rest and Work—Business Principles—
Ready-money Payments—Avoidance of Law—Thrift—Freedom
of Speech—Fox-hunting—Early Rising—Raising Prices—Views
on Catholicism—Letters to his Son and to Count Guicciardini.

LINNELL presents so many strong and individual
traits of character that it will not be amiss to point
out some of his more striking peculiarities. Nearly
everyone who has heard of him has been made
acquainted with his thrifty habits, and, indeed, in
this respect he was one in ten thousand. As we
have seen, at the age of twenty-five, when he
married, he had £500 in the funds, and the sum
was ever afterwards being added to, and never
diminished, to the day of his death.

He states in his 'Autobiography' that he early
adopted such habits as were best calculated to save
time and worry. Those habits were of the simplest.
He wasted no time in frivolous amusements, his
very relaxations consisting of what would be called
by others hard work. But when he had worked
enough he gave up, and did not force himself to
continue his labours when he was tired. Hence it
arose that he was enabled to do so much work of a

uniformly good quality. He gives some of the results of his experience in this respect in a letter to his son William while at Paris. It belongs to a date some years in advance of the period we have reached.

'Just received yours of the 17th. I am surprised to find you measuring your powers of progress in your work by James. You have plenty of time, if you could only remember not to " Billy-Dixonize " over it and judge of your work with a tired brain. The small picture for F—— should not hinder the large one, as it could be used as a means of getting a fresh eye. The time that is generally lost is through going on when you should leave off, and painting too soon after dinner, and in a deficient light. Now, only be alive in these matters, and you will succeed, I doubt not. . . .

'The house had better be deferred till you are here, as the consideration now would hinder your work, and that is the one point to secure. I think I gave your address to ——, but will do so again soon. James is quite right, I think, to give up the large picture, as he has one of his best of sufficient size, " Wales." I expect to have three long " kit-cats," etc.

'Your Π.'*

Three of the artist's sons were now successful painters, and in a way friendly competitors with their

---

* It should be explained that in writing to members of his family the artist frequently signed himself Π, or Πρεσβυτερος (Presbuteros), signifying ' elder.'

father for public favour. James began to exhibit in the Royal Academy in 1850, his brother William in 1852, and Thomas, the youngest, a few years later.

When at Porchester Terrace, Linnell had a billiard-table in his studio, and frequently when he had a sitter he would break off work and propose a game, though on no account would he play for money, or allow others to do so in his house. By this means he rested both himself and his subject, and was enabled to get two sittings in the place of one. At the same time he obtained a needed bit of exercise.

He showed similar business tact and diplomatic ability in most of his dealings. Thus, when he built his house in Bayswater, he made agreements with all the firms who supplied the materials, and with the master-builder also, that they should take part-payment—half, two-thirds, or whatever it might be —in pictures or portraits. By this means he was enabled very considerably to reduce his expenditure upon the house.

Another habit which he early adopted, and thereby saved himself much time, inconvenience and annoy-ance, as anyone who has not done the same will admit, was that of paying for everything in ready money. Nor was he to the last above doing a bit of 'haggling' with a tradesman in order to secure a bargain. Then he always avoided going to law, considering it better to suffer than to fall into the lawyer's hands. His endeavour was ever to keep himself free and unembarrassed, so that there should be the least possible interference with work. Thus, on one occasion in his younger days, when he was drawn for the militia, he preferred to pay a substitute to wasting his time soldiering himself.

His saving of money by superintending the education of his children himself in place of sending them to school has already been referred to. Perhaps there never was a man of means whose school-bill for his children came to so little as his.

Many stories are current implying that Linnell's thriftiness verged upon downright meanness; as, for instance, that on one occasion when he received £1,000 for a picture, he demanded the price of the case in which it was packed, and so on. But there is no foundation whatever for these stories. Linnell undoubtedly drove close bargains; he kept a tight hold of his money, too, but he stinted no expenditure that was for the good of those about him, and in many cases he acted with rare generosity, as, for example, in his dealings with his friend Blake.

On one occasion when a gipsy woman was taken in the pains of labour on a plot of land—a favourite spot for gipsy encampments—in the lane near his house, he sent his own doctor to attend to her, afterwards paying his bill, and in other ways saw that the poor woman did not want.

On another occasion he gave a substantial amount to the National Life-boat Fund. But he was no believer in indiscriminate charity, and he acted up to his conviction.

As in the case of most men of his strong character,

the defects of his qualities were very pronounced, and they became more so as he grew older. He spoke his opinion with great freedom, and naturally sometimes offended by so doing. He never spared those whose views were opposed to his own, nor allowed any latitude to what he considered wrong, even though the matter were of comparatively minor importance. Thus, he was opposed to the decoration of churches on festive occasions, and he would not allow holly to be gathered on his grounds for that purpose. He held it to be a matter of allegiance to the truth not to be a party to any such observance. Once he was asked by a Redhill churchwarden for a gift of evergreens for the church. Linnell refused, and the circumstance led to an exchange of letters between the artist and the churchwarden. The artist regarded the matter as so essentially one of principle that, *more suo*, he threw his opinion on the subject into the following aphoristic form :

'An answer to the churchwarden's request for cuttings of holly and ivy to decorate or ornament the human building of dead stones, called a church, but which name only properly belongs to God's building of living stones, which he alone can ornament with the graces of his Spirit :

'The true ornaments of a church are the graces of the Spirit,
Ornaments that flesh does not inherit,
Ornaments to be had by the Church through the Divine lessons
    taught her,
Ornaments not communicable to bricks and mortar.
        Alas ! alas ! how great the folly,
        To substitute for grace ivy and holly !

December 16, 1868.'

Another of Linnell's pet aversions, though of a more secular character, was his dislike of fox-hunting. He was so determined in his opposition that he was always up in arms when the hunt threatened to trespass on his estate. Once reynard took refuge in a disused pit near the house, and the hunters wanted to dislodge him, but the artist refused to allow them to do so. He declared that they should not touch the poor fox if they gave him £50, and they did not.

On another occasion a stag, which was being followed by the hounds, took refuge in his grounds, and finding the house-door open, entered the hall. One of the artist's daughters immediately shut the door to keep out the hounds. Linnell at first refused to let the huntsmen touch the poor creature ; but as it was not a very safe guest to have in a house, they were permitted to secure it and take it away on the Master of the Hounds agreeing to pay the damage the hunt had done by trampling over the cultivated ground and breaking some glass.

More than once when the fox-hunters wanted to cross his grounds the artist got together everybody about the place capable of bearing arms, put rakes, hoes, and such-like weapons into their hands, and then bade the red-coated huntsmen 'come on if they dare.' All this, of course, was only for show : a more peaceful man than John Linnell never lived.

At times he manifested a brusqueness which gave those who came in contact with him an unfavourable idea of his character, and one which was not borne out by subsequent acquaintance.   He had an objection to taking cheques in payment for his pictures, and would not accept them from any but known and tried customers.   Once a friend took a gentleman with him to see Linnell's pictures.   The stranger was so pleased with a landscape he saw that he decided to buy it and carry it away there and then, offering to write a cheque for it at once.   But the artist replied, ' No ; bring me notes or gold, and you shall have the pictures, but not before,' greatly, of course, to the would-be purchaser's amazement.

Subsequently the gentleman met one of the artist's sons, whom he at once recognised by his likeness to his father.   He told him the circumstance of the cheque, saying : ' I never had such a facer in my life, my cheque always having been held good for any amount ; but I took it in good part, setting his manner down as one of the oddities of genius.'

Linnell always paid with gold or notes himself, never keeping a banking account, but investing all his money in the funds, except what he needed for current expenses.

He was always an early riser, invariably lighting his own fire, and often getting to work before others were up.   He was never one to require others to do for him what he could do for himself, in this being true to his democratic principles ; and this habit of lighting his own fire in the winter time he continued almost to the very last, until, in fact, he was forbidden by his physician to do so any more.

Linnell probably acquired his shrewd business

habits from his father, who, having once failed, was ever afterwards careful to make no bad debts, and to keep strictly within his income. From him he learned the beauty of cash payments, and the wisdom of maintaining a watchful observation on the doings of the business world.

Busy as he always was, he never failed to have an eye to the fluctuations of the market, and to the aspect of affairs generally ; and whenever he perceived a chance of benefit for himself he was quick to take advantage of it. If business generally was brisk and prices improving, he raised the price of his pictures. He has expressed his views in this respect in some of his pithy and humorous verses, and I cannot do better than quote them, as showing his particular point of view better than anyone else could put them :

> "'Tis a fact I avow,
> Which I'm sure you'll allow,
> And which no one could dare to deny,
> Tnat in war or in peace
> We always increase
> And exceedingly multiply.

> ' Whether in China or in Japan,
> We blow up the natives as well as we can
> Or lick the Russian bear into shape,
> Till stopped by the coils of home red-tape ;
> And then o'er the sea,
> Where they're trying to free
> And emancipate the nigger,
> They've guns in store
> Of the greatest bore,
> And they're always getting bigger.

> ' So to keep on a level
> With every fast devil,

I must raise my prices
    At every crisis,
Taking care all the time to be civil.
    Crying, " Double or quits,"
    Though you go into fits,
    Or your heart should go pit-pat
    For every " Kitcat."

' You've only to pay,
And you have your own way :
    Then come let us try,
    I sell and you buy,
Any fine day.'

His prejudices were of the strongest. Amongst
them was a deep-rooted dislike of the Roman
Catholic Church, out of which he could not be made
to believe that any good whatever could come. This
was based upon his belief—which he held so firmly
—in the one priesthood of Christ, any other priest
between God and man being non-existent. But if
he held the Romanists in keenest detestation, he
had a positive contempt for the Ritualists—those
' hypocritical imitators of the Roman system of falsehood ' — and treated them often with but scant
courtesy, as in the following lines, which he entitles
' Pope-Awry ':

' Ye mongrel monks, ye snobs of Rome,
Who in old England, happy home
    Of all true-hearted men,
Do play your superstitious pranks,
Using our liberty with little thanks,
    But granting none again,—

' Counterfeits ye are, for all ye say ;
Ye are not even genuine papists for a day.
    The popery ye practise ye deny,
And play so awkwardly the trick,
Ye make us laugh or make us sick,
    And all ye do is naught but Pope-awry.'

On one occasion this feeling against the Catholics
caused Linnell to refuse to meet Cardinal Wiseman.
The incident arose out of his acquaintance with the
Dowager Lady Mostyn, who for some years was a
near neighbour, living in a house near Redhill
Common, and who was a frequent visitor at Redstone.   She was a Catholic, and she and the artist
had many arguments on religious questions.   But
being no match for the latter in the discussion of
these subjects, Lady Mostyn suggested that he
should have a talk with Cardinal Wiseman, who, she
said, would be able to explain matters of doctrine
and faith better than she could.   For this purpose
she proposed that she should take an invitation to
the Cardinal to call and see Linnell's pictures.   But
the artist would not consent ; he felt that he should
be no match for the erudite prelate in the subtleties of
dialectics, and so the two never met.   He and Lady
Mostyn, however, continued their discussions whenever they met ; sometimes, indeed, Linnell carried
his into the region of letters, as will be seen from
the following epistle, which is a good specimen of
the fearless—and one might add ' gloveless '—way
in which he dealt with the doctrines of Catholicism :

' Dear Lady Mostyn,

        ' Believe me, I shall be glad to find that you
are able and willing to pay me a visit, and hope you
will do so whenever you please. You shall be at
liberty also to say what you please to me ; but I
shall, without asking your permission, tell you some

truths you are prevented from hearing elsewhere—
prevented by the ignorance of the truth, or want of
zeal for it, in those you associate with—prevented
also by your own want of allegiance to the holy
fountain of truth and your deference to the authority
of men whose motives for keeping you in ignorance
of the truth ought to be, and would be evident, to
you if you did not willingly yield your conscience,
faith, and understanding to them, instead of to God,
whose precious Word you have in your hand, and
which you reject by substituting human inventions
scarcely possible to speak of without profanity. Why,
the words in your last note, " Our Blessed Mother,"
read to me like the commencement of a parody on
the Lord's prayer, which He gave as a model of
that brevity so becoming to us children of an omnis-
cient Father, but which said model is generally set
at naught. Yes, Lady Mostyn, you are not, and
your friends called Catholics are not, the only people
who set at naught God's wisdom on this point. The
Divine Word says (Eccl. v. 2), " God is in heaven
and thou upon earth, therefore let thy words be
few." And how is this regarded ? Is not the ex-
cess of disobedience rewarded as the greatest virtue,
and those who repeat certain forms of prayer
the greatest number of times reckoned the best,
though the Lord Jesus said, " Use not vain repetitions "? All this proceeds from the want of conscience towards God. But my conscience towards
him requires of me that I should tell you plainly
this one thing, that "at the time when you ought to .

be teachers you need to be taught the first rudiments
of God's Word" (Heb. v. 12). If, however, you
desire to be taught, let the holy Apostles teach you.
Read their inspired teachings, and give no heed to
anything that is contrary thereto, and you will soon
find that you are taught of God. As to the Mortara
case, as it will in all probability be publicly handled,
I need say only that you have not produced any
case like it amongst Protestants. What you can
mean by St. Malachi and his prophecy of the Pope
is beyond my utmost guess. Pray tell me the
chapter and verse. Surely you cannot appropriate
a prophecy of the Messiah to the Pope. I fear,
however, this must be the case.

' Yours, etc.,

' JOHN LINNELL.'

When the artist's son William went (in the
beginning of October, 1861) to Italy to study, he
was troubled all the time with the fear lest he should
be beguiled into joining the Church of Rome, and
was not satisfied until he had finally prevailed upon
him to quit Italy. But at this time he was getting
very old ; combined, too, with his own anxiety, there
was the failing health of his wife, and her natural
desire to see her son again before she died, to aug-
ment his wish for his son's return.

Linnell was not what would be called a good
letter-writer. He did not carry on much correspondence, and what he did was mostly of a business
nature. But his letters were always characteristic,

and some of those received by the dealers with whom he chiefly dealt, peculiarly so. In not a few of these he made sketches of the pictures which were the occasion of his writing. Many of his letters to Messrs. Agnew and Son, the dealers, were in this respect very striking.

His letters to members of his own family, however, best show the character of the man, because they show the whole man. In nothing, perhaps, does a person mirror himself so fully and so truly as in his letters, and this is especially true of Linnell, who was always perfectly natural, and never made use of any sort of artifice in order to show off or to appear to be other than what he really was.

On October 30, 1861, he wrote as follows to his son :

'DEAR WILLIAM,

'We are glad to hear from you, and hope you will write for your mother's sake as often as you can. Your letters are meat and drink to her, and a glass of wine to me. I hope, however, you may be able to add some literal wine to the treat before you leave Italy. I will pay for all letters, so do not spare in number on account of expense. We have had one letter on your arrival in France, one from Paris, one from Marseilles, one from Nice, and now one from Pisa.

'I am glad you took the road by the coast, and have no doubt but you have the best of it. The

weather here, however, is very fine, and the foliage
is only just beginning to change colour. Our wood
this morning was looking so fine I wondered if you
were likely to see anything better. I hope you
will not let such things pass without some mem-
oranda, however slight. Words will not suffice :
all the young lady travellers can supply plenty of
the finest, new and old. No day without a line.
Everything here is much the same. . . . A——
has paid for my drawings, so there is cash at home
if you want to buy a palazzo or a prize bull at the
cattle show at Florence. You had better save your
money, though, *if you can*, and go softly. Remember Italy is volcanic, and there are strange
rumbling noises heard even here.

'Be wise, and look at the invisible as well as the
visible.

'I enclose you extract of *Times*—a sufficient dose.
I wish you could see the paper, but you have
sufficient in my extract to get at the rest.

'Remember me to Count Guicciardini, and tell
him I shall esteem it a great favour if he will put
you in the way to procure some of the best Italian
wine of more than one sort and send me samples
with price in cask and in bottle.

'Write again soon, and tell us if you stay at
Florence long enough to get another letter, or you
can arrange with your friends at Florence to forward
your letters to Rome if you go there. Naples, I
fear, is not safe enough yet. I see by a letter
to-day that an English captain was stopped in the

public street by a man who presented a pistol. The captain threw up the thief's arm and kicked him in the stomach, and only left him because some accomplices came up. You see, therefore, the place is not safe. You should avoid going out alone, especially at night.

'Your mother was horrified at your account of using Child's nightlights for anointing your face, in order to prevent mosquitoes biting you. She says that all those candles are made with arsenic, and you may poison yourself badly. Olive-oil and camphor or without camphor is best.

'Yours,

'J. L. AND Co.'

The Count Guicciardini who is frequently mentioned in this correspondence was one of the Plymouth Brethren, and the leading light of an Italian branch of the sect in Florence. He was a direct descendant of the historian of the same name. The following characteristic epistle is to the Count himself :

To Count Guicciardini.

'Redstone Wood, Redhill,
'Surrey, England,
'*December* 27, 1861.

'DEAR FRIEND,

'Permit me to address you by this title, as it is your friendship that I rely upon to assist me in my endeavours to obtain what it is almost impossible to accomplish without such help. You are in a position to help me to procure some genuine first-class wine, and I understood from my son when he wrote from Florence, that you kindly offered to attend to my solicitations on this subject. And in a letter just arrived from Rome my son advises me to write to you direct, that you may be in no doubt respecting my wishes. I have many reasons for applying to you to assist me to obtain some of the best wine of Italy. First my wife requires such for her health, and that which I got from Madeira is nearly gone, and no more is to be had from that place. I have no hope of obtaining any such from wine merchants here, and, if I could, their price is so exorbitant that I find it out of my reach. I find in wine, as in most other matters, that unless I can get near to the fountain-head, there is little chance of being able to obtain the best. That which I imported from Madeira was Sercial, and I have never tasted any wine so good. It was a wine of body and strength, though pure and delicate in flavour. I name it to you as a guide in your selection of any wine for me. I am told that Marsala is to be had from Italy direct of a very superior quality to what is sold here by the merchants. One quarter cask (about twenty-three gallons) may be sent of the best quality of this wine as a sample; pale wine, if to be had, I find generally best, though I have never seen pale Marsala. But as I am unacquainted with Italian wine, I would gladly leave it to your judgment to order for me what you think best, from the grower, if possible, or as near to that point as convenient, for I fear every step from the grower through the mercantile department.

'I trust that if you should be able to send me two or three small casks of the best wine in the first place as samples of what is to be had, you will at the same time introduce me to the channel from which I can procure more without again troubling you. In the first instance, however, I am compelled to intrude my want upon your attention.

'I am sorry to find that a struggle is requisite to enable one to obtain anything pure and true in this life, and even the Word of life itself is the most adulterated by man ; but, thanks be to God, we have direct access to the Father through the Son, and do not rely upon man in this. What a predicament, however, are those in who rely only on those who make merchandise of their souls !

' Mr. Berger will, I have no doubt, assure you of my ability and readiness to pay for everything forwarded to me in any way directed by the party sending the wine. As to the sort, I can only say as Weber said when he was asked what sort of music he liked best. " I like," said he, "*good music*" *:* so I say I like good wine. Let it be good of the sort, and wine that will keep in this climate, for we drink but little at a time. It is really for stomach's sake more than for appetite that we require it.

'If you should find it practicable to serve me in this matter, I shall not forget your kindness, but be always your obliged servant,

' JOHN LINNELL, SEN.'

The following characteristic letters are to his son :

'We were all glad to get your letter dated October 25, from Olevano. We hope you may realize your harvest some day, though you say you have only just set your hand to the plough. What thou sowest, that shalt thou reap. Your answer to my remarks shows that you have missed my meaning. The qualities I spoke of had nothing to do with a knowledge of Italy, or of the people, but of Nature and Art in general. Many go to the grandest scenery in the world, and they bring home capital information, not so good, however, as photos. I would rather have some good photos of Italian romance—the wildest—wilder than any modern pictures of Italy I have seen. It will be wise of you to get all the photos you can of scenery and figures, such as are only to be seen in Italy. As for the wonderful skies that young ladies talk of, I never expect to see them on canvas. I see them, however, at Redhill, and other things finer than anything brought or sent from Italy yet. . . . I shall not offer any more advice unless asked for as to returning. Mr. and Mrs. Stewart I expect will have found you ere you get this ; they take colours to you, etc. . . .

'Yours,

'Πρεσβυτερος.'

'*November* 30, 1861.

'I have sent a letter to Florence for you merely to say that we shall be glad to hear from

you as soon as you can.   We have not received any
letter from you since yours from Rome with post-
mark November 4, the first and only one from that
city. . . .

'I hope I shall receive some wine from Italy
soon.   Ask Mr. Severn about it.   Perhaps he may
be able to do more than anyone we know.   What I
want is first-rate wine at the growers' price, and not
the dealers' or merchants' prices, and if shipped from
the growers the price should be low.   It is like
buying a picture of the artist instead of the dealer,
as to price, and also as to what is more important,
quality.   The nearer to the source, the better in
everything that is good.   Prompt payment, say
as soon as the wine is received and found all right.
Sample and price to be sent first if possible, or only
a small cask as sample ; but I should like to have
samples of several sorts of the best. . . .

'J. LINNELL, Paterfamilias.'

The Mr. Severn above referred to is the friend
of Keats, whom Mr. W. Linnell met at Rome, as
Mr. and Mrs. Palmer had done years before during
their stay in Italy.

'Redhill,
'*February* 2, 1862.

'Your letter to your mother and others was
received to-day, and we are made both sorry and
glad by the contents : sorry to find that you have
suffered as I suspected (for there was a touch of
fever in your former letter), but glad to find you

are safe through the peril of that dire disease small-pox. I am glad we did not know of your condition before, for it is certain some of us would have suffered more than you who are blessed with courage that enables you to go through the wave which threatens to overwhelm you. Fear is undoubtedly the thing of all others to be afraid of in many cases ; caution, however, is wisdom. I think you run too many risks, one in walking late into the country after sunset. The air is unwholesome here, and fifty-fold worse, I am told, in Italy. Then that is the time for robbery and the stiletto. . . .

'There is room for all of us, but if anyone is to refrain from exhibiting, I can best afford to do it, as my work is nearly done, and if I have time to set my house in order before I sleep, I shall be content. I wish you could see how plain the course is open before you to do well, and even better perhaps than by any other by avoiding all political connection with any academy or corporate body.

'It is better to keep to the εν σωμα και εν πνευμα καθως και εκληθητε εν μια ελπιδε. So far as the exhibition is concerned, I am not likely to be sorry for any hindrances respecting elections, though I suspect the advice given you to keep where you are was with reference to that matter.

'Mr. Cameron, the War Secretary to Mr. Lincoln's Government, U.S., has been sent off as Ambassador to Russia, because he was enthusiastically troublesome for abolition, which the hypocritical Federal Government intend to avoid if possible.   We shall see if God intends the liberation and exodus of the slaves by the U.S. Government being compelled to adopt it as their only safety. It is the common policy of all crafty politicians to send away on some foreign expedition whoever they consider in their way.   However, like Joseph's brethren, what they intend for mischief often turns through the grace of God to the benefit of those meant to be lost.

' I am now most thankful I did not attain to the degrading honour, or rather distinction the wrong way, of A.R.A.   I should not have been at Redhill, or even alive.   Let the men who cannot obtain a living any other way seek and get those worldly distinctions ; but when God has so far blessed our labours as to put us on a level with the best, it is to me ungrateful not to be content and to leave it evident that it is to God we owe our success more than to man.   "*Lest thou shouldst say, I have made Abram rich.*"   Reliance upon God throws us into communion with Him, and gives power to all our efforts.

' Yours,

' J. L.'

' *March* 6, 1862.

'. . . . Either I failed to express what I intended, or you failed to see my meaning as to the R.A. question.   I do not regret your being at Rome ; I only meant to say that, *if* you were right in trying for the election, your being at Rome

might interfere with it. I am more than ever
convinced, however, that you are better as you are
—"even as I." You will not find out what the
cost is until too late ; no one tells the secret of his
own degradation, any more than fagging at public
schools is denounced by the sufferers. Scarcely
any of the men in the Academy are, I fear, awake
to the great argument upon which my conclusions
are based. Then, again, we ought to be contented
with the success granted to us. There is not to us
the excuse that so many have had of want of purchasers of our works—that great object for which
the distinction was at one time, and is now, by
many sought. It was for this chiefly that all the
machinery was set up, and all the time wasted at
meetings of business and ceremony. Glad would
many an R.A. have been, I have no doubt,. could he
have had the constant employment that we have,
free from all bondage arising from the rules and
influence of a sort of monastic order, and free also
as to the choice of our subjects and artistic style—
more free in this last matter than if we were inside.
I have arrived at a point of view from which the
whole subject is to be more clearly seen than at an
earlier period of life, and I have no doubt but that
you will, if you arrive at the same point, see with
me, whether you are in or out. . . .

'J. L.

'It is settled now that I send my large picture of
"Carrying," and James his "Haymakers"—one
each. . . .'

The picture referred to above as 'Carrying' is his 'Carrying Wheat' (39 by 54 inches), exhibited in the Academy in 1862. It was subsequently damaged by fire, and was brought to the painter and repaired in 1874. It shows a harvest-field, with a waggon and horses in the foreground, and men loading wheat. There is a distant view beyond, with the sun setting in a cloudy sky. In 1867 it was sold at Christie's for 1,650 guineas.

'*April* 10, 1862.

'We have just received yours dated April 5, and hasten to reply, though I think I have already said my say upon the one subject which seems uppermost in your mind, and sends it wavering about in an unstable state. I remember suffering the same anxiety, to which I saw no end ; and I had no peace until I made up my mind to give up all endeavour to obtain a distinction, which, though it held some worldly advantages, was fraught with evident and latent mischief. Longfellow's words on this subject are : " Better for them and for the world in their example had they known how to wait. Believe me, the talent of success is nothing more than doing what you can well, and doing well whatever you do without a thought of fame. If it come at all, it will come because it is deserved, not because it is sought after ; and, moreover, there will be no misgivings, no disappointment, no hasty, feverish, exhausting excitement." The struggle has shortened the lives of many of the R.A.'s, and would have shortened mine had I been elected. Far better if one can be content to wait for such results from our labour as God shall please to produce, taking everything as from Him through man's agency. It is only when contented that we can work our best, and to be contented we must feel possessed of real good—the best good—and feel so rich as to be satisfied. We should be rather terrified at the consequences of success, and, as greatness is thrust upon us, the more humble our-selves. It appears to me that all which a man should desire to do is now within your reach by only working contentedly, and waiting for results. . . .

' Yours,

' J. L.'

In June, 1862, the anxious father so far prevailed that his son returned from Rome, remaining in England until January in the following year.

CHAPTER X.

Correspondence respecting a Picture by Giulio Romano—W. M.
Rossetti and Blake's Life—Letters by Mrs. Sarah Austin—Jean
Ingelow—Correspondence with William Henry Hunt—His Death.

LINNELL having, in 1859, learned that there was
a valuable work by Giulio Romano for sale, and
being deeply impressed with the need of having as
many fine specimens of the old Italian masters
available for study as possible, wrote to his friend
George Richmond, representing to him the importance of securing this picture for the National Gallery,
and asking him to exert what influence he could in
the right direction. The following is Mr. Richmond's reply :

'*August* 5, 1859.

'MY DEAR MR. LINNELL,

'The first thing I did on receiving your note
was to enclose it in one to Sir C. Eastlake, stating
that, although I did not myself remember the picture
of Giulio Romano, I took it as a strong recom-
mendation that you did, and was at some pains to
secure its being purchased for the nation. I now
send you Sir Charles's answer, which I received last
night, and am on my way to the National Gallery
to see if the picture is arrived there yet.

'I beg my kindest remembrances to Mrs. Linnell and your whole party, and remain,

'Yours very faithfully,

'GEO. RICHMOND.'

Sir Charles Eastlake's letter was as follows :

'7, Fitzroy Square, W.,
'*August* 4, 1859.

'MY DEAR SIR,

'On my return last night from Cheltenham, after having bought the Giulio Romano, I found your note enclosing Mr. Linnell's. You will now be able to tell him that the picture is secured for the nation.

'There will soon be a change in the arrangements of the pictures when the temporary galleries at South Kensington are used, and I suppose any new acquisition will not be exhibited till the alteration takes place.

'Sincerely yours,

'C. L. EASTLAKE.

'GEO. RICHMOND, ESQ.'

Linnell replied to Mr. Richmond as follows, under date August 6 :

'MY DEAR SIR,

'I return you Sir C. Eastlake's letter, with many thanks both to you and Sir Charles. We are all much gratified to find that a picture so full of beauty and without any alloy is now the property of the nation.

'I hope you will see the picture soon, and then run down here and tell us what you think of it.

'I am, dear sir,

'Yours sincerely,

'J. Linnell, Sen.

'Geo. Richmond, Esq., A.R.A.'

In 1862 some correspondence took place between William Michael Rossetti and Linnell relative to Blake. Rossetti was compiling his catalogue of Blake's works for Gilchrist's Life, and he applied to the artist for information on the subject of his labours, as Allan Cunningham and Gilchrist had done before him. Like them, he received valuable aid; and in one of his letters he refers to 'the minute and useful answers' which he had received to his queries, and which were compiled by the artist's eldest son from the various documents in his father's possession.

One of Rossetti's questions had reference to a story about the origin and inspiration of Blake's dragons, the authority for which appears to have been a Mr. Rivière, of Oxford. According to this veracious witness, Blake at one time did heraldic painting, and derived his information in the department of 'unnatural history' relating to griffins and dragons from coats-of-arms and the like recondite sources. Linnell's answer was as follows:

'Dear Sir,

'Thanks for the information about the Blake story, which I have no doubt is a mistake built upon

a criticism.   I never heard of Mr. Rivière before,
or anyone of that name who knew Blake.   I knew
a little of an artist of that name who was the brother
of Mrs. Bishop, the celebrated singer; but he was
certainly not intimate with Blake, if he knew him
at all.   I hope after this the story will not make its
appearance in the Life, for I can find no one who
believes it.   Mr. S. Palmer has the same wish that
I have for its suppression.   The criticism upon
Blake's dragons would apply just as well to Turner's
for his picture of Jason in the National Gallery,
where the dragon is quite as heraldic in its character
as any of Blake's, and even more so.*   But the fact
is, dragons are rather uncommon.   There are none
in the Zoological Gardens.   They are traditional, and
all have been drawn from the same type, or nearly
so, and hence unavoidable similarity.   Blake, however, has given a sublimity of character to his
dragons and serpents which we look in vain for
elsewhere, and those who could not see the grandeur
of Blake's conceptions were always spiteful in their
criticisms, from a desire to bring that down to their
low level which they could not reach.   I believe it
is in art as in the highest knowledge.   The ψυχικος,
or sensuous man, receiveth not the things of the
spirit; they are foolishness to him, and he is unable
to know them because they are spiritually discerned.
                   ' Yours,
                        ' JOHN LINNELL, SEN.'

* I remember another picture in the National Gallery by Turner
which has a terrific dragon in it, high up on a rock.

Before answering as above, however, Linnell had put the question to Samuel Palmer in the following humorous form :

> ' L. WILL BE OBLIGED TO P.
> TO ANSWER QUESTIONS 2 OR 3.
>
> ' Does he know, or can he guess,
> Not who wrote of the oil mess
> That Blake, he said, made in his printing,
> But who told how (no malice stinting)
> Blake took all his griffs and dragons
> From the coats-of-arms on flagons.
> The Muse is tired, so off she goes
> To rest herself in common prose.
>
> ' Did P. ever before this hear of the story of Blake's herald-painting?
> ' Did P. inwent it or propagate it?
> ' Did P. furnish Mrs. G. with the story?
> ' Does P. know who did, and will he tell?
> ' Blake's reputation demands that this story be tested. The public will be ill-treated if it is not set right.'

It will have been seen from the letter to Rossetti that Samuel Palmer gave as little credit to the story as did Linnell.

It may possibly have been this correspondence—stirring up as it did the foundations of memory—that first gave John Linnell the idea of writing down the autobiographical notes which he commenced in 1863, and from which I have been allowed to draw very largely in this Life.

Another very interesting series of letters, from a well-known personage in her day, claims a few pages at this point. Reference has previously been made to Mrs. Sarah Austin, the authoress, two portraits of whom Linnell had painted twenty years before. It is to these portraits that the earlier letters refer.

The daughter spoken of, for whom she wanted a copy of one of them, was, of course, Lady Duff Gordon. In other respects the letters speak for themselves.

'London,
'*April* 8, 1862.

'Dear Mr. Linnell,

'I don't know if you have still any recollection of one who is hardly to be reckoned among the living, having lost more than half herself. Yet as an old sitter, as well as an old neighbour and admirer, I will urge my claim to be remembered. I have a little request to make to you. Besides the finished portrait, which Mrs. Empson very kindly gave me after her husband's death (and which was the source of infinite pleasure to my dear husband), you made a little sketch of me. This my daughter has always esteemed the most perfect likeness of me in existence, and has always desired either to possess it or to have some true copy of it.

'You probably do not know that we have been for two years and more in the greatest alarm about her, and that she is at this moment at the Cape of Good Hope, whither she was sent as a last resource. God be thanked, it has proved successful, and in six or eight weeks we hope to have her back in renewed health, though still to be watched with infinite care.

'Now, it would give me great satisfaction to be able to gratify her wishes.

'Will you allow me to have a photograph, a lithograph, or any sort of copy of the sketch in question taken? Or are you disposed to part with it?

'My own health is very much broken—sorrow and anxiety have done their work—and before I depart I should like to give my dear child the only likeness of her mother she is fully satisfied with. Her father was entirely satisfied with the other, and continually expressed his pleasure in the possession of it.

'I write to you from London, but my home is Weybridge, where I have often and often wished for you to see some of our beautiful heath and wood scenery. If ever you are inclined to look at it, pray remember that there is an old rambling cottage at which you would be very welcome. I hope all goes well with you and yours.

'Very truly yours,

' Dear Mr. Linnell,

' S. AUSTIN.'

The likeness above referred to is the one from which the portrait of Mrs. Austin on page 297, vol. i., was taken.

Linnell does not appear to have kept copies of his replies to this and the following letters, although of all letters of importance he invariably made and carefully preserved copies. The other letters need no comment.

' Esher,

'*April* 16, 1862.

'DEAR MR. LINNELL,

'Thank you for your compliance with my request. But before I urge it further, I must be

sure that we mean the same thing, which appears to
me questionable. The portrait I mean was certainly
a sketch in oil. I was leaning forward one day,
talking, when you asked me to remain in that
position while you made a sketch of me, which was
done. You had your palette and brush in your
hand. To the best of my recollection, I never sat
for that again. And this is the likeness which my
daughter always preferred to the finished picture,
now in her possession. When this doubt is cleared
up, I shall be happy to avail myself of your proposal
on your own terms; I don't even know what a
"negative" is in any but the grammatical sense.
But I am sure you would make no stipulation that
would be unpleasant to me.* Is the picture at Redhill or in London? I should like much to see it.
If it is in London, nothing is easier; and if at
Redhill, I should be tempted to drive over in my
little pony-chaise and give myself the pleasure of
seeing not only that, but the contents of your studio,
and still more yourself. Your exhibited pictures I
have, of course, seen and admired with all the
world, and have felt a constant interest in your well-
merited success. I am at this moment at Esher
with my dear son-in-law and the children, but after
Monday I shall be at home. Weybridge, Surrey,
is all the address necessary. I gave none in town
because I was there but for a few days. I wish you

---

* Linnell had written Mrs. Austin to the effect that she might have
a photograph of the portrait by paying the expense and allowing him
to retain the negative.

would think seriously of a little visit to Weybridge.
I could show you lovely spots. But I dare say you
know them all.

'Yours, dear Mr. Linnell,
'Very truly,
'SARAH AUSTIN.'

'Weybridge,
'*June* 14.

'DEAR MR. LINNELL,

'I shall be very much obliged by your
sending the photograph (together with all charges,
etc.).

'My dear daughter is on the ocean, and may
arrive in a few days, or, more probably, in three
weeks. All my visitings stand over till this intense
anxiety is at an end. I have to thank you very
much for the remarkable and interesting lines you
sent me. You are very happy in being able to
satisfy yourself so completely that you understand
that wonderful and mysterious book. I feel that I
want more of that inward light which alone can
solve all difficulties.

'Yours very truly,
'S. AUSTIN.

'I am told Joubert's photographs are excellent.
Have you seen any?'

'*June* 17.

'DEAR MR. LINNELL,

'I should be a traitor if I said that photograph is good enough for your picture. I shall be
content with nothing less than the best that can be

done. Since I wrote I have seen several of Joubert's, which are really beautiful. Why not get him to do it? Nevertheless, I am very much obliged to you for the one you have sent me. It only makes me the more sensible of the merits of the picture, which I positively must go to see.

'Thank you for the books; I had no idea you were such a Biblical scholar and critic. I am in no danger of being priest-ridden. My difficulties will never come from that quarter. You say the mystery is told: told, yes; but not explained—at least, not to my poor understanding. But this is no subject for a hasty note, so pray believe me,

'Very truly yours,

'S. AUSTIN.

'What an extremely pretty picture it is! The arrangement is so free and graceful.'

'*August* 20.

'DEAR MR. LINNELL,

'I beg your pardon for so long delaying to answer your inquiry. The truth is, that in the hurry and agitation of my dear daughter's second departure (she starts to-day for the Pyrenees, and then Egypt) I entirely forgot it, which I am sure you will allow for. My son-in-law never had anything to do with the "Duff Gordon Sherry" trade, which, owing to his father's death, passed into other hands when he was a boy. His brother had a share in it for some years, but retired from it some years ago, and has now nothing to do with it. I fear, therefore, I can be of no service to you in the way you mention. I do not even know the names of the present successors to the business.

'Summer is slipping away without affording me one opportunity of realizing my plan of a visit to Redhill. My daughter has spent only one month among us. I only returned last night to Weybridge, where I shall now be stationary for some time. I still do not quite despair of my little journey, but am very uncertain.

'Yours, dear Mr. Linnell,
'Very truly,
'S. AUSTIN.'

'DEAR MR. LINNELL,

'Miss Ronalds was so kind as to send me a very friendly invitation to Redhill, and though I told her I feared I could hardly accept it at present, I am now so strongly tempted that I write to you for the indispensable information· when you are to be found at home. And likewise, whether Miss R. is still inclined and at liberty to have me.

'My project is to drive in my pony-chaise, spend the whole following day at Redhill, and return the third day.

'Your account of railroad speed does not tempt nor profit me, for I am not (thank God) in London, and the way by Guildford supposes being transhipped four times at least.

'As for my dear daughter—alas! since July I have not seen her beloved face.

'After two years of torturing anxiety, I parted from her that she might go to seek health, or at least life, at the Cape.

'I am now daily expecting the letter that is to announce her return—with what feelings, I need not say.

'I am sure Miss Ronalds will be kind enough to write and tell me her plans and yours, and give me exact directions where and how to find her house.

'I am by no means certain of coming. I never am, for, added to the usual precariousness of weather, I have now that of very feeble and uncertain health ; but my wishes are strong.

'Yours, dear Mr. Linnell,

'Very truly,

'S. Austin.'

Another of Linnell's lady friends and correspondents was Miss Jean Ingelow. The friendship appears to have grown out of a mutual appreciation of each other's works. Under date September 24, 1863, Linnell wrote as follows :

'Dear Jean Ingelow,

'Your having expressed a sympathy with my works, and having at the same time sent me a copy of yours, is just one of the pleasantest things that has happened to me for a long time. Believe me, the liberty I have taken in addressing you as an intimate friend arises from a fellowship I cannot help feeling with such thoughts as are expressed in your poems.

I hope that you practise my art as an amateur, for
I find generally that those who do, or at least
endeavour something, know and feel most. And
that you may see that I follow my theory by
practice, I send you one of my endeavours to
express in language what I feel. Lest, however,
you should think I am nothing if not critical, I
promise to show you my studies from nature if
you will favour me with a visit, spending a long day
at Redhill with any companion you may choose to
bring.

' Yours gratefully,
' JOHN LINNELL, SEN.'

Three days later the artist received the following
letter in reply :

' DEAR MR. LINNELL,

'Your note was put into my hands two days
ago, and I am much pleased that you should respond
so kindly to my little offering. I should also much
like to make your personal acquaintance and see
those sketches from which result the pictures that
have so much delighted me. If, therefore, nothing
unforeseen should prevent it, and you do not write
to tell me it would be inconvenient, my brother and
I hope to come and pay you a call on Wednesday
or Thursday in next week.

' I thought your poem very original. Unfortunately, my admiration for your genius is not so
intelligent as I could wish, for I have no technical

knowledge of art. I can feel it intensely, but my pleasure in it is derived chiefly from the love of Nature, not from any power to paint.

'I am yours very sincerely,
'JEAN INGELOW.'

The 'poem' here referred to appears to have been the following, which was appended to the artist's letter as a sort of postscript :

'We hope you will come early,
And if you will stay till the sun is down
And the deep gloom set in,
You shall see the owl fly across the dell,
In a way that will cause your heart to swell,
When he enters the shade
By the thick leaves made,
With well-poised loitering wing.'

Amongst a number of other letters there is one of a later date than the foregoing, which concludes as follows :

'We have been reading the " Life of Blake " with great delight. My brother, who has long admired his works, bought his illustrations to Blair's "Grave" some time ago. You cannot think how pleased I am at the place you hold in it, and how glad I am to discover that the painter whose works I have so admired for years is as kind-hearted as he is great.'

Linnell lived to see most of the artists whose careers began about the same time as his fall off one after another. John Varley had died in 1840, Wilkie in 1841, Haydon in 1846 (by his own hand), and William Collins in 1847. Mulready followed in

1863, and William Henry Hunt in 1864. The death of the latter is rendered particularly interesting in connection with Linnell from the fact that shortly before his death he recalled his former fellow-student to mind, and opened a brief correspondence with him after years of silence.

In 1858 Wethered the dealer had taken Hunt a quince which Linnell had plucked for him from the garden at Redstone. From this Hunt executed a drawing, with grapes, etc. This Wethered bought, and afterwards showed it to Linnell, who, in exchange for it, gave him a sketch of his own. No correspondence, however, at that time passed between the former fellow-students, Wethered, who was doing business with both, being the medium of communication.

Then, after a further silence of a year or two, Linnell received the following letter from Hunt :

'62, Stanhope Street,
'Hampstead Road, N.W.,
'*November* 16, 1863.

'FRIEND LINNELL,

'I herewith send you a *carte de visite* of myself at a venture, if you care to have the same. I only know that I should prize one of yourself if you will grant me the favour of one. I should like those of your sons.

'How long ago is it since I met you at the Royal Academy Exhibition ? I did not think how different we look to what we did when I had the advantage of sketching with you opposite Millbank.

What fine things you would have made in the old town in France, and of the fishermen and boats, if you had gone over the water!

' I hear of you sometimes through Wethered, and I dare say he has told you how lame I am all through falling off some four or five steps. I fear it's quite out of the question my ever seeing your beautiful place. Wethered tells me you have said you would like to see me there. I should so much like to see you, should you ever be able to favour me with a call.

' From yours truly,

' W. HUNT.

'J. LINNELL, ESQ.'

To this letter Linnell replied as follows :

'Redhill,
' *November* 17, 1863.

' MY DEAR FRIEND WILLIAM HUNT,

' Your sincere, kind, friendly epistle, received this morning, gave me great pleasure, as it not only contained the photo of your outward man, but an intimation of the workings of your inner self. You refer to old times and associations which are interesting and good to chew the cud of sometimes ; but, alas ! there is so much of melancholy in all that has passed away that it is better to press on towards a glorious future, " forgetting the things behind." This future is within your reach, only act in this matter as you have done successfully in your art—go to the fountain-head—study there. As you have studied and faithfully copied Nature, the work of God, now study God himself. Be his disciple, and beware of all ecclesiastical help ; beware of the Pharisees and their counterfeit humility.

'Your wish to see me is gratifying every way, and I shall make a point of paying you a visit, not, however, to tease you, but to see you and your work.

' I enclose photos of myself—one for you and one for Mr. Wethered, when you see him. Keep which you prefer best. These photos were taken in my old shop at Bayswater, which I little thought, when I built it, would be used for such a purpose. I am right glad, however, to be here and not there, and shall still hope to see you here next summer, if not before.

'God bless you, my dear old friend, and believe me,

'Yours faithfully,

'JOHN LINNELL, SEN.

' P.S.—There is another photo of you, I am told, said to be better than the one you have sent. I shall try to get it, though I like this much. Perhaps Mr. Wethered will procure me the other photo of you. Ask him.'

Perhaps the following epistle, addressed to Mr. Wethered, which was at this time in Linnell's possession, may account somewhat for the tender tone in which the foregoing letter is couched. What a striking difference it reveals between the writer and the old friend who, nearly sixty years before, had

commenced with him the ascent of ' Fame's rough
steep'!

' Bromley,
'<i>June</i> 18, 1860.

' FRIEND WETHERED,

    ' I am astonished to find you have had any
summer weather. As to going on with the drawing
of the house and the roses, it is quite out of the
question.   I could do nothing in my painting-room
unless I kept a good fire.   There must be some
mistake in the order of the seasons.   Moore says
there will be nice hay-making weather in August ;
then perhaps I may be able to do something out-
doors.   Until there is really some warm weather I
can only make small drawings.   The primrose
blossoms, the apple and the may blossoms, are all
over.   I would try my hand at a cow, but it's too
cold even to sit in a cowshed.   Still, I am not, nor
do I intend to be, idle.   I fear that I shall not be
able to make two drawings for Mr. Gillott until there
is some large sort of fruit, such as melons, pines,
grapes, etc., which can be done in town, the latter
end of the summer, when it comes.   We have had
to-day more or less rain and cold north wind, so
much indeed that I could not stay out-doors to hear
the Ranters preach about Christ being the only name
that can save sinners.   But what's the use harping
upon it Sunday after Sunday?   You would be
amused to hear how they harp upon being washed
in the blood of Christ.   What a very singular
destiny !   I will not forget to do something for you ;
(I do not quite understand what you mean by the

large drawing for Mr. Gillott) ; and then I can make the other two for him.

'From yours truly,

'WM. HUNT.

'W. WETHERED, ESQ.'

Linnell received the following letter, dated December 9 (1863), in acknowledgment of a second photograph :

'FRIEND LINNELL,

'In return for your second portrait I send you another of myself, on, I think, a rather larger scale. What a beautiful situation your house must be! My country retreat is an old farm-house near Basingstoke, Hants, and that I rent.

'I still work very hard at grapes and apples ; but I wish persons would like the drawings as bits of colour instead of something nice to eat.

'With best respects to Mrs. Linnell and family,

'I am, yours truly,

'W. HUNT.

'J. LINNELL, ESQ.'

This was the last communication our artist ever had from his friend. On February 10, 1864, he received the following from Mr. Wethered :

'MY DEAR SIR,

'I am sure you will with me much regret to learn our dear old friend Hunt died this morning early.

'Believe me, very faithfully yours,

'WILLIAM WETHERED.'

CHAPTER XI.

Additional Correspondence—Aphoristic Wisdom—Views on Work—
Views on Art—' Beware of Americans !'—Mr. and Mrs. Cropsey
—Death of Mrs. Linnell—Premonitions of his own End--Letter
from George Richmond, R.A.'

AMONG the letters written by Linnell to his son
William during his second stay in Rome there are
many which have an exceptional interest, inasmuch
as they are replete with ideas on art. Here and
there, perhaps, prejudices crop up—the prejudices
of a man who has never visited Rome, the Mecca
and Medina as it were of art, and who, though
always staying at home, has yet discovered there,
at his very threshold, what the most laboriously
travelled has seldom found with all his wandering.
It is not to be wondered at, therefore, if he fails to
appreciate the value of foreign study, and sees all
the evils and none of the advantages derivable from
such change.

But, besides this, the letters are full of wisdom—
worldly, and other-worldly also. Nor are they lack-
ing in wit. In many of the letters, not otherwise
of general interest, are interspersed gems of this
kind that are well worth quoting. Thus, in a note
dated October 7, 1864, occurs the following :

'What you say of your transition state reminds me of a certain blackbird that we heard trying with all his might to whistle a well-known English tune ; and he succeeded up to a certain point, when he became but half blackbird, but he finished by whistling his " native wood-notes wild." I suppose when he was half-seas over he was in the transition state. Am I to account for your letters being so difficult to read on the same principle ? If so, I wish you would get over the transition state as soon as possible, and write plainer.'

In another letter, wedged in between a lot of dry business matters, occurs the following parody on Shakespeare's well-known lines (*Julius Cæsar,* Act IV., scene iii.) :

'There is in man's affairs a tide
Which leads to fortune if descried
And taken promptly at the flood ;
But if through laziness or blindness lost,
He may be in the tempest sadly tost,
And finally left sticking in the mud.'

In another saying he retorts upon La Rochefoucauld's 'No man is a hero to his own valet' with the aphorism, 'No man is a hero to his own valet, because valets are not judges of heroes, and cannot tell when they have found one.'

The following characteristic views upon work were written to his eldest daughter :

'According to your own account, you are very busy with household matters. Here is some advice from an idle person who is often detected poring

over books, or even dozing in the daytime. You
know the difference between a work of art and a
mere heap of matter, or jumble of things without
arrangement? Well, try and consider your day's
work, or your week's work, as a work of art.

> ' Begin the work of the day
>   As if you had to play
>   A piece of music grand and glorious,
>   And you your utmost skill
>   Intended, with good will,
>   To use so as to be all-victorious,—

trying to resolve the unavoidable discords into
their proper harmonies by some lucid touches here
and there, using some touches also of melody in
the midst of the recitative of directions and com-
mands.

> ' Yet of crotchets be aware,
>   And quavers, too, for they breed care,
>   If out of time at all ;
>   But breves and semibreves are best,
>   Sedate and calm, with many a rest,
>   As sweet as evening fall.'

The following letters to his son in Rome need
no comment :

> ' Redhill,
>   ' *May* 2, 1864.

' I am just arrived from the Royal Academy
Exhibition, where I saw G., who was so gracious
that I guess he will allow you anything. I expect
him here this week, and will tell him what you say,
and write to you. If you want to be in Rome again
in the autumn, you should certainly be here in the
summer, for very many reasons—more than I can
state. From what you say, I think it quite necessary

for you to return here as soon as you can arrange
it ; only, if you bring your large picture and frame,
do not think of taking it again to Rome. Your
" Banks and Braes" is on the line in the middle
room. James's are all low, but look well. One of
mine is too high, and looks nothing. My other kitcat, " Haymakers," is on the line in the great room,
and looks something. There is nothing first-rate ;
most of the great guns have either missed fire or
not put in powder enough. Well, as to difficulties
of a moral sort, I pray not for you to be taken out
of the world of vice that you are in, so much as that
you may be kept from the evil.

' Were I with you, I should in all probability
throw up my cap for a peep at Sicily, though if it
should appear on inquiry that the autumn is the
best time for that, why, then I should come here in
the summer, and return early enough for Naples
and Sicily. This is a good time to finish off your
lust of travel. You can best judge what is practicable, and I will not attempt to direct, and only
say be sober, be vigilant ; remember what your
adversary is, and remember also the helps—the
λειτουργοι, who are your companions, though unseen.
I will do what you wish as to money, etc., only let
me know in time. I have much to do just now.
James's house is to be enlarged—Chart Lodge also ;
and in painting also I have something to do.

'Yours,

'J. L., SEN.

* * * * *

'Comfort yourself as to the evils about you that there is a man with an inkhorn who sets a mark upon those who honestly groan at the sight. Beware of the spite and revenge, however, of those who may, through your counsel to the simple, be disappointed of their prey ; so be wise as serpents.

'In your letter, supposed from Olevano, October 15, you offer a scorpion to Tom in exchange for something better than an egg—Luke xi. 12. I won't say anything about the spirit of your observations upon Redhill ; but, according to the letter,

'There is no one here but a fogey old,
  For the rest they are only chits,
With Bell, and Shoe, and Oxtoby bold,
  Oaks, and nubbly bits.

'The excitement of the discovery of the brass Hercules accounts for your writing in the " Hercules vein," smashing us poor Redhillians with your club, and roaring as you used to do when you acted lion under the table. That Olevano letter is a terrible one, with the handwriting on the wall. If your photo had been in the position of mine by M. and P., we could have made pictures of the subject.

'As far as I am concerned, I say :

'Send no more photos, photos send no more,
  They are deceivers ever,
Fading at last if not before,
  And satisfying never ;
So when they show, just say, " No go,"
  And be you blithe and bonny,
Pooh-pooh the sellers' notes of woe,
  And keep your ready money.'

'Redhill,
'*May* 9, 1864.

'Your letter came this morning, dated the
3rd; the same day one was sent to you, and one
the day after, both of which you should have by
this time. The questions you ask in this last are
all answered in ours of the 3rd and 4th. It seems
to me that, as your pictures must be brought here
either in a finished or unfinished state, you may as
well do the last winding up here, as they are to be
seen in English atmosphere, and there is some
danger of your working to suit the Roman light,
which I think led to most of your trouble in "The
Gleaners." You are as capable of judging what is
best, and in a position to know better than I am;
but I feel sure you ought to return some time
before the summer is over. We will attend to your
wishes respecting the captain and the pre-Raphaelite
Wallis.

'Look out for squalls in the political horizon.
Money is scarce, funds very low—all which, I suppose, you see. If you are flush of cash this summer,
I may want to borrow some to pay for additions to
Chart Lodge, which I have nearly settled to do. I
am to have six per cent. in rent; but as Palmer's
house has swallowed up all my savings, I am
getting short, and loath to sell out at such a loss as
three or five per cent. A. has not been or written
lately. Everyone is cautious and shy, so we must
wait. If peace continues we shall prosper, but war
is very probable, I fear; so be prepared, and do not

leave anything in Rome when you return here if you can help it. Try and arrange so that you can give up your studio when you please. I hope you will come before the Royal Academy Exhibition closes, and on your mother's account. You ought to see her before long, lest you should regret the omission. I have many irons in the fire, some getting " werry ott." You should be here with your sledge-hammer to lend us a rap. You shall have some beer, I promise you ; for I am going to brew in a day or two, while this north-east wind lasts.

' Yours,

' J. L., Sen.'

' Redhill,

' *Saturday, October* 8, 1864.

' In your letter of last April you asked for my counsel, so I venture to give it now. The pictures for G. I expect he will like, as he has, I think, good reason to be satisfied, as I doubt not they will sell well, and he will want more. The group of goats I think capital, and many other points ; but the thing I want to tell you is, there is, I fear, a theatrical scene-painter alloy creeping into your work that you will not get rid of in Italy, because it is the vice of the place. It is in every artist who goes to Rome, and most go through the love of that quality. It is not the beautiful they seek to accomplish, but novelty, the sensational, the melodramatic. Hence the pigmental colouring of drapery. These things,

however, soon tire, like fireworks. Beauty never
tires—qualities which affect the inner man. There
is, I fear, a bad style of art and criticism in Rome
of a contagious kind, rather Cropseyish, and worthy
only of the name "slang." I cannot help feeling,
notwithstanding the many good things in the two
pictures sent, that you have left your first love.
Your English subjects I like better ; even the
costume is more humane—not so savage. The
majority of artists who go to Rome think to make
up for the deficiency of power to express beauty by
seizing novelty. . . .

'I could not urge you to come here into frost
and snow, when you are just where most people
would like to be for the winter. If you stay, I have
no doubt but it will be far more profitable to make
studies from nature than to paint pictures. Finish,
or nearly so, your large picture, and no more; spend
the rest of your time in getting valuable matter
such as can be got nowhere else, and then, like a
good bee laden with sweets, come to your hive,
only don't you sting us if we are a little curious to
see your store. G. would see the small picture, and
wished to have it when you had retouched it. I
told him it was intended for A., and if A. did not
come soon and see it, or if he did not wish to have
it, I would let him (G.) know, when he said he
would write to you about it. I did not mention any
price. . . .

'Slight pictures, unless there is some peculiar
grace in the execution, are not good to send out ;

so I recommend more work upon the small picture when you come here.

'Yours,

'J. L., SEN.

'The disease which appears to me to be in Rome infects all the painters who go there—costume pigmentally coloured ; scene-painting style ; novelty, and not quality, uppermost. I write strongly to make what I mean clearer. There is, I fear, an atmosphere in Rome unfavourable to improvement, though the finest examples are to be seen. The men, however, who produced them did not go after novelty, but painted their own country, and what they were used to ; hence, in my opinion, they were affected more by what is permanently beautiful than what is striking, because new. Beware of Americans, North and South. They are repudiators of debts ; so, whatever you do, expect nothing again. I will attend to all you wish, but can't judge here—*you can*. This winter in Rome ought, I think, to suffice for you ; and you should be home in time to retouch your large picture here that you intend to send from Rome for the Royal Academy exhibition. There is such a thing as drifting out of a good track—a *taint* is soon acquired.'

The Cropsey referred to in the foregoing letter was an American artist who had spent some time in Rome, and who, as the result (as Linnell thought), inflicted upon the world a lot of 'painty' and rather meretricious work — a description which

Linnell held in abhorrence. About this time (1864) Mr. Cropsey and his wife sought an introduction to the artist, and after a first formal visit to Redhill there was some correspondence, preliminary to a second visit with friends. A letter from Mrs. Cropsey called forth the following humorous reply :

'DEAR MRS. CROPSEY,

'Monday will do for me beautifully—if you can only get the day to be beautiful. You are sure to look so yourself, and your party also, if you only look as usual. How could you be so cruel as to dub me R.A. on the cover of your letter, and so envelop me in an honourable distinction to which I have no pretension ? I am so far *infra* such a *dig*. I shall write you Wicountess Cropsey, I think, when I am disposed to retaliate. Perhaps, however, you meant something else than royal scholastic honours. R.A. may stand for many things—for Right American, or for 'Rong American, adopting the orthography of Sir William Curtis, who gave as a toast the three R's—reading, writing, and arithmetic. I am not sure that in my case R.A. might not stand for Ragged Artist, seeing that I am more allied by sympathy and habit to the ragged schools than to any others, and such let the meaning be. I shall, therefore, so take it in future, and subscribe myself,

'Your obedient servant and ragged artist,

'JOHN LINNELL.'

The following is from a letter undated, but having the post-mark October 22, 1864 :

'Thanks for the *fotografs*, as the Italians spell it.
Very few of the best things seem to be done.   Are
there no *fotos* of the wonderfull bulls, rustic waggons
and figures, or are we to have those in words only?
I hope you will not return without studies and fotos
to back up your description, which is sure to fall
otherwise into the Bill Stumps style.   I should be
glad also for once to see something to correspond
to the boasted Italian sky ; the pictures sent are—
though very nicely finished—only English skies,
and not the best of those.   The old vice in the
tints, proceeding, I suspect, from some red used
which increases in force after painting, or through
not mixing the light first and then refraining from
the addition of red or any warmer tints, except in
distinct features ; but, after all, the eye ought to
detect the fault and correct it before the stains have
accumulated, and by a better method of mixing
relative tints first, the fault I speak of ought to be
almost impossible, even if painting by lamplight.
I know by so rigid a process you would be shut out
from some varieties which are natural, but they
could be added safer than attempting them at first.
Then, again, when strong colours are in costume,
great care should be taken that the shadows and
middle tints are true, and evidence the influence of
the phenomena about.   Without great attention to
this the figures will look like coloured prints in
children's books.   *Fotos* will not help here—only
careful observation of facts in the circumstances
represented in the picture.   There is a red garment

on the centre figure of the squares and of the two
pictures sent which is open to this criticism in my
opinion. The figure is sitting on the ground—a
man with a crimson cloak, or something of that
sort. You see nothing like it in any of the great
masters, only in the modern clap-trap Italy-mongers.
It is not colour in the true artistic sense—it is colour-
shop.

'We all remark how like Wales the mountains
are in the last picture—not better, to my mind. I
hope to see something yet which we may say could
only be got in Italy, or is worth going for. However, you must not in your search for this forget
the brigands, who, I find by letters in the *Times*,
are now infesting the Roman States, and go from
there to the Italian. The French pursue, but
seldom catch them. You are ignorant in Rome
of the extent of the evil, as the Government hides all
and publishes nothing. Only to-day, October 13,
there is a letter to that effect, which has disturbed
your mother's mind not a little. Gambart says that
the banditti are very numerous, but they only rob
the English; they do not carry them off. So you
may think yourself well off if you only get robbed,
which you had better permit quietly if they fall in
your way.

'I think it is the Indian red which James has
just procured for you that spoils your cloud tints.
I remember that Mulready and all I knew avoided
that pigment as one that showed itself in a most
obtrusive and offensive manner after the work was

dry, and could only be used by the coarse portrait-painters of the regular old R.A. school. Vermilion is safer, I have no doubt, and will not appear in the tints beyond the time of the working. As the tints appear when first put on, so they will remain, whereas the Indian red comes out in stains afterwards. Scarlet extract and yellow ochre, or red chrome, are best for lights on clouds when well mixed with white lead. . . .

' I think it will be wise to return early next spring, and leave nothing behind you. Make a clean sweep of it, and trust to finding a place to suit you when you go again, which may not be so soon as you expect. However, if you wish to keep your studio, it will only be the loss of so much money ; but it would be folly to risk the loss of your studies, so do bring all those with you. Stirring events may be expected before long.'

' Redhill,
' *November* 21, 1864.

' We are all much relieved from anxiety about you by the receipt of yours to-day, dated from Rome the 16th. The accounts of brigandage are so frightful, all about Rome it is said, so, if you do not know it, look out. . . . I shall write to Count Guicciardini soon, and tell him what you say. I do not remember your former message, but I dare say it was sent. I paid nothing to Horne, who has behaved liberally in refusing to take anything for all the trouble we gave him about the case sent to Mackraken. You may as well repeat your message, which you say you asked me to give to C. G., as I can better tell if it was attended to. You should remember what a task I have to perform at my age. I have, besides providing soap, candles, oil, and stone blue, etc., etc., to earn enough to pay all expenses with no better materials to study from than the "nubbly bits of Redhill, Oxtoby, Bell, bitch and donkey." You really ought to contribute some sensational figures that I might turn to account. Some swinkamswash, melodramatic vagabond to place on a bridge over a cataract just about to throw a hinnocent babby into the foaming gulf. Oxtoby, Bell and Co. might be looking on and form a pleasing contrast. Next package you send I hope will contain something to give us some notion of what Italy is like.

'We expect Mr. Adams* here in a day or two, and he will take out to you the mounted photo of Mary and Phœbe. I enclose you Sarah's. I hope Stewart will be with you before you get this, and Adams soon after.

' Yours,

' J. L., Sen.'

' Redhill,

'January 7, 1865.

'. . . . Your mother improves, and I have only lumbago, as much as I can well stand under, though I can't understand it, seeing that I wear woollen vests, and take care of myself. I begin to

---

* Mr. Adams Acton, the sculptor.

think I am getting old, or older than I was some years ago, though I doubt that sometimes. . . .

'Do, pray, write more at leisure, and as soon as you get my letter, instead of writing just before, and in a hurry. It is incredible that you should not be able to find time to write all that is requisite. Candles are not scarce, I guess, in Rome surely. I should have sent £100 this time, had you been more attentive in acknowledging the last, so do not omit this time.

'Yours,

' PATERFAMILIAS.'

' Redhill,
'*January* 18, 1865.

'. . . . Now, put this and that together, as Bill Stump would say, and then you will be able to stump up some day. In the meantime as much stumpey as you want shall be sent. In your letter from Olevano you say I need not infer from your remarks about everlasting oaks, nubbly bits, with " Bell, Shoe, Oxtoby, bitch and donkey," that you have "lost your taste for England." Why, from those remarks it would seem there was not much to lose, though, as you have painted such successful contradictions to that idea, we shall set down your remarks to another account. As they stand, however, without the picture commentary, they look too like the common claim set up by the admirers of the man-stealers of South America, when, after praising them for qualities which brigands may possess, and

calling men chivalrous who sell their own offspring
for slaves, these sympathizers with the slaveocracy
pretend they are as much opposed to slavery as you
who denounce the whole set.

'I am glad to find by your last that the Stewarts
have reached Florence. I hope they are with you
now. Send the wine as soon as you please. I
shall drink your health with that of the senders—
Stillman, Pendegrass and Co.

'Can't you fish out some prime old store?
Though I suppose the Cardinals are such knowing
ones on that subject, that there is no chance of the
very best being procurable by such heretics as we are.
Severn could help in that matter *if he would*. See
growers yourself, if possible, and go into their cellars
and ferret out some reserved sample. You see how
I want something Italian.

'Π.'

'Redhill,
'*February* 10, 1865.

'We received yours dated February 1, 1865.
That is as near as I can make it out from your
masterly touches. I suppose I must be content,
though I would rather that all such matters as dates
should be given and written plain. . . .

'Thanks for inquiries after lumbago. I have had
as much as I could well get on with, and now a cold,
but not more than I can bear easily. I have such a
sense of the great blessings I possess in the knowledge of Divine Wisdom and the gifts of her left
hand that I am supported through much bodily

weakness. Not that I am weaker than usual, but I have a sense of the trials that threaten at times to be too great for me. By faith, however, all is possible, and so I walk. I hope poor Mr. Stewart can find comfort that way. If you write to him or Mrs. S., could you not give him or her a note of introduction to Count G., who would do him good ?

' Mr. Grece wants a *foto* of Aristotle's bust in the Capitol ; I forget if I named it before. He has just read to us an interesting article by Taine in the *Deux Mondes*, a description of Rome, very original and evidently true. He reads in English from the French book. He would be a more valuable ally if he received τα του πνευματος. We must not, however, forget that we were once in darkness, though now Φως εν Κυριω. As children of light let us walk. These are some of the thoughts which help me through the long nights here, which I now pass alone in a room that should extort thanks from anyone. The beautiful things to be seen from the window even in the worst weather ; but the worst weather seems to have been everywhere but here. We have had nothing to speak of bad, and some delightful days. The snow has been seven and ten feet deep in the North, with many disasters to travellers. . . .

' I shall be glad to get the wine you mention, that Mr. Stillman will send. And what about the other from Mr. Pendegrass ? I enclose you another copy of the group, which you can do as you think best with; also one of the miniatures of your mother.

'Yours,

' Πρεσ.'

' Redhill,
' *March* 1, 1865.

'Notwithstanding what you say about Redstone habits leading to isolation, I believe that I am the most really sociable person in the family, and the best employed, for, in spite of the Hebrew roots and Greek constructions, I am enabled to do as much painting work as you, if not more, and, if price is any test, I can get enough and do get it—enough to justify my boasting (παραφρονων λαλω) ; and, though I do not visit much, others visit me, and I give them the result of my studies by telling them as much precious truth as they would hear in all Portman Square in a week, especially if they are priests or priest-defenders. These studies, however, can't be very unprofitable, as you say you "hope to get at it." If instead of no one knowing his neighbour, as you say, they secluded themselves as I do, I think they would be more neighbourly and know each other better, not so much κατα σαρκα, perhaps, but more profitably. After all, however, there is a deal of visiting here, more than I could find room to tell.

'If the wine is shipped I ought to have the bill of lading, especially as you have paid for the wine. You are right in not ordering more till we taste the first. I fear it is useless for you to write to Mr.

Stewart, as the last we heard of him is that they were at Leghorn, and he was not expected to live. I forwarded a letter from Gambart to you; say if you have it. . . .

'Fitz has not kept his engagement, but I have another string to my bow in Morley, who has just arranged for a kitcat and a 30 by 20 inches. . . . The kitcat is from one of my Balcombe subjects, very woody (a scarce quality in Italy I fear now). I guess you will have to borrow of Redhill now for oaks, if not for 'nubbly bits.' Don't forget that pictures depend more upon phenomena and expression for their effect than upon the matter or topographical character. The difference between Turner and Stanfield lies there.

'Yours,

'Π.

'This paper (*i.e.*, that on which the letter was written) was cut off your last.'

The following letter, although undated, evidently belongs to May 17, 1865 :

'Your picture of " Banks and Braes " is level with the eye, and for height could not be better. It is liked, and cannot easily be " licked."

'You should write again when you get our letter, in order to get the step which, like an unskilful walker, you have lost. Wait for our letter, and then write at once instead of writing just before you get ours. We got yours dated the 10th on the 17th (to-day), and write immediately. If you go to the mountains, write from the mountains, and beware of brigands. I shall not be able to send a ransom for you without selling three per cents. I must sell stock to get you out of the stocks. You can have some cash if you want it, as I have some coming in a few days. I have just sold a small picture of " Feeding Chickens " for 250 guineas—and something to Fitz. Chart Lodge is not let, but I intend to put it into a letting state. My " Disobedient Prophet " sold at Christie's for 950 guineas. I cannot tell what is best for you. No one here can see what you can see ; you must judge for yourself— only remember your mother.

' Yours,

' J. L., SEN.'

As will have been seen from the foregoing letters, Mrs. Linnell had been in failing health for several years past, and her husband could not but fear the worst, which took place on September 15, 1865, a few days after the return of her son from Rome. She died of heart disease in her seventieth year. If she had lived two years longer, the aged couple would have been able to celebrate their golden wedding, so that their marriage lost nothing of the character of durability by the simple secular ceremony in presence of the Edinburgh magistrate of forty-eight years before.

In Mrs. Linnell the artist lost a helpmate such as it is the lot of but few men to possess. She was the personification of gentleness and piety ; her patience had no end ; and through forty-eight years of married life she devoted herself to her husband and family with unwearying fortitude and inexhaustible affection.

Although Linnell was destined to live many years yet, he seems about this time to have had an impression that his own end was not far off. He refers to this feeling in a letter written to his son in April, 1865. In it he says :

'I have been relieved of my sufferings from rheumatism and sciatica, or nearly so. I am now putting all I can in order, though I fear being beaten by time ; a sense of its value seems the last thing that is learned. Your mother is certainly some steps lower down towards release, and I feel the shadows of evening are lengthening, and I feel also the great value of the knowledge, though small, of that πανοπλια with which all the assaults of the evil one are to be defeated. Hence, then, the melancholy of the flesh. Tell me not of death, of churchyards and God's acre ; I am in love with Life, sweet maid, and I will take her, as she is given me from her Father's portal to be mine for ever, making me immortal.'

A letter received by Linnell from his old friend George Richmond, sympathizing with him on the death of his wife, will suitably close this chapter. It is dated Holwood, Bromley, October 16, 1865, and is as follows :

' My dear Mr. Linnell,

'It was not from want of sympathy with you in your great loss that I did not write to you directly we heard of dear Mrs. Linnell's death, for both my wife and I thought much of you, and of the true friend whom we had also lost; one with yourself, when our fortunes were very low and our friends few indeed, who always received us with kindness— a kindness which neither time nor separation ever shook, and the givers of which I believe we shall always remember with most affectionate respect.

' Dear Mr. Linnell, we see very little of each other, but if the company of an old friend would be any pleasure to you now, I shall be only too pleased myself to run down and see you. With kindest remembrances to all of your house,

' Believe me, in true sympathy,

' Very faithfully yours,

' Geo. Richmond.

' John Linnell, Esq.

' P.S.—I return to town to-morrow.'

CHAPTER XII.

Refusal to become an Academician—Why was Linnell not elected
R.A.?—What he himself thought—Urged by Creswick and
Herbert to put down his Name—His Reasons for Objecting—
Again urged by Stanfield—Royal Commission on the Academy—
Correspondence between Mr. Horsley, R.A., and Linnell--Letter
to the *Athenæum*—Mr. Cope's Reply.

REFERENCE has previously been made to the fact
that for many years Linnell applied in vain for
admission to the Royal Academy, and something
has been said of his opinions as to the reason of his
being passed over. But the question why he was
not elected in the days that he sought the honour,
though often asked, has never hitherto been satisfactorily answered. For something like twenty years
(1821-1841) he regularly went through the pre-
scribed form of setting down his name as a candidate
for the Associateship; and for twenty years he was
as regularly passed over in favour, for the most
part, of inferior men. It could not be because his
work was not known, since, as we have seen, during
all those years he was a constant and honoured
exhibitor on the walls of the Academy.

The Academicians have more than once shown a

strange infatuation of blindness, as in the case of
William James Müller, one of the greatest of modern
painters, who, like Linnell, was not only not elected
to their ranks, but never even got the shadow of
fair treatment at their hands.   But as regards Linnell, there was no such excuse as blindness to his
merits, for the undoubted powers displayed in his
works from the first were almost universally acknow-
ledged, while the Academy never grudged him space
upon its walls.

Why, then, was he not elected?

Was it, as he always averred, because he held
unpopular religious and political opinions—opinions
that were not relished by the powers that were?
In other words, was it because he was a Noncon-
formist and a democrat?   We have seen what
were his religious opinions.   His politics were of a
similar decided and uncompromising stamp.   He
never mixed up much in public affairs; albeit he
voted steadily and consistently on the popular side.
But he was in political opinion somewhat of a re-
publican of the old Puritan type; and he never
cared to disguise his views. Can it be because those
views, both in regard to religion and politics, were
not liked, that he was not elected?   Or was it
because, as Collins put it, a man who is a ' Sabbath-
breaker ' is capable of any wickedness, and therefore
not a fit person to associate with Academicians?
Or are we to believe that it was because he did not
pay enough attention to his dress, and was not
enough of a courtier, as Mulready said?

Possibly all these various reasons may have had
their weight in the formation of the prejudice which
kept him outside the ' charmed circle ' of the Forty.
For that prejudice was the cause of the injustice is⁻
unquestionable.   Can anyone doubt that it was prejudice, and not lack of talent, seeing the walls of the
Academy year after year covered with the bald,
conventional, and insipid canvases of such men as
Witherington, Lee, and others of the like stamp, who
were preferred before a man whose brilliant pictures
riveted alike the attention of learned and unlearned
in art by their wonderful qualities ?

The list of those who were elected Associates
during the time that Linnell continued to be a candidate contains many notable names, such as those
of Etty, Leslie, Eastlake, Creswick, Grant (afterwards President of the Academy), Clint, etc. ; but
these form barely a fifth of the whole number.   Of
the remaining four-fifths, the majority, as regards'
painting, have passed out of the record as unimport-
ant entities in the history of British art.

What, then, was the reason of his non-election ?
Can it possibly be that he relied too much upon his
art as the necessary passport, and that if he had not
done so, but had seconded it with some of those
electioneering devices which were so repugnant to
him, the result might have been different ?   It was
broadly hinted to him more than once in his earlier
days that he should play the courtier more, make
himself acquainted with the Academicians, and solicit
their votes, etc.

Anything of that sort, however, as we have seen, Linnell resolutely refused to submit to, thinking that to an academy of art a man should be elected for his art alone.*

When he had ceased to put down his name as a candidate, it became, after a time—when, having relinquished portraits, he was exhibiting landscapes more and more—a common thing for Academicians to advise him to do so, telling him there was every chance of his being elected at the next vacancy, and so on. This, he afterwards believed, was the custom and policy of the Academicians, in order to keep men hanging on to the skirts of the institution, judging, and doubtless rightly, that so long as they had any hopes of being elected they would not set themselves in opposition to the Academy.

At all events, this was the way in which Linnell accounted for the perseverance with which, after he had decided no longer to seek honour at the hands of the Academicians, he was solicited to re-enter the competition. In 1843, especially, William Collins was urgent in his appeals to him not to omit to put his name down, representing that he was almost sure to be elected. The persistency of these demands had the effect of putting Linnell's back up, remembering how often the same thing had been said, and how often he had been deceived, and to

---

* One Academician remarked that the probable reason why John Linnell was not elected was that Academicians generally did not know his line, as he exhibited portraits, landscapes, figure-subjects, and was even known to engrave. Surely that was a strange reason—to be debarred because of the universality of his genius !

one Academician who thus importuned him, he is reported to have replied impatiently, ' The Academy can make me an R.A., but it can't make a fool of me !'

But whether the remark was made or not, it is certain that about 1843 he resolved to seek election no longer.

It was not resentment that caused him to come to this decision. He had at this time resumed his critical Biblical studies, and, in order to prosecute them to the best advantage, he wanted all the calmness of mind and freedom from external worry that it was possible to secure. And, though so frequently solicited to re-enter the competition, he never wavered in his resolve.

Among others who thus entreated him were Thomas Creswick, R.A., and John Rogers Herbert, R.A., the one in 1847 and the other a year later. When Herbert thus solicited him his picture of ' The Eve of the Deluge ' was in the Royal Academy exhibition.

Recording the incident later, Linnell wrote :

' Herbert tried even to pull me downstairs to set my name down in the list, and asked me to let him do it for me. But I refused, for I then saw clearly that it was degrading to be chosen only to be an Associate.'

He goes on to say that, when he had been convinced that it would be hurtful to him as a man, as a Christian, and as a painter also, to be a full member of the R.A., it was not likely that he could ' submit to the insult of being admitted to the ante-room only.' He adds : ' There were men among the full members who have been pretty generally set down in the public estimate as inferior in attainment as artists to me.'

Another by whom he was urged again to submit his name for election was Stanfield. This was in April, 1852. The R.A. sent a message to him by Wethered the dealer, requesting him to call and see him. He accordingly paid Stanfield a visit at Hampstead, where he was then living.

Linnell had that year sent in three landscapes, which were accepted and hung. They were ' The Timber Waggon,' ' Barley Harvest,' and ' Sere Leaf.' The first-named, the size of which is 34 by 56 inches, represents a dell surrounded by rich wood-land ; in it a number of men are leading a waggon with timber, while a distant landscape is seen through the trees to the right. This picture is remarkable as being the last painted of the artist's middle period. It was begun before he went to Redhill, from which time dates his later style. It is warm in tone, rather Titianesque in colouring, with a focus of rich blue sky and deep green trees. It was, as has been already observed, painted from studies made at Under-River, near Sevenoaks.

' The Timber Waggon ' was painted for Mr. Oxenham, the dealer, of Oxford Street, by whom it was sent to the Paris Exhibition of 1855, and for which he received 'the gold medal, the chief prize for landscape. The medal, however, never reached

Linnell's hands. The picture subsequently went into Flatow's possession, who sold it to Mr. David Price for £1,000.* It was lent by the latter to the Old Masters Exhibition of 1883.

'Barley Harvest' (36 by 43 inches), which was also at the Royal Academy Winter Exhibition (lent by Thomas Jessop, Esq.) along with the last-named, shows one of Linnell's troubled sunset skies over a woody background. In the foreground are men loading a waggon, while an empty wain is coming along the field to the right. 'Barley Harvest' was sold to Gambart for 300 guineas, and was at the Paris Exhibition of 1855. At the sale of the Gillott Collection in 1872 it was sold for 1,630 guineas.

'The Sere Leaf' shows us the middle of a wood, with pools of water in the foreground, and near them two men, one tying up a faggot, the other carrying one on his head; on the left are some children at play under a tree, on the right a horse and cart and other figures; the distant landscape is darkened by mist. The picture is somewhat brown and dark, with a Poussin-like quality of mystery about it. 'The Sere Leaf' was purchased by Mr. Oxenham, and was in the posthumous exhibition, lent by Mr. Wakefield Christy.

These pictures, when exhibited on the walls of the Academy in 1852, were greatly admired by all the Academicians, and Stanfield took occasion to point to the fact that the painter of them was still

* At the sale of Mr. Price's Collection (April 2, 1892), 'The Timber Waggon' was sold for 3,100 guineas.

an outsider. Sir Charles Eastlake, Leslie, and others, declared that it was disgraceful to the Academy that such was the case, and a general opinion was expressed that someone ought to see Linnell and inform him that it was the general wish of the Academicians that he should put his name down for election.

It was to communicate this desire that Stanfield sent for him. He told him what a great impression his pictures had made, that he himself had got up and made a speech in his favour, and that there was a general feeling of regret that he had not put his name down.

Linnell expressed his gratitude to the members of the Academy for their high appreciation of his land-scapes, and said 'that if he did not put down his name it would be for reasons allied to the fear of the mischievous effects of titles.'

'When I told him' (he writes) 'that I thought all titles were bad and unwholesome, quoting the Gospel of St. John: "How can ye believe that receive honour one of another, and seek not the honour that cometh from God only?" Stanfield put his hands upon my shoulders, and, looking in my face, said: "Oh, do you think so? Well, it is a much grander thought, and if I could be sure that it was so, I would lay down the title at once."'

One is inclined to smile as one reads this, because, good Catholic as Stanfield was, one can hardly imagine him retiring from the Academy on such a conscientious scruple.

Later the same day Linnell went to see Mr. Webster, R.A., who expressed the same views about his pictures, and said he would be elected if he put his name down. Mulready, whom he also saw, expressed the same opinion as Webster, and said all the landscape men would vote for him.

Referring to this invitation to accept the Associateship at a later period, Linnell wrote : ' I had arrived at that conviction, and through it resisted the enticement then offered to set down my name, with apparently a first-rate prospect of being chosen. I did not then know that probably all was insincere, and it was only to keep me as a follower, which, it is evident now, it has always been the policy of the R.A.'s to do with such as I was then.'

Thus the position remained until 1867, when, as a result of the Royal Commission on the Academy (1863), an alteration had been made in the method of electing Associates, it then being no longer necessary for an artist to inscribe his name as a candidate. Mr. J. C. Horsley, R.A., was deputed, or took it upon himself, to ask Linnell whether, if he were elected, he would accept the honour which he in earlier years had so greatly desired. Of course, after the position Linnell had taken up, there could be but one answer.

Mr. Horsley's letter was as follows :

' MY DEAR SIR,   '*January* 13, 1867.

 ' You are perhaps aware that the mode of obtaining a list of candidates for the degree of

Associate at the Royal Academy is now altered, and that it is no longer required that artists should themselves put down their names, but that it is the members of the Academy who are called upon to put down the names of those who they think should be elected.

'In the list just sent to me of names obtained in the mode I have described above, there is one of a man who, it can be safely asserted, is considered by all who have any knowledge or love for art as one of the most distinguished artists this country has ever produced, and whose exclusion from the Academy years ago is, I believe, the *one great* blot upon their election annals.

'The miserable reasons which led to this exclusion, no one cares to know now or inquire about; but it is believed that there would be the most hearty desire upon the part of a large majority (it may be said a unanimous desire) of the institution to rectify this wrong, and to give this honoured name the *full* honours of the Academy at the earliest possible day. There is an election for Associates on the 31st of this month, and there will be one for an Academician in June next at latest (a vacancy existing now). Need I say that the name I refer to is that of "John Linnell, Senior"! It is very probable that your name has been put down without your knowledge or consent, but *being down*, I trust that you will sanction its appearing.

'Nothing (artistically speaking) would give me

more satisfaction than to see the ranks of the
Academy honoured by the addition of your name.

'I repeat (and I do so after due reflection) that I
believe this is the only omission to be charged
against the Academy, but it is *such* an omission that
all its true friends will rejoice to see it atoned for.
I am of course aware that you declined a few years
since to let your name appear in the list, but I trust
you will alter that resolve now ; and you have given
lately such an unmistakable proof of feeling your
years to rest lightly upon you (let me sincerely con-
gratulate you upon the event to which I allude!)
that I hope you will exhibit similar juvenile feelings
in matters academic.

'My old friend (and yours) and neighbour Webster
begs me to say how heartily he endorses all I have
said.

'All I have to ask is whether you sanction your
name going to election on the 31st inst. With kind
regards to you and all your circle,

'Always faithfully yours,

'J. C. HORSLEY.'

To this Linnell replied as follows :

'Redhill, Surrey,
'*January* 17, 1867.

'MY DEAR SIR,

'I thank you sincerely for your letter containing so many kind expressions of professional
approbation and asking me to allow my name to
stand, with my sanction, in the list of candidates for

the degree of Associate of the Royal Academy. I am gratified also by your saying that Mr. Webster endorses your request, and that a good majority might be expected in my favour. I am thankful for all this kindness, as it affords me an opportunity and a justification for stating my reasons for not following your advice, as well as my reasons for not having myself put down my name for the last twenty years, though I had done so previously for as many, or more, without success. I agree with you that "the miserable reasons which led to this exclusion no one cares to know or inquire about." But though I do not wish at present to examine the reasons for not electing me, I do wish to state (as you kindly afford me this ground for so doing) what my reasons were for discontinuing to put down my name. First, then, the jealousies and falsehoods that my endeavour to become an Associate gave rise to. I saw that heartburnings, calumnies, and injurious conduct beset everyone struggling in that direction, and affecting some to the extent of shortening their lives. I felt all this to be so destructive to the peace necessary to successful study and work, so destructive to all peace, and especially that peace which surpasseth all understanding, that I determined to abandon the contention for distinction and privilege, and to take the result of only endeavouring to deserve them. I did so, and I am contented with the result, and thankful exceedingly that I did not succeed in my effort to become an Associate, as I am convinced that if I had succeeded I should not have been found in the happy circumstances I now enjoy.

'One great cause of the heart - burnings and jealousies seems to me to arise from the uncertainty of ever arriving at the full membership of the R.A. ; but being detained and fixed for life in a degraded position of servility, alike degrading both to R.A.'s and Associates. I never heard that any of the foreign Academies of Art required an artist to solicit for full or half membership, but I have heard of full honours being conferred upon some without their knowing it until it was done. Honour thus conferred without seeking for it honours both the giver and receiver. But to elect a man to a position of servility and inferiority of privilege, and make his elevation to full honours dependent on the will of those who have already degraded him, is in my opinion a disgrace to all concerned in the act. I cannot therefore, it is plain, sanction my name being placed on the lists as candidate for what I consider a degradation.

'I am, yours faithfully,

'JOHN LINNELL, SEN.

'P.S.—When I think of that assembly which of all others is the chief, if not the only one really desirable to belong to — the real true Christian Church, to which 3,000 were in one day admitted to full membership—when faithful men established a school in which there were only official distinctions, and when I think of the sad usurpations afterwards established whereby the people were robbed of their privileges God had bestowed upon them—when I think of the pretext urged for the lording it over God's heritage, I see in all a sad but somewhat amusing type of the doings in such societies as the Royal Academy.

'To J. C. HORSLEY, ESQ., R.A.'

That Linnell did not make too much of the 'servility and inferiority of privilege' to which the Associates are elected may be seen by the evidence of David Roberts, R.A., before the Royal Commissioners.   He said :

'The drawbacks to the present system are really so great that I think it renders not only the Associates themselves very wretched, but makes the Academicians feel very uncomfortable. . . . I do not see anything to compensate for the pain it causes the Associates in the event of their not becoming full members.   There are some of the Associates who have been upon the list upwards of twenty years whose chances of becoming Royal Academicians are hopeless, and who would have been much better off if they had never been elected Associates.'*

He goes on to say :

'Whilst it (the Associateship) lasts (and it does so for life with some), I cannot conceive anything more painful to a sensitive mind ; and that all men

* It is worthy of note, in this connection, that Clint, after being an A.R.A. for twenty years, resigned the 'position of inferiority,' the degradation of which he could no longer support.

of genius are sensitive will be readily admitted.
Murmur at his hard fate he dare not ; but he must
appear happy and contented, with sometimes a
heavy heart.'

Linnell subsequently wrote the following letter,
which explains itself, to Mr. Horsley :

'Redhill,
'*February* 18, 1867.

' MY DEAR MR. HORSLEY,

'I was much pleased to hear from Mr. A.,
who, I suppose, is good authority, that I had not
forfeited the friendship of the R.A.'s by my conscientious answer to your very kind letter inviting
me to sanction the insertion of my name in the list
of candidates for A.R.A. I hope this is true, and
that I am not to be looked upon as an enemy
because I have said what I believed to be the truth.
I had no other wish, I assure you, than to say what
I felt ought to be said by somebody, and the occasion seemed to me to justify the utterance of that
unmitigated expression of my opinion. But as along
with that expression I fear there was something
said by me that might have appeared ambiguous,
and imply more than I meant, I crave your indul-
gence to explain that in asserting my belief as to
the custom of foreign Academies conferring full
honours at once upon those they deemed worthy,
and that without solicitation, and in my adding that
I thought the bestowing honour so gratuitously
honoured both giver and recipient, I only meant to
state a fact in opposition to what I condemned. I

did not, however, for a moment intend it to be guessed that I only wanted such honour to be conferred upon me.   And I should not have written again upon the subject but for the fear that I might possibly have been so misunderstood ; for allow me to assure you that I have no wish for anything of the kind from any society whatever.   I am fully content with my position ; and if my works obtain their fair share of attention in the hanging, I shall be thankful, and esteem it a favour, though I think I may claim somewhat in that direction, inasmuch as the Royal Academy does occupy the place of a national institution.

' I am, yours truly,

' JOHN LINNELL, SEN.

' P.S.—Years ago I was told that it was considered *infra dig.* for an R.A. to visit an outsider like myself who did not court the honours of the Royal Academy, and it is a fact that I have had scarcely any visits from R.A.'s, though often promised.   One R.A. did come as far as my doormat, but could not be induced to penetrate beyond that apparently enchanted circle, or rather square. Now, what say you, Will you dare to come within the circle where I am casting my pictorial bullets ? If not, what prevents you?   Ask my old acquaintance, Mr. Richmond, who should not be forgot—ask him if he will come with you ; he has not been since he was R.A.   Or will both of you see me hanged first ?

'To J. C. HORSLEY, ESQ., R.A.'

Mr. Horsley replied as follows :

'*February* 28, 1867.

'MY DEAR MR. LINNELL,

'Please always direct to me *as above*, otherwise letters perform postal gyrations (as yours did
the other day) before they reach me.   I have also
been away, otherwise I should have replied to your
letter long since.   There was, I assure you, but one
feeling amongst the members of the Academy, and
that sincere regret at your decision.   Several blamed
me for communicating with you at all, expressing
their belief that if nothing had been said, and you
were elected—as, doubtless, you would have been
in the most unanimous way possible — that you
would not have declined the election.   It would be
a lamentable position for me were this the case ; but
I feel confident from the tone of your first letter
that *nothing* would induce you to alter your decision.
Webster and I agreed that it was only right towards
you and the Academy simply to state that you did
not wish your name to go to election, and I trust
that we verily and in deed acted according to your
fixed determination by so doing.   You must be
joking in what you say about R.A.'s not calling
upon you!   Do you really believe that there is an
artist worthy of the name who would not think it
an honour to be welcomed under the roof of John
Linnell ?   If you do, you have very little notion of
the estimate put upon you.   The cares and troubles
of this mortal life prevent all of us from doing a
tithe of what we would do ; but I can truly say that

I scarcely ever pass Redhill without looking at your roof peeping above the trees, and wishing I could have the pleasure of a chat with you, and the delight of seeing some sterling good art. Well, I trust this year will not pass without my beating up your quarters, and trying to convert you from what I venture to consider the erroneous views you entertain about the Academy. Think of two things —that the Academy for *one hundred years* has educated the whole body of artists of this country *entirely gratuitously* (besides spending thousands charitably upon others, and treating themselves, the members, in the stingiest fashion), and that the *only real artist* not included in their ranks during that time—*the only one*, is John Linnell; and admit that the institution has done well, and justly to some extent.

'With kind regards to you and yours,

'Ever faithfully yours,

'J. C. HORSLEY.

'I will give your message to Richmond.'

The two letters signed 'John Linnell' (but without the postcripts) appeared in the *Athenæum* on June 8, 1867, with the following explanation :

'Since those letters were written, I sent four landscapes (39 by 28 inches) to the Royal Academy Exhibition, expecting they would be hung as usual, or a request to withdraw any one or more would have been made to me during the hanging, as on a former occasion, when my picture was afterwards hung well, as I declined to withdraw it. This time, however, I found my picture (No. 1 in my list) among the rejected pictures in the hall of the Royal Academy, with a label bearing my name stuck in the frame, on Wednesday, May 1, the varnishing day ; and when I complained of this treatment to one of the hangers, he said he thought a letter had been sent to me. But that was not done. A letter came three days after, requesting me to send for the picture. This letter is dated May 3, and I had taken the picture away on May 1.

'These are the facts, upon which I refrain from making any remarks. Others will form their opinion as to whether there was any connection between my letters and the determination not to hang my picture, judged by myself and friends to be my best work of the season, and marked in my list accordingly as No. 1. The picture had been painted for a collector, who had hung it in his room with unqualified approbation ; but he became so disgusted and annoyed by the rejection of the picture from the walls of the Royal Academy, that I was induced to take it back, and return the money he had paid me for it.

'JOHN LINNELL, SEN.'

To this Mr. W. C. Cope, R.A., replied as under :

'*Mr. Linnell and the Royal Academy.*

'19, Hyde Park Gate South,
'Kensington Gore.

'Mr. Linnell has written to the *Athenæum*, June 8, complaining of the treatment he has received at the hands of the Royal Academy. I do not propose to follow him through his two letters on another subject with which I have no concern ; but as he insinuates a grave charge at the conclusion of his communication, I think it my duty as one of the " hangers " to notice it. He says, " Others will form their opinion whether there was any connection between my letters and the determination not to hang my picture." In other words, he implies that the Royal Academy is capable as a body not only of wishing to injure Mr. Linnell professionally on account of those letters, but that they had desired the Hanging Committee to manifest their displeasure by rejecting one of his pictures, and that the Hanging Committee was capable of consenting to carry out so base a suggestion.

' The simple facts are these : Mr. Linnell sent four pictures for exhibition, all of which were accepted. The hangers had placed three of them in excellent positions, and the fourth was reserved to ornament the North Room. After repeated efforts to hang it upon the line, it was found impossible to do so without displacing other works of merit, many of them by younger artists who had not been so fortunate as to get even one picture placed.

' Under these circumstances, the hangers concluded that it would be more respectful to Mr. Linnell to return the picture (with the usual letter expressive of regret), so that it might be available for exhibition on a future occasion, rather than place it in a position inferior to what its great merits demanded.

' Mr. Linnell also complains of not having received
the letter until May 3.   This might have occurred
from press of business in preparing the catalogue ;
but I presume that it was issued at the same time
as other similar letters.   I would have written to
Mr. Linnell had I known that it had been done on
a previous similar occasion, and for this neglect I
hope he will accept my apology.

' In conclusion, I have only to express my regret
that it was found impossible to place a picture we all
so much admired, and to remark that it was detained
until the last moment in the hope of being able to
find it a place in the North Room, which was the
last to be arranged.

' Begging you to allow the insertion of this
(personal) explanation, and apologizing for its
length,

' I remain, etc.,

' C. W. COPE, R.A.'

Subsequently (1869) Linnell published this correspondence in a pamphlet, entitled 'The Royal
Academy a National Institution,' in which he set
forth at length his criticisms upon the Academy.   ·

But the more personal aspect of the matter as
regards this episode in his career is well set forth in
some remarks on honours and titles in general at the
close of his Autobiography, the following excerpts
from which may fittingly be given here :

' When you have found that nugget of wisdom '
(he writes), ' " To know my end and the measure of

my days, and to know how frail I am," then from
that point of view all may be seen in its true light.
God's estimate of worldly things becomes your estimate.   This is the vantage-ground of truth that
Lord Bacon speaks of in his "Essay."   From this
point of view how vain and contemptible the strug-
gles for distinction seem!   "What is the chaff to
the wheat? saith Jehovah," and you see it bears no
comparison, though you see thousands preferring the
chaff.   And truly it is a very sad sight, from this
vantage-ground of truth, to see how elated even the
highly-educated are with the baubles and toys of
worldly ceremony and ostentation.   We are not
surprised to see young children taken with toys, but
we expect them to grow out of that taste.   We are
sadly mistaken, however, for it is only changing one
toy for another more vain and frivolous, and generally baneful and pernicious. . . .

'But the true Christian man flies to his vantage-
ground of truth, and forms his estimate of worldly
things from that position. . . . With such perceptions these toys are not to his taste.   He has no
doubt about the wisdom of rejecting them; and
when any officious friend reproves him for disre-
garding his interest and the steps to his worldly
prosperity, he feels there is a snare in his path; the
counsel is from one who regards not the things of
God but of men. . . .   No, let this mind be yours as
also was Christ's, who emptied himself of the glory
he had, and became a slave, suffering crucifixion as
the path to exaltation.   If we are exhorted to follow

this example, how can we pursue those toys? If reputation for well-doing follows us, let us be thankful and accept the result in all honesty, as far as fair remuneration for our work is given, but not in the shape of those intoxicating, empty, worthless forms of titles, badges, or marks of any kind, which are often only marks of the beast.'

CHAPTER XIII.

Linnell's Culminating Period—'Noonday Rest'—'The Hayfield'—
'The Moorlands'—Replica of 'The Storm in Harvest'—Biblical
Subjects—'The Disobedient Prophet'—'The Journey to Emmaus'
'Abraham'—'Sunset'—Scene in the Academy—The Artist and
the Critic—'Sleeping for Sorrow.'

WHEN his correspondence with Mr. Horsley took
place respecting the Royal Academy, Linnell had
long since passed the term of three-score years and
ten. But, thanks to his careful living, hard work,
and abstemious habits, he was, though in his seventy-
fifth year, still hale and hearty, and able to wield his
brush with almost undiminished vigour of hand and
eye. In grasp of mind and vigour of invention there
was no sign of falling off. Perhaps the culminating
period of his power was a little before the Royal
Academy correspondence took place, that is, roughly
speaking, between the years 1862 and 1866, when
he was painting such landscapes as ' Noonday Rest '
(1862), 'The Hayfield' (1864), and 'The Moorlands' (1865), all exhibiting a mastery such as in
their several ways the artist had seldom excelled.

The first-named (38½ by 54 inches) shows a par-
tially-cut cornfield under the bright noon sunlight.

In the foreground three men are lying asleep in the
shade of some sheaves of corn, while beyond others
are busy harvesting. Nothing could better convey
the idea of shimmering sunlight and heat.

In ' The Hayfield ' (28 by 39 inches), which was
exhibited in the Academy in 1864, we have a wide-
spreading upland meadow, with a group of figures
seated in the foreground and others making hay
beyond. An expanse of uncut grass stretches towards a distant plain on the horizon. Here again
we have that pearly freshness of a mid-day sunlit
landscape for which Linnell, perhaps more than any
other painter, is famous.

' The Moorlands ' (28 by 39 inches) shows us
another aspect of nature—a wide expanse of rough
heath under a sunset sky, with overhanging, threatful clouds of purple hue. In the foreground is a
pond with horses and cows watering. It is one of
the artist's favourite themes, in which oft-repeated,
magnificent struggling skies meet the eye with all
the charm of novelty. Moreover, it is replete with
the poetry of upland solitudes.

All these pictures exhibit the master-hand at its
best, and the artist's touch with nature as the most
intimate and sincere. And when the statement is
hazarded that after this period Linnell's work began
to show signs of decadence, it must be taken with
considerable latitude and with many allowances.
For whilst here and there, in works executed after
this time, there are indications of less firmness of
hand, of less clearness of sight, they are for some

THE STORM IN HARVEST-TIME.

(From the 'Magazine of Art,' by permission of Messrs. Cassell and Co.)

years to come so slight as almost to escape detection save by the most experienced eyes. Even then the best judges may sometimes doubt whether their own eyes do not deceive them when they see such a picture as the replica of 'The Storm in Harvesttime,' which was executed after this time (1873), and is undoubtedly one of the grandest pastoral subjects the artist ever painted. It depicts the uprolling of a black thundercloud, the central nucleus of which seems just about to burst over the heads of a party of harvesters. It is almost terrific in its grandeur. The execution is no less masterful than the conception. The original, upon which it shows some slight variations (and in some respects it may be said for the better), was painted in 1855 and 1856, and purchased by Sir William (now Lord) Armstrong.

Among other pictures belonging to this period, and displaying a mastery in which it would be difficult to point out positive signs of failure, the following may be noted: 'The Woodlands' (panel, 27 by 39 inches), 'The Wood-Cutters' (panel, 18 by 24 inches), 'Sheep' (canvas, 27 by 39 inches), 'Surrey Woodlands' (canvas, 38 by 54 inches), 'Milking-time' (canvas, 35½ by 55½ inches), 'The Dusty Road' (canvas, 27 by 38 inches), and the 'Baptism of Christ,' all of which belong to the years from 1863 to 1869 inclusive.

Not much has hitherto been said about Linnell's Biblical pictures. Being, as they undoubtedly are, subsidiary in importance as works of art to his more purely landscape subjects, they do not appear so much to require chronological treatment. And yet it would be a grave mistake to pass them over as minor matters, and not calling for special remark. The artist himself ranked some of them amongst his most important works, and they are undoubtedly of great importance as showing in a peculiar manner the limitations of his art.

Some of those pictures which must be classed amongst his Biblical subjects owe their distinction very largely to their mastery as landscape studies. Such, for instance, is the case with 'The Eve of the Deluge,' 'The Disobedient Prophet,' 'Christ and the Woman of Samaria,' 'David and the Lion,' and several others. In these the subject was suggested by the landscape, which was afterwards overruled, and given additional interest to, by the figures. The key-note of 'The Eve of the Deluge' was struck by the angry and threatful sky, which suggested a drama of deep and world-moving import; while in 'The Disobedient Prophet' the noble qualities of the landscape, with its sombre pines, inspired the idea of wedding it to a suitable historical subject. Hence the figures of the lion and the ass, and that of the disgraced prophet, were introduced.

In both these pictures, as well as in the 'Christ and the Woman of Samaria,' there is sufficient realism in the figures to give dramatic interest and to fill out the theme supplied by the background.

This, however, is not the case in all the artist's Biblical subjects. Their common fault is that they fail in not exhibiting that realization and truth of nature for which his landscape and pastoral subjects are remarkable. The figures in too many of them are flat and weak, not having sufficient realism to give dramatic interest. They were painted more from his inner consciousness, and as an expression of his poetical and religious ideas, than from that outer aspect of nature his triumph over which in his own peculiar line had been so signal.

The 'Journey to Emmaus' is something of an exception. That picture was painted to some extent from models, his future son-in-law, Samuel Palmer, having sat for the younger disciple in the straw hat. This was—probably in consequence—the most popular of his subjects, and was purchased by the Art Union in 1838 as a prize picture, and engraved by the artist for presentation to their subscribers. The head of Christ was painted from an oil study of a Polish Jew having a remarkably fine type of feature, who happened to call upon Linnell while he had the picture in hand.

In his other Scriptural subjects, as a rule, he used no models. The exception is his picture of 'Jacob's Well,' for the woman in which he made a careful study from life.

These subjects were painted for the most part late in life, when, apparently, the artist no longer had the patience to work from models. He was satisfied to paint from memory, or from what was in his mind. This is strange, because it is so opposite to the methods he pursued in early life, and which he recommended as the true ones to the end of his days. Hence, though poetical, his Scriptural subjects do not interest us by their life-like and dramatic qualities.

His 'Gethsemane' is a good example of his weakness in this respect. The landscape is a beautiful one, and, though not Oriental, is suggestive of a solemn theme ; but the figures are flaccid and unreal, and do not rise by any means to the height of the 'vast argument' of the subject.

In short, most of John Linnell's Biblical themes are more like ideal studies for figure-subjects than actually worked-out pictures.

This may be said in especial of perhaps the most notable of his purely Scriptural subjects—his 'Abraham.' In this the character of the Divine being is wholly dramatic and solemn in effect, and is founded upon the artist's deep spiritual perception of the subject, which gives grandeur and force to the work, although the figure is not realized entirely as it might have been by one of the Old Masters, like Michael Angelo or Raphael.* And yet it has a deep religious and spiritual import which makes it unique. In this picture there is something of the peculiar imagination and grandeur exhibited in Blake's symbolic pictures.

This and one or two others, including the ' Philip baptizing the Eunuch,' have a special significance,

---

* It should be noted, however, that the text says, 'a furnace and lamp of fire passed,' etc. This will probably account for the indefiniteness here.

THE BAPTISM OF CHRIST.

(From an oil-painting by John Linnell, 1867-69.)

as embodying a particular interpretation of the
Scripture text. In the latter baptism has been by
‘complete immersion,’ a doctrine he held to with
great tenacity. The same truth appears to be en-
forced in the ‘Baptism of Christ,’ which forms a
rather striking picture. The Saviour is represented
standing on the bank of the stream, and John the
Baptist in the water, holding a branch with his left
hand ; the figure of a dove appears in a ray of
light above. The composition is very simple, yet
dignified. The treatment, however, is somewhat
hard, and the colour hot, while the landscape has
not the charm of some of his other ‘ religious ’
subjects.

The picture which called forth the correspondence
in the pages of the *Athenæum* Linnell himself did
not consider one of his best ; and his indignation
was aroused more by the neglect to let him know
that it was not hung, than by the fact. of its not
finding a place on the walls of the Royal Academy.
The ‘Sunset’ is, nevertheless, a fine picture. It
represents a landscape aglow with the fires of the
setting sun—one of those scenes in nature, in short,
which never seemed to lose their hold upon the
artist, and which he was never tired of painting.
It was sold for £700 before it was finished ; but
when the gentleman who had purchased it found
that it was not hung, he wrote to Linnell, saying
that he bought the picture in the belief that it would
be exhibited on the walls of the Academy. In
short, he wanted to cry off. Linnell at once re-

turned him his money, and had the picture on his hands for several years.

A good deal has been made of the 'scene' which is said to have taken place at the National Gallery (where the Academy then held its exhibitions) when Linnell went there on varnishing day and failed to find his favourite picture of the year, his No. 1 as he styled it, upon the walls. The artist is reported to have gone stamping from room to room, amid R.A.'s, Associates, exhibitors, dealers, and porters, demanding to be informed where was his 'Sunset,' and indignantly fulminating against the Academy and all its works.

Various versions of the occurrence are current; but, whilst all are more or less dramatic in conception, they are all equally devoid of truth. The simple fact, as narrated by an eye-witness, appears to be that, having failed to find his picture on the walls, he demanded of one or another in authority to be shown where he could find it. He was finally conducted to the basement, where he discovered the missing picture amid a host of others.

It should be said that whatever indignation the artist may have shown on this occasion was aroused by the exceptional character of the annoyance, and was soon over. Although he oftentimes received but indifferent treatment at the hands of the hangers—his splendid landscapes being often 'skied,' or stowed away in corners, or in the architectural room, as was his 'Hawthorn,' while banalities of the Witherington and Lee type occupied the line—yet it was not his habit to complain, but to take what he got and be thankful. He had his compensation in the knowledge that he obtained prices for his works that very few of his academical rivals could emulate.

In his later years, when the dealers had come to vie with each other for the possession of his works, he had less cause for complaint. His landscapes were then so well known and admired, that even the most independent of hangers would hardly dare to hang badly what the instructed public had come to regard as among the first treasures of the exhibitions.

How little resentment he felt in regard to the rejected picture will be seen from the following letter, dated May 3, 1867, and addressed to his son William, who, having married, was then residing in Paris :

' I have been with Marian to the private view of the R.A. to-day. . . . I saw lots of people, R.A.'s, and all very friendly, except two R.A.'s, —— and ——, the hangers, who wouldn't hang my " Sunset," but sent it down in the passage along with the rejected pictures. I found it there, and brought it home on Wednesday. I said some plain words to —— and —— and they are sulky. Not so others.

' Mr. Knight, the secretary, told me the P.V. tickets were voted me by the Council with acclamation—this, of course, as a set-off against my " Sunset." My other pictures are well placed. . . .

' I had lots of applications for the pictures hung.

. . . My eyes are weak, but are better for rest, so you will excuse scribble.

'J. L.

' Lots of bad pictures in the Exhibition. Hook's are excellent, and he is most hearty. I am going to see him. Redgrave also is very friendly. He has an exquisite picture of trees and water—no figures. Webster, Herbert, Creswick, and Cook all hearty and congratulatory. Sir F. Moon, ex-Mayor, and Mr. Field, who introduced me to Tom Taylor, have promised to come and see me.'

Tom Taylor paid his promised visit, which gratified Linnell, who greatly admired his poems and satirical writings in *Punch*. This was the only occasion, however, on which the art critic of the *Times* visited Redhill, and the two probably never met again. Taylor appears to have been a genuine admirer of Linnell's landscapes, and generally had a good word to say in their favour. One year, however, in writing of the Academy pictures, he ventured to be less complimentary than usual, and the artist was at once told by some of his friends that there was something wrong, and that he ought to send the critic a cheque for £50. A strange reflection, surely, on the supposed relations between painter and critic!

However, Linnell did not act upon the suggestion. For one thing, he did not set much store upon newspaper criticism, and even if he had he would have been one of the last to buy it. Perhaps some-

one had given him such a hint when, in 1864, the
Times, referring to his 'Hayfield' (previously referred to), spoke of it as 'a poem of rural nature.'
This brought out the following bit of humorous
verse :

> 'The *Times* says my picture is a poem—
>   Tooral-ooral-lay !
> A poem of rural nature—
> Oh, the dear old crayture !
>   Tooral-ooral-lay !
> The *Times* is surely growing better,
> Obligation upon me to lay ;
> If so I must remain his debtor,
> For to such I never pay.
> Rural tooral-ooral-lural,
> Wide awake I say !'

It should be explained in regard to the 'private-
view' tickets referred to in the foregoing letter, that
prior to this year Linnell had never been favoured
with invitations to the private view of the Academy.
His friend George Richmond called attention to
the fact, and henceforth to his death tickets were
regularly sent to him, and he valued the attention
very highly.

Among other works belonging to this period
may be mentioned 'Southampton Water,' 'Feeding
Sheep,' 'Chalk,' 'Harvest Showers' (the two latter
were exhibited in 1867), 'The Lost Sheep,' and
'Sleeping for Sorrow' (1870).

The history of the latter picture is peculiarly
interesting. At the Manchester Art Treasures
Exhibition his sons saw and afterwards described
to him a picture by Bellini, entitled the 'Sleep of

Sorrow.' He was greatly struck with the subject, and shortly afterwards began to work upon a picture that had shaped itself in his mind. This work is still upon the walls at Redstone Wood, Redhill. It exhibits great dignity and force of treatment. Upon a dim hillside are recumbent figures, over which the last evening gleam still shows a shaping light, while heavy clouds overhang and darken the scene.

Some years after this picture was painted Linnell saw at the National Gallery the original, the description of which had suggested his own ; but it was so different that no one would suppose that the one was in any way the outcome of the other.

In one respect there may be said to be a certain amount of sameness in Linnell's later pictures. In his earlier works he introduced Welsh, Derbyshire, and other scenery, with which he was then familiar, and with which—that of Wales in particular—he had been so deeply impressed. The background of his 'St. John preaching' is Derbyshire scenery, with a palm-tree introduced. But the subjects of the pictures of his last period, that in which he had attained to a style peculiarly his own, are derived chiefly from Surrey scenery, of which he had always been especially enamoured, and in the midst of which he had, as it were, taken root during the latter third of his life. In nothing was he more successful than in his treatment of woodland and of timber generally ; and his woods are essentially Surrey woods. But even with this sameness there is the greatest possible variety, as may be seen by a comparison of some of his later works, amongst which may be mentioned 'The Ford' (1872), 'Woodcutters' (1874), 'Woods and Forests' (1875), 'The Hollow Tree' (1876), and 'Autumn' (1877), all of which were exhibited on the walls of the Academy.

CHAPTER XIV.

IN the month of September, 1866, consequently
when he was seventy-four years of age, Linnell
entered the bonds of matrimony for the second time,
taking for his wife Mary Ann Budden, an old friend
of the late Mrs. Linnell and the family, and a former
member of the Plymouth Brethren. The marriage
took place in the simplest possible manner, before
the registrar of Reigate, thus showing what an
immense change had been effected in the marriage
laws since the artist's first wedding experience,
forty-nine years before. He thus makes entry of
the event in his journal :

'Sept. 18, 1866.—To Reigate to Mr. Hart's
office at 9.30 with Marian and her sister, E. L.,
J. T. L., etc. Received certificate of marriage
(which see). To St. Leonard's with Marian by
11.10 train.'

On the following day the venerable bridal pair
visited Ecclesborne and, on September 20, Fair-

light, returning to Redhill the same day. One or two friends held up their hands in dismay at these late nuptials, prophesying ill ; but Linnell took no notice of them, and declared that he had become rejuvenated thereby, and such in truth seemed to be the case.

In the ' Life of Richard Redgrave ' (recently published) an amusing story is told about this second marriage, and it has every appearance of being true. The anecdote is quoted from Redgrave's diary, and is as follows :

' On the occasion of his second marriage, the Reigate registry-office was put in requisition. The wedding took place not from the lady's own home, but from Redstone, where she had arrived about a week before. When someone objected to the old painter that this was contrary to received custom, he said : ' There is full authority for it. Rebecca came to Isaac. Why should not Mary Ann Budden come to John Linnell ? The only difference I see is that Rebecca brought all her worldly goods on a camel, whereas my bride's belongings came by Pickford's van.'

Another story told by Redgrave is not only ill-natured, but has not the merit of being *ben trovato*. ' Linnell's son John ' (the narration goes) ' asked his father to give him some painting tools, of which the old man had an abundant supply. " Nay ! nay !" said the painter ; " recollect, my boy, your mother's first words to you, ' Bye-bye, bye-bye—buy-buy !' " '

Redgrave gives the story as having been told by

another Academician, and adds that it 'showed truly Linnell's habit of making the most out of everything and everybody.' There are several reasons for affirming that Linnell could not have said any such thing. He never used the negative, 'nay,' and he never said 'my boy.' Moreover, the person represented as being chiefly concerned has no recollection of such an incident ; but he and all other members of the family bear emphatic testimony to the fact that the artist never begrudged anything to his sons and daughters that was necessary for their studies or their welfare.

Redgrave ought to have been the last to put such a story on record. He was Linnell's friend, and he bears testimony to his generosity as a host ; but the latter remembered to his dying day an act of gross inhospitality on Redgrave's part. They were, in a . sense, neighbours, the Academician having a cottage at Abinger, near Leith Hill ; and Linnell one day, when he was very old, drove over in his pony carriage to see him. Redgrave came to the door to speak to him, and did not so much as ask him to step in.

A writer who paid a visit to the veteran painter shortly after his second marriage, and who saw him at work, says that, though his ' hand may not be as strong as it was sixty or seventy years ago, it shows no diminution of vital energy, or of the cunning that it has so long possessed.'

The picture he gives of him, as seen at this time, is interesting. ' Dressed in a close gray suit, with the chosen one of a score of broad-brimmed hats shading his brows, Linnell sits at a clear, easy distance from his easel, holds his brush at arm's length, and takes a view over his left-hand, as a mariner by a point out at sea. Then, with a short, sharp, nervous, incisive movement of the hand and brush, he lays down his living mark of colour.'

Linnell's hand in his prime was so firm and steady that he hardly ever used a maul-stick. Nor, if we may judge from his neat, small handwriting, which hardly showed signs of tremor to the last, did that firmness of touch ever become much impaired. A letter now lying on the writer's table, which was written in 1865—when, therefore, he was seventy-three years of age—will not be easily paralleled among septuagenarians.

'He never leaves his domain' (the description proceeds) 'except for a drive in the neighbourhood; and very often is not tempted over the threshold of his house, unless there is a cloud which must be looked at, or Nature holds out some such special enticement to this most loving child of hers.

' " Just see those rooks," he says, when you follow him into that holy of holies, his studio. He points to a fresh picture now upon the easel. " I *saw* that. I saw those rooks come boiling up over a cloud, and then, while you stood looking, came another posse, rushing past you like tigers." '*

The picture in question is among the best he painted, and is an exceedingly beautiful one. Its

* From an article in the *Dublin University Magazine*, Nov., 1877.

only fault is that it is a little too gray in tone.   It
shows a broad landscape, with a glint of water in it,
and some figures and a dog in the foreground.   But
the rooks certainly form the central interest of the
picture.   They are full of life and vigour, and seem
literally to *boil up* over the hill.

After his second marriage Linnell became more
than ever tied to Redstone.   In his little domain,
with his sons and daughters and his grandchildren
about him, he was content to spend the remainder
of his days.   He now seldom left his own grounds,
except occasionally for a drive in the neighbourhood when the weather was fine.   He spent much
time out-of-doors, however, driving, or having
himself driven, to and fro in a little donkey-chaise,
somewhat in the style of William Henry Hunt, the
companion of his younger days.   Later he dis-
carded the donkey, and had himself pulled about by
his man Bell, who, he used to declare, was the stub-
borner donkey of the two.

Always a man of marked individuality and originality, these traits seemed to come out in a still
stronger light in these later years.   In many of his
opinions there was something of incongruity when
considered in conjunction with his views on other
subjects.   For instance, although strongly Liberal,
and even democratic, in his general tendency of
thought, yet on some subjects he was not only at
variance with the popular current of Liberal sentiment, but quite Conservative, if not altogether
reactionary.   As an instance in point, I may men-

tion that while he was in substantial agreement with Mr. Gladstone's Liberal views in regard to general reform, he did not support his foreign policy. He had been a great admirer of Lord Palmerston as Secretary of Foreign Affairs, and regarded Lord Beaconsfield as his natural successor in that department. In short, he was no 'peace at any price' man, but was ever for upholding the honour and supremacy of England by vigorous action. Hence the Afghan war had his hearty approval.

Some of the measures of reform also that came to the front during his later years did not have his entire sympathy. In short, he was of an older generation, and could not trim his sails to every fresh wind that blew. Most striking of all was his lack of interest in Mr. Forster's Elementary Education Bill. He soon became utterly weary of hearing about it, and could not hear it spoken of with patience.

It is not difficult to understand this lack of interest if we consider that he had never been to school himself, and that all the education that he ever possessed he had practically obtained by his own unaided efforts. He, too, with the assistance of Mrs. Linnell, had directed the education of their children in the rudiments of learning, and had been the inspirer of their later self-education, which it is not surprising if he considered the best. Indeed, he looked upon the home as the true school, and in a large degree he was doubtless right. The fact is, the artist was losing more and more his touch with the everyday world. His thoughts were on other things. The life to come seemed more real to him than the physical life about him, and he was contemplating that, and meditating upon it, with the tranquillity of one who has long been perfectly assured of its imminence and reality. Indeed, the last few years of his life were characterized by a perfect Christian calm, untroubled by doubts, and free from worldly ambitions or cares. He had for years been accustomed to turn to his Biblical studies for rest, and for the purpose of escaping from the minor worries of life. While thus occupied he was as it were translated, an enfranchised being. Truly has it been said by a writer who had met the subject of whom he was writing:

'A man like this, who can feel in the life around him an inner depth for which the generality have no eyes, may well observe that men choose to live in a dust-hole when they might have the best room in the house. With him, as, indeed, with every true seer, artistic or otherwise, "everything," to use his own words, "is duplicated and full of more meaning than itself." The "Open thou mine eyes, that I may see," with him refers not only to prophetic vision, but to deep sight artistic.'

That this inner vision of Linnell's had something of real depth in it may be gathered from one bit of criticism which was the outcome of his study of the Psalms, which now became his favourite relaxation. In Psalm civ. occur the words:

'O Jehovah, how manifold are thy works !
In wisdom thou hast made them all ;

The earth is full of thy riches ;
So is this sea, great and wide in its shores,
Wherein are things creeping without number,
Living creatures both small and great.
There go the ships, there is that Leviathan,
Whom thou hast made to take his pastime therein.
These all wait upon thee,
That thou mayest give them their food in due season.'

Most thoughtful readers of the Bible have noticed the incongruity of the ship occurring amongst the creatures that God had made, and to which he gives their 'food in due season.' The commentators and Biblical critics have, of course, called attention to the difficulties of the passage, albeit without showing us any way out of them. It is all the more interesting, therefore, to see how a man of Linnell's imaginative insight would solve the enigma. For 'ship' in the ordinary sense he reads 'nautilus,' the little 'Portuguese man-of-war,' as it is called by seamen, the ship of the Almighty's own making.

The point is not one of great vital moment, like some of those questions to which Linnell had formerly given so much attention, and many persons perhaps may not see any particular interest in it beyond a happy suggestion. But it is just in this gift of suggestiveness that the critical intellect, coupled with spiritual perception, is so potent in solving difficulties, and in harmonizing the various parts with the whole. And how happy in this case is the result! The picture presented by the magnificent passage is now complete. We behold the fruitful earth and the wondrously peopled sea; the latter with its great whales and the tiny and delicate nautili in their shells of iridescent hue, all the work of his hand, all needing 'their food in due season.'

Such was the way in which Linnell approached the great Book, which he took so literally, and by which he had endeavoured so sincerely to shape his life.

For the Psalms in especial he had ever had the greatest love and admiration, and it was now his delight to compare the Authorized Version with the original, and to make such emendations as he thought were necessary for a more perfect rendering. He had some idea of having the Psalms published as thus edited or emended by himself, but he did not live to complete the work. Some of his suggested alterations or corrections were very happy, and showed that the critical acumen and the clear perceptions which had guided him in his earlier and more important studies of the Hebrew text had not yet lost their brightness and vigour.*

How strong and clear his perceptions continued to be, long after attaining the age of threescore years and ten, is evidenced by a letter dated November 3, 1867, written to his nephew, Mr. Chance, on a subject which was always uppermost in his mind. It is as follows :

* Apropos of this love of the Psalms, Linnell used to relate with much pleasure how a gentleman, who had purchased several of his works, once told him that *looking at one of his pictures did him as much good as reading a Psalm.* The artist, naturally deeply gratified by such appreciation, replied that the compliment was the greatest that could be paid him.

'MY DEAR CHANCE,

'I have read the report of the discussion with much interest, and from the circumstances you mentioned respecting his history, I guess he must have been as industrious as Dr. Lee, the carpenter who became the Professor of Hebrew, etc., at the University of Cambridge. Mr. Booth has, it seems to me, much light and much honesty, which I expect will lead him into more truth. I care not for the question between Prayer-book and Missal, or Ritualism, as the Prayer-book Protestantism is, in my opinion, only Romanism or Popery diluted. The mother-tincture is at Rome, and the dilutions are in England. For us, however, if we thirst for it, there is the pure river of the water of life, and the unadulterated Word, if we are disposed to prefer it to poisoned streams.

'I wish you would get a tract by Catesby Paget called, "Can Ritualism cast out Ritualism ? A Letter to Earl Shaftesbury " (London : Marlborough and Co., Ave Maria Lane). Give the tract to Mr. Booth from me, and I will pay you for it.

'I am sorry for the Appendix to Mr. Booth's report, as it seems to me to partake of the equivocation so common with Popery, and somewhat reduces my estimate of Mr. Booth's sincerity. But what is a man to do who has error to defend? It was so even with the inspired Apostles. See Gal. ii. 12, 13, where Paul relates how Peter dissembled, and Barnabas was led away with the *hypocrisy of Peter* and the Jews. Now, what can a man do who has the Prayer-book to defend? He must equivocate and dissemble. How can he honestly defend infant-sprinkling, falsely called baptism, and the pretended regeneration, should he be connected with it, and the sponsors, etc. ?

'And then the priesthood, which alone condemns the whole system. Why, priesthood is a denial that Christ has come in the flesh, and so is really Antichrist. Bishops, I know, and others, impose upon the ignorant by telling them a falsehood, viz., that presbyter and priest are the same in the New Testament. (See the Bishop of London's Charge to his clergy.) Then the whole ceremonial, according to the Prayer-book, is ritualistic and popish—only a pot-and-kettle question of degree ; the vestments and the titles usurp the glory of God ; even the common title of *reverend*, assumed by Mr. Booth, is robbing God, to whom alone it belongs (Ps. cxi. 9). I exhort Mr. Booth to lay down this presumptuous sin, as Mr. Spurgeon has publicly done.

'From all this a Christian should separate at any cost. And that that cost may not be a hindrance I recommend Mr. Booth to stick to his bench still, and do as the Thessalonians were exhorted to do by the Apostle. See 2 Thess. iii.

'Your uncle,

'J. L., SEN.

'P.S.—If Mr. Booth comes to Redhill I shall be glad to see him, or if you like to bring him some day to tea, at four or five o'clock, do so.'

The following letters to Count Guicciardini present a striking contrast to the above :

'Redhill, England,
'*October* 12, 1868.

'MY DEAR FRIEND COUNT GUICCIARDINI,

'Will you be kind enough to remember me as a dependent upon your kind assistance to procure some more of the Priorata wine, which I hope this year's vintage will produce in abundance and perfection? As soon as this year's wine is fit to move, I shall be glad to have 100 gallons either in two casks or four, as the last. I venture to ask this favour of you again, as I fear to attempt to alter the channel of application to the merchant or grower of the wine, and as I can only write English I fear I should not be successful. I hope the happy events in Spain will tend to facilitate business rather than otherwise.

'The book you gave me about the doings of Christian Brethren in Italy I got translated, but I have lost both book and translation. I beseech you to give me another copy. I always speak of the Brethren in Italy as the best examples of Christians in Europe. I trust they progress and increase.

'I am, yours truly,
'JOHN LINNELL, SEN.'

'*October* 28, 1868.

'MY DEAR KIND FRIEND COUNT GUICCIARDINI,

'Thanks for your friendly note with offer to obtain the best wine for me. It is very desirable to procure the true and pure in all things in food and drink, as well as knowledge. There is a mental satisfaction in drinking good genuine pure wine ; one feels there must have been veracity and conscientiousness in the minds of all concerned in the making the wine, and one feels grateful not only to God, but to man, and the mental satisfaction is as beneficial as the wine.

' My only reason for choosing this year's vintage was that I supposed the season to be the best which had occurred for years on account of the great heat, which I always thought produced the richest wine ; but if you think there is better Priorata wine in store than this year's vintage will turn out, I leave it to you to procure me the very best, and what will keep.

' If the price of about a franc the bottle applies to the white pale Marsala, my son will be glad to have a quarter cask (24 gallons) of that, and one cask of the red Sicilian, called Vittoria, which you intimate will keep by saying it is good when old. The Priorata has reached me *viâ* Liverpool by rail, and I have paid the duty and expenses to the Liverpool firm of Bahr, Behrend and Co. This plan suits me best, as I have not to employ any agent in London to clear the wine at the docks, etc. Now, if the Marsala can be sent by the same route, I shall prefer it much. I am told there is an article in Marsala that never finds its way to England, but is much superior to that which is usually sent ; they say it is much paler. If there is any superior

Marsala, I should be glad to have some ; that which I had before from Florio was only the usual sort, and no better or cheaper than I can get in London. You may order 100 gallons of the best Priorata in two or more casks, as may be most convenient ; and if this year's vintage makes very superior wine, I can wait till next year to receive it. I do not want to pay for age, as I can wait and keep the wine till it is old ; all I want is best quality, and such as will keep. Payment shall be made as you direct, and when you please.

'I am, yours truly,
'JOHN LINNELL, SEN.'

In 1869 occurred a correspondence with a gentleman in Manchester, apparently a dealer in a small way, who sent the artist a picture which he called an early work of his, with a request that he would do something to it. He wrote :

'I think it would be of greater interest if you painted a few sheep in, and worked on the picture a little—I know not what else to suggest.'

On the receipt of the picture and the letter Linnell wrote :

'*May* 21, 1869.

'DEAR SIR,

'Had I not had previous business transactions with you, I should have required the usual verification fee, and a guarantee against being called to give evidence on the point of originality of the picture. All, however, I require now, before I say

aught of the work, is that you give me an assurance
that I shall not be called upon except to give a
written opinion of the work you have sent me.   If I
am expected to say what I wish upon the work, I
think I may claim from you some account of where
it came from, from whom you had it, and how much
you gave for it, if it is your property, and if not, to
whom it really belongs.   As soon as I receive from
you a satisfactory reply, I will write all that is
requisite.

'I am, yours truly,

'J. LINNELL, SEN.

' ——, Esq.,
    ' Manchester.'

In reply, the gentleman wrote that he had bought
the picture at Huddersfield, and had paid under £20
for it.   He also said :

'Had there been a doubt about its genuineness I
would have sent the fee.   (I can do so now if you
desire.)   The foreground is so transparent, you
may see pencil-drawing previous to painting and
the impasto.   What little there is, is Linnell all
over. . . .

'I've had great experience in pictures, ancient
and modern, and am known to understand them.
I've no desire to do anything unfair or shabby.   I
thought a few sheep or geese would improve the
picture, and perhaps the tree on left-hand side of
picture worked up a little.'

To this letter Linnell replied under date, May 24,
1869, as follows :

' DEAR SIR,

' I fear from the confidence you speak with of your experience, etc., you will scarcely believe my account of the picture you sent to me the other day. But I beg to say that I never saw it before. Of its merits I forbear to say aught but that I do not feel flattered by your admiration and assertion that it is " Linnell all over." Indeed, I think it would soon be " all over" with Linnell if your account of the matter were right. Now, I suppose, after this from me, you will not either part with the picture or keep it with a forged signature on it. Will you allow me, before I return the picture, to erase the forgery, and so have the evidence that it does not leave my room with a falsehood as if I had sanctioned it ?

' I shall require nothing more, but that you will believe me to be,

' Truly yours,
' JOHN LINNELL, SEN.'

The desired permission to erase the forged signature was not given, and the picture was finally returned, followed by the annexed letter :

' Redhill, Surrey,
' *May* 26, 1869.

' DEAR SIR,

' I have sent the picture as you require with the false signature on it, just as it came to me, and beg to say that whoever now sells the picture with that name on it will be liable to prosecution for forgery, as Mr. Clöss was, who was sent to Newgate for the same thing in 1857.

'I am, yours faithfully,

'JOHN LINNELL, SEN.

'P.S.—I hope you will let me know if the name has been erased, for it will be highly disgraceful if the person who keeps the picture does not erase the name after my declaration of its falsehood.'

In regard to the man Clöss above referred to, there appears at one time, when the demand for the artist's pictures was at its height, to have been a systematic manufacture of spurious 'Linnells,' and from time to time he was called upon to decide as to the genuineness of pictures said to be by him. There was never any difficulty, however, in detecting the counterfeits, the imitation always being crude, and of the shallowest surface quality. Clöss was one of the spurious manufacturers, and was prosecuted for passing off a copy with a forged signature.

A curious point of law turned up on this occasion. Although it was proved beyond question that the culprit had signed Linnell's name to his own work, yet technically he could not be convicted of forgery, because the signature was upon canvas, and not upon paper or parchment, as by law it should be to become a felonious act. Clöss in consequence got off with a nominal sentence.

CHAPTER XV.

Cornelius Varley — His Death — Letter by Mr. Gladstone — The Chantrey Bequest—Proposal to purchase one of Linnell's Pictures —Correspondence—Last Days—Visited by Mr. Holman Hunt— Death.

CORNELIUS VARLEY, who has been previously mentioned as having had so important an influence upon the life and character of John Linnell, he having been the first to introduce him to the Baptists, outlived his elder brother John by upwards of a quarter of a century, dying in 1873 (October 2), in the ninety-second year of his age. He presents, in his life and achievements, a striking contrast to his brother, and exemplifies perhaps as well as anyone could the advantage of talents over genius. John Varley was a genius, with many of the eccentricities, and all the possibilities of running an ill-regulated course, that are among the only too well-known attributes of genius. Cornelius, on the other hand, with many talents, was as regular as a watch, to the business of making which he was first put. He subsequently devoted himself to the study of mechanics, chemistry, and optics. After learning the trade of an optician, he gave it up to follow

in the footsteps of his brother, as did also the third
brother, William Fleetwood Varley, becoming a
water-colour painter, and making several visits to
Wales, and one to Ireland, in the pursuit of his
calling.   But he subsequently settled down again
to the making of optical instruments, and to the
study of science generally.   He was the author of
many articles, and one or two works on subjects
connected with mechanics, optics, and allied subjects.

His invention of the Graphic Telescope has
already been referred to.   The Colosseum, it would
appear, owed its origin to this instrument, Mr. T.
Horner, after satisfying himself of its capabilities,
having erected an observatory on the dome of St.
Paul's, where he fitted up a Graphic Telescope, and
traced his magnificent panorama of London, for the
reception of which the Colosseum in Regent's Park
was built.

In 1850 Mr. Varley was elected chairman of the
committee of exhibitors in Class 10 for the Great
Exhibition of 1851, and received a prize-medal from
the jurors for his telescope, forty years after its
invention.   A fellow-member of the Society of Arts
who had known him for many years has described
him as 'a most conscientious man, a true friend, an
excellent philosopher, and an able mechanic and
optician.'

In 1871 John Linnell had occasion to write to
his old friend as an expert in the last-named capacity,
when his letter brought forth the following reply
with its double postscript :

'337, Kentish Town Road, N.W.,
'*October* 2, 1871.

' FRIEND LINNELL,

'Though spectacles were largely made by excellent machinery in London, yet latterly they have all migrated to Sheffield, from whence nearly all the dealers obtain them. So I reckon you can be as well supplied in the nearest town to yourself as in London, you stating size and focus that will suit you. But I recommend pebbles as being more transparent and harder than glass, and not so liable to be scratched.

' Yours truly,

' CORNELIUS VARLEY.

' P.S.—I don't think we have seen each other since you banished yourself from London. I am nearly through my ninetieth year. How much younger are you?

' 2nd P.S.—I think it was you who gave me a small coin found in the Red Hills many years ago. It represents the beginning of the twelfth chapter of Revelation—a woman clothed with the sun, the moon under her feet, and a crown of twelve stars on her head. The moon regulated all the Jewish feasts, particularly the Passover. It is her foundation and support ; the sun her clothing of righteousness ; the stars her honours, the twelve Apostles. On the reverse is the woman and man-child whom the dragon has always sought to destroy by floods out of his mouth. Witness the many thousand books which the clergy have poured and still are pouring forth.   It has become a separate trade to deal in clerical books only.'

This and a letter dated nearly twenty years previously are the only ones, in the mass of Linnell's correspondence, from Cornelius Varley.   The letter, written from 1, Charles Street, Clarendon Square, and dated July 2, 1853, is as follows :

'DEAR SIR,
        'I cannot distinctly say I have practised photography, though we have fitted up several sets of apparatus for others.   Two of my sons who were making themselves acquainted with it have now got profitable engagements very far from home, so at present we are not pursuing it.   Yet for any profitable engagement I could go through the processes sufficiently to communicate the same to others.
        'The Photogenic Society have an exhibition of excellent sun-pictures, and works in the Royal Academy show that photography is doing much good to the arts.
        'I cannot fix any day in the ensuing week to give you a visit, but may be able in the week after, if you are determined to go heartily into play with the sunbeams, the most glorious associate the arts have ever had.
                    'Yours very truly,
                        'CORNELIUS VARLEY.
    'J. LINNELL, ESQ.'

In 1873 Linnell sent to Mr. Gladstone, through Mr. George Richmond, a copy of his engraved portrait of Sir Robert Peel, which called forth the following reply from the Liberal leader :

'11, Carlton House Terrace, S.W.,
'*May* 21, 1873.

'My dear Mr. Richmond,

'Acceptable as must be the engraved portrait you have kindly deposited here, both for its own sake and because it proceeds from Mr. Linnell, I must not hold it in fraud ; and therefore I hasten to acquaint you that Mr. Cardwell is the fortunate possessor of the picture of Sir R. Peel which it represents.

'I mentioned the work to Mr. Cardwell, and had our respective positions in respect to the blessing of offspring been reversed, I might perhaps have made the acquisition, about which he was most considerate.

'I am happy enough to possess a picture by Mr. Linnell, which I greatly value.

'Had not my name been placed in error on the ·print, by Mr. Linnell's kindness, I should at once have forwarded it to Mr. Cardwell, and I think I had better do this as it is, unless I hear from you to the contrary effect.

'Yours sincerely,
'W. E. Gladstone.

'I ought to add that I have sown my wild oats, and am now a reformed character in regard to purchases.'

In the year 1876, when the Chantrey Fund became available for the purchase of works for a national collection, there was a feeling amongst some of the Academicians that a portion of the first money at their disposal under the bequest could not be better expended than in the purchase of one of John Linnell's famous landscapes. George Richmond made a proposal to that effect, and he was heartily supported by Mr. Webster and others. The suggestion, however, does not appear to have been taken up very earnestly amongst the Academicians generally, or it must have resulted otherwise than it did. Opinion was in favour of a picture of Linnell's second period, when he was undoubtedly at his greatest, and Mr. Richmond was commissioned to see what was in the market. In the course of his inquiries he made a journey to Redhill to look at the pictures still in the artist's possession.

The following correspondence has reference to the proposed purchase. The first letter is dated January 1, 1877, and was from Mr. Thomas Johnson, a dealer of Manchester:

' MY DEAR SIR,
    ' I cannot resist wishing you and yours every good wish for the New Year.
    ' I think you will be equally gratified with myself to hear that the Royal Academy think of purchasing one of your finest works out of the " Chantrey Bequest." In short I was asked if my friend Mason, of Bradford, would sell the " Last Gleam before the Storm," which I bought last year for £2,500 guineas, and which originally belonged to

Mr. Eden, of Lytham. I have named the subject to several R.A.'s, and they strongly approve of the purchase, notably Webster, who told me this morning that he sincerely hoped it would be accomplished. Raeburn's portraits in the Academy are much admired. I trust you keep fairly well.

'Yours truly,

'THOMAS JOHNSON.'

On the receipt of this letter Linnell sent it with the following note to Mr. Richmond :

'DEAR MR. RICHMOND,

'Enclosed is a letter received this morning, and as you so kindly interested yourself in the matter, I send it to you for perusal and return, with my wish that you máy remember my two R.A. pictures, 1875, 1876, are both with me, price £2,000 each, a price I was offered for one, but refused.

'I am, yours truly,

'J. LINNELL, SEN.'

The pictures referred to are 'Woods and Forests' (41 by 57 inches), which was sold at the Neck sale at Christie's in 1890 for 1,900 guineas, and 'The Hollow Tree,' subsequently purchased by Mr. McLean for £1,600.

Linnell's reply to Mr. Johnson, dated January 4, was as follows :

' Dear Mr. Johnson,

'Many thanks for your kind letter. The subject is not new to me, for my old friend Richmond, R.A., had last year interested himself in the matter of the proposed purchase of one of my works for the Chantrey Fund Collection. Mr. Richmond recommended my 1875 R.A. picture as one, or the 1876, but the committee seemed to wish for one of my middle style. If you are referred to, will you kindly remember that both my R.A. pictures, 1875 and 1876, are still in my possession, price £2,000 each. The amount I refused for one, but would now for such a purpose feel gratified by the sale at that price. Hoping you will come and see them the first opportunity,

'I am, yours truly,

'JOHN LINNELL, SEN.

'THOMAS JOHNSON, ESQ.'

The following letter from Mr. Richmond completes the correspondence on the subject, and nothing more seems to have been done in the matter.

'20, York Street,
'Portman Square, W.,
'*January* 2, 1877.

'Dear Mr. Linnell,

'I heartily join with Mr. Johnson (whose note I return) in wishing you, and all yours, a very happy New Year ; and I can think of very few things of a professional kind that would delight me more than that the trustees under the Chantrey Fund should make their first purchase in a picture of John Linnell, sen.

'This I stated in Council when I first entered upon the duties two years ago, and the last time we met before going out of office, I rose to urge this with all the earnestness that I felt. This was on December 12 last.

'Your picture exhibited in 1875 I mentioned as one that I should like to purchase, but I see that many of the Academicians incline to a work of your middle time.

'I asked Woolner about the picture that was his, and which was sold at Christie's last year, and he said he would inquire if the possessor was willing to part with it. So stand matters now. And such is the uncertainty of things in which several persons are concerned, that I should not be surprised if no agreement is come to, and no picture purchased for some time to come. But still I heartily hope that it will not turn out so, but that purchases will be made soon, and that a picture by you will be the first that is purchased for the collection which is eventually to be the nation's.

'I remain,

'Dear Mr. Linnell,

'Very faithfully yours,

'GEO. RICHMOND.'

It would have been a graceful act if the Academy, which ignored Linnell so long, had seen its way to do him the honour of selecting one of his noble

landscapes as the first to form the nucleus of a
national collection under the Chantrey Fund ; but it
was not to be—the spirit which had ever been
against him was against him still, and though his
friends in the Academy did their best for him, their
efforts were in vain.   Mr. Richmond in particular
never ceased to regret the failure of this endeavour
to do an act of well-merited honour to the octo-
genarian painter.

Linnell continued to paint almost to the last ; but
in his latest works he shows a gradual falling off.
He becomes somewhat mannered and less simple,
more large and general in his treatment, with less
of that definition and detail which give to his
earlier works some of the finer qualities of Dutch
art.   Then his touch became less firm, with the
result that his pictures began to show a certain
amount of 'wooliness.'   Along with the weakening
of his hand came a gradual failure of sight, so that
he had to take to stronger and stronger glasses.
Among the latest exhibited of his works was a
small 'Woodcutter.'   A man is seen standing on
the felled trunk of a tree in the act of swinging his
axe.   It was painted from a sketch made at Hampstead while he was living there, but it was not
finished till towards the close of his career.   Then,
on account of the talk about Mr. Gladstone's fond-
ness for tree-felling, he used to call it his 'Gladstone.'   It cannot, of course, be reckoned amongst
his best productions ; but it is, nevertheless, a suf-
ficiently remarkable picture, when it is considered

that it was painted when the artist was considerably over eighty years of age. The last painted of his pictures were ' Sweet fa's the Eve,' ' The Heath,' and ' Sunset on the Common.'

Finally, during the last year or two of his life, in consequence of the gradual decline of physical power, he was obliged to give up painting altogether. It was a trial to him ; but this, as well as his growing physical infirmities, he bore with exemplary patience. Happily his mental perceptions remained undimmed to the last, which was a source of great thankfulness both to himself and to those about him.

It was during this period (1881) that Mr. Holman Hunt, being on a visit with Mrs. Hunt to Mr. William Linnell, who was now living at Hill's Brow, the house built for him on the estate by his father, called upon his old friend. He thus describes what occurred on that memorable occasion.

' He was then very feeble from advanced age, not seeing people under ordinary circumstances. To me it seemed a characteristic and noble earnestness which made him abruptly appeal to me on my approach in exhortation on the importance of mastering the teaching of the New Testament as the first important duty of life. He would not allow me to evade the question, but appealed to me for a direct answer whether I had done this. The scene was a very interesting one in my eyes. He recognised that he had come to his last days, and that there would never again be an opportunity for

him to deliver his sacredest message of all to me;
and he would not fail, although, when he regarded
my reply as failing in thoroughness, he had to
reproach me, which he did unsparingly.'

The venerable painter had the Bible in his hand
when Mr. Hunt entered. He held it aloft tremb-
lingly as he spoke, asking him if he had made sure
of his eternal salvation. To him then nothing else
appeared of any importance, and he insisted upon
the momentousness of the question with the earnestness and solemnity of a man with one foot in the
grave.

This is almost the last glimpse we get of Linnell
from an outside source, and it shows him as he had
ever been—direct, fearless, and sincere, thinking
more of the real, the true, and the eternal, than of
that which is merely ephemeral and conventional.

He finally passed away, the physical powers of
his nature quite exhausted, on January 20, 1882,
being then ninety years of age all but five months.
He was conscious to the last, and had but a few
minutes before taken leave of the members of his
family, most of whom were gathered by his bed-
side.

CHAPTER XVI.

Conclusion — Sixty Years a Contributor to the Royal Academy — Linnell's Fortune — His Monument in his Works — Estimate of his Powers — His Place in British Art.

THERE are but few more words to be said before closing this imperfect record of a remarkable career. As he had lived, so John Linnell died, true to the principles he had espoused in early manhood, and from which, through all his years of toil and struggle, he had never swerved. There is hardly another example in the whole history of art of a life so uniform and consistent in its aim—of a devotion so entire and so unflagging through a career of eighty years.

For sixty years he was a regular contributor to the Royal Academy exhibitions, and during that time exhibited something like 170 works, being an average of nearly three per annum.* Only about twice during the whole course of those years have we a record of pictures which he sent for exhibition being returned to him unhung; and if the works from his brush to be seen in our public galleries are,

---

* He also exhibited, from 1808 to 1859, about eighty-two works, that had not been exhibited elsewhere, at the British Institution.

as regards size and numbers, inferior to those of many of his contemporaries, they are so because as soon as his art became known, almost to the day of his death, he sold as quickly as he could paint, and for the greater part of the time obtained such prices as few contemporary artists did.

In a worldly sense, the result of his industry and his painstaking perseverance through years of unflagging endeavour was the accumulation of a fortune such as it has been the lot of but few of his profession to emulate. Artists in their confidential moments are apt to hold their breath when speaking of the fabulous amounts which it is currently reported John Linnell was enabled to amass. A common figure at which his savings are put is £300,000. This, of course, is an exaggeration ; but had he not invested largely in land; and settled handsome sums upon his sons and daughters, his fortune might have reached something like two-thirds of that amount.

In accordance with that shrewd business tact, however, which had characterized him through life, he disposed of most of his fortune long before his death, so that his personal property at the time of his decease was comparatively small.

It is a remarkable fact, and one worthy of record in this connection, that, according to his own statement, often repeated, he never in the whole course of his career made a single bad debt, except it might be in a very few instances of a trifling character. The fact is almost astounding, and speaks volumes for those business principles of his, from which, established early in life, he never deviated.

In accordance with another principle upon which he had always acted himself, and upon which he wished to see others act in such matters, his family had his remains interred in the unconsecrated portion of the Reigate Cemetery, with no other monument to mark the spot save the usual headstone, with a suitable inscription.

His monument, as he believed all men's should be, is in his works; and a noble monument it is— one which we may well believe will last so long as sincerity in art is honoured; for whatever may be the ultimate judgment upon it, it can never be said that John Linnell's art was other than sincere. It is, perhaps, too early yet to estimate his influence on landscape art, or to give him his true place in the ranks of English artists. On the morrow of his death the *Times* spoke of him as 'the most powerful of landscape-painters since Turner died'; and though the world generally has not yet accorded him such a high place—and it might seem presumptuous in his biographer to claim it for him— still, that he will by universal consent be recognised as one of the foremost of British artists no one can doubt who has once had the opportunity of judging of his work as the works of other native artists are capable of being judged—that is, by a selection of his best works being made available in a national collection.

Perhaps in the course of time other specimens of his art may be bequeathed to the national collections, or purchased for them. Since his death the appreciation in which his works are held has increased rather than declined, and this is what we should expect ; for John Linnell's art is of that kind that comes home to men's hearts the more they know it. We may travel in foreign lands, and be pleased and delighted ; but the time invariably arrives when native scenes and native skies offer an overwhelming attraction.

In this lies the strength of Linnell's art. It is so English that it must ever be doubly interesting on that account. It is as English as Gainsborough's, as ' Old ' Crome's, as De Wint's, or as David Cox's. It is on that account somewhat circumscribed as compared with the works of men like Turner and William H. Müller ; but it is rich in variety, nevertheless, and may be said to cover the whole ground of English landscape.

During his time John Linnell saw many changes among contemporaries, and beheld fashions in landscape art rise and decay. But throughout he remained uninfluenced by them, and preserved as striking an individuality in his art as in his character. It is this unbroken unity in his strongly pronounced landscape-painting which has placed him somewhat apart in the lineage of art. No one has been able satisfactorily to trace his artistic pedigree. He imbibed so much from others, but assimilated it so perfectly, and made it so thoroughly his own by interfusing it with his own perceptions, that though it is not difficult to trace similarities and points of contact with men of many schools—with the Poussins and the Claudes, with the Hobbemas and the Cuyps, with the Gainsboroughs and the Morlands, etc.—yet from none of these can a clear descent be made out. It was a fairy gift rather than an inheritance that he derived from these men. Indeed, as has been shown, in seeking his true relationship, we must look to the older Masters rather than to those of a later age.

Although, in regard to composition, Linnell's pictures seem to owe something to the Poussins, in colour their inspiration is derived more from the splendours of Rubens, Titian, and the Venetian School generally than from any other source.

In respect to contemporaries, Linnell exhibits more points of resemblance with John Crome and De Wint than with anyone else. But in order to understand him aright we must look at him as the child of Nature that he was, with a peculiar and oftentimes deep insight into her ways and mysteries, and with a rare power of reproducing her in all her simplicity and truth.

It was owing to this gift, and to the perennial freshness of his contact, that Nature and Art in his works are rarely dissevered, but are ever one and inseparable. In the same way he never separates humanity from nature. His landscapes are always peopled. They do not reveal merely the beauty of nature ; they tell also the story of man's connection therewith. Moreover, what he sets down is never mean or trivial, but wholesome and dignified. In all this he was loyal to the best traditions of English landscape art, and for that we owe him much.

As regards composition, if he does not emulate the complexity and magnificence of Turner, he is at least harmonious and symmetrical. In his lines and masses there is always dignity and proportion, in which respect, and in the general simplicity of his method of composition, he is again allied to the Old Masters.

It is questionable, perhaps, whether Linnell possessed the power to have become a great figure-painter. There is not much in his works to suggest that he could; and yet indications are not wanting, faint it may be, but yet indubitable, that had he enjoyed the opportunities as a young man, in place of being kept so closely to portrait-painting and engraving, he might possibly have shone in figure-painting.

It is useless to find fault with him that his power was not broader and more general—that he did not paint rugged mountain scenery, the sea, and Nature as a whole in her wilder and more savage moods: he painted what he could, and he painted it so well that few before or after him have done what he did, and done it better.

APPENDIX.

LIST OF PICTURES, ENGRAVINGS, ETC.

THE following lists form a catalogue, as nearly complete as possible, of John Linnell's landscapes and other paintings and drawings ; also of his engravings. It also gives the more important portraits that he painted.

ENGRAVINGS.

The sizes, when named, are those of the engraved work.

Portrait of John Martin, Pastor of the Baptist Church, Keppel Street, London. Engraved (in etching and line) from the artist's oil picture (1813).
Replica of the Head, small vignette (in dry point and line), signed 'J. Linnell, 1817.' (Gale and Fenner, Paternoster Row.)
Portrait of Rev. J. M. Bletsoe, head-master of Loughborough Grammar School (6 by 4 inches), 1814.
Portrait of Mr. G. Phillips (head) from the artist's own drawing, 1814.
Two Views in the Island of Elba. Small etching for 'A Tour through the Island of Elba' (one not used).
A View of the Source of the Ebro for General Maitland. Etching on copper, 12 by 20 inches, 1814, 1815.
A Girl at a Well (8 by 6 inches), etched on copper for Mr. Cristall, 1815.
'A Landscape,' small; engraved for J. Varley, 1816.
A View of Woody Mountains called 'Taleh Rudbar' (6 by 6 inches). Etched for Sir Wm. Ouseley, 1816.
'Ruins near Morghun' (Persia). For Sir W. Ouseley, from a drawing by Col. D'Arcy, 1816.
Two Views of Mountains, with Huts. For Sir W. Ouseley, 1816.
Portrait of Mr. Spence. Small etching for Mr. Rickards, 1816.
Portrait of Dr. Chalmers. Etching, small, 1817.
Bust of the Princess Charlotte, drawn on stone for Mr. White, engraver, December, 1817.
Portrait of Mrs. Whiting (7 by 5 inches). Etched from the artist's pencil-drawing for Miss Doig, 1817.
Waterfall in a Wood (6½ by 5 inches). Etched from a drawing by Robson, 1818.

'Interior of a Ruined Abbey' (4½ by 3½ inches).   Etched from a drawing by J. Constable, 1818.

'Mid-day' (4 by 8 inches), 1818.   Etched on copper from his picture painted the same year.

'Woodcutter's Repast' (4 by 8 inches).   Etched on copper from his sketch in Windsor Forest, 1818.

Portrait of James Upton, pastor of the Baptist Church, Church Street, Blackfriars Road (10 by 7½ inches).   In line and dry point from the artist's own picture, 1818, 1819.   Linnell employed William Blake to begin and lay in this portrait.

Landscape by Ruysdael (6½ by 9¼ inches).   Etched from the picture for Mr. S. Woodburn, 1819.

Portrait of Wilson Lowry, F.R.S., M.G.S.   Vignette, engraved (in line) by J. Linnell and William Blake from Linnell's drawing, 1824.   (Hurst, Robinson and Co., Cheapside.)

Portrait of Thomas Chevalier, F.R.S., F.S.A., F.H.S., Surgeon-extraordinary to the King, and Professor of Anatomy and Surgery to the Royal College of Surgeons.   Vignette, engraved (line) from the artist's own drawing from the life, 1825.   (Colnaghi and Co.)

Figure (small) from the centre panel of the triptych by Van Eyck (3½ inches square).   Etched for Mrs. Aders as a specimen of style for a prospectus for the publication of the whole work, 1825.

Triptych, by Van Eyck—first panel (20 by 7 inches).   Engraved in line for Mrs. Aders, 1826.

Views in Norway (6 plates containing 8 subjects).   Etched from drawings by Mr. Edward Price, 1827, 1828.

Portrait of the Rev. George Pritchard (vignette, 9 by 5½ inches).   From the artist's own drawing, 1827.   (Wightman and Cramp, Paternoster Row.)

Heads, various (8 plates, 6½ by 10 inches), etched for J. Varley, and published in his 'Treatise on Zodiacal Physiognomy,' 1828.

Michael Angelo's Figures on the Ceiling of the Sistine Chapel. Facsimile copies of old line engravings.   Six plates of single figures 6 by 4½ inches, 1828.

Portrait of Robert Gooch, M.D. (11½ by 9½ inches).   In line from the artist's own picture, 1831.   (W. J. White, Brownlow Street.)

'Feeding the Rabbits,' by W. Collins, R.A. (15 by 12½ inches). Engraved for the artist in mezzotint, 1831. (F. Collins, 52, Great Marlborough Street.)

'Saul' (15 by 22 inches). Engraved in mezzotint from John Varley's picture, 1831. (Albert Varley.)

Portraits of Rev. Rowland Hill, M.A. (1827); C. Babbage, Esq. (1832); and Rev. Wm. Marsh, M.A. (1831). Engraved from portraits by Miss Sheppard.

'Boys in a Boat' (6½ by 5½ inches). Engraved in mezzotint from the picture by W. Collins, R.A., 1831.

Portrait of A. W. Callcott, Esq., R.A. (13 by 10 inches). In mezzotint from the artist's own portrait from the life, 1832.

Portrait of Wm. Bray, Esq., of Shere, Surrey, in his ninety-seventh year (14½ by 12¾ inches). Mezzotint from the artist's own portrait, 1833. (Colnaghi and Co.)

Portrait of the Rev. T. R. Malthus, M.A., F.R.S., Professor of Hist. and Pol. Economy at the East India Co lege, and author of the 'Essay on the Principles of Population,' etc. (14 by 11½ inches). Mezzotint from the artist's own portrait, 1833. (Colnaghi and Co.)

Portrait of James Stephen, Esq, one of the Masters of the High Court of Chancery. Mezzotint from the artist's own posthumous portrait, 1834.

Portrait of the Rev. John Marshall (small). Mezzotint, 1834.

Portrait of Edward William Wynne Pendarves, Esq., M.P. (15 by 12 inches). Mezzotint from the artist's own picture, 1835. (Colnaghi and Co.)

Portrait of Pelham Warren, M.D., F.R.S. (15 by 11½ inches). Mezzotint from the artist's own painting, 1835.

Portrait of 'The Right Hon. Thos. Spring-Rice, Chancellor of the Exchequer,' etc. (14½ by 12 inches). Mezzotint from the artist's own picture, 1836. (Francis Graves and Co., Cockspur Street.)

Portrait of Mrs. Daniel, mother of the Rev. E. T. Daniel (8½ by 6½ inches). Etched from the artist's drawing, 1836.

Portrait of Mr. Zachariah Langton (15½ by 13 inches). Mezzotint from the artist's picture, 1836.

Portrait of the Rev. John Leifchild (15½ by 12¾ inches). Mezzotint from the artist's picture, 1836. (Leifchild, 13, Piccadilly.)

Portrait of Thos. Norris, Esq., F.R.A.S. ($15\frac{1}{2}$ by $12\frac{3}{4}$ inches). Mezzotint from the artist's own picture, 1837.

Facsimiles of Original Drawings of the Frescoes by Michael Angelo on the Ceiling of the Sistine Chapel   These drawings were made at the time of the paintings, and before the fresco of 'The Last Judgment' was executed.   Originally the subjects were on one sheet of paper, forming one whole, similarly to the frescoes of the ceiling.   Forty-one plates, engraved in mezzotint, and published at first in six numbers, containing (with the key plate) seven plates each.   The first number was issued to subscribers, April, 1833 ; the others as completed, the last being finished February, 1837.

Portrait of 'The Right Hon. Sir Robert Peel, Bart.,' etc. (16 by 13 inches).   Mezzotint from the artist's picture from the life, 1838.   (Thos. Boys, publisher.)

Portrait of Richard Whately, D.D., Archbishop of Dublin (12 by $9\frac{1}{4}$ inches).   Mezzotint from the artist's picture from the life, 1838.   (B. Fellows, 39, Ludgate Street.)

Portrait of the Rev. Joseph Hallet Batten, D.D., F.R.S. (16 by 12 inches).   Mezzotint from the artist's portrait from the life, 1838.

Portrait of the Rev. George A. E. Marsh, A.M., Rector of Bangor (12 by $9\frac{1}{2}$ inches).   Etched from the artist's drawing, 1835.

'The Journey to Emmaus' ($13\frac{1}{2}$ by 18 inches).   Mezzotint from the artist's picture, 1839.   A proof impression of this print, from the picture selected by the Committee of the Society for the Encouragement of British Art in the year 1838 was presented to each subscriber for the season 1839.

Landscape by Titian—Herdsman driving cattle (7 by 6 inches). In mezzotint for 'The Royal Gallery of Pictures.' (Jas. Bohn, 1840.)   The original is at Buckingham Palace.

Portrait of William Otter, D.D., Bishop of Chichester ($16\frac{1}{2}$ by $13\frac{3}{4}$ inches).   Mezzotint from the artist's portrait, 1841. (W. H. Mason, Chichester; and Welch and Gwynne, St. James's Street.)

Portrait of Major Beamish ($14\frac{1}{2}$ by $11\frac{1}{2}$ inches).   Etched from the artist's drawing, 1838.

Portrait of the Rev. Robert Clarke Caswall, LL.B. (10 by 8 inches).   Mezzotint from the artist's painting from the life, 1847.

Portrait of Robert Peel, Esq. (cousin of Sir Robert Peel), (size 15¾ by 13 inches). Mezzotint from the artist's picture, 1841.

Portrait of the Rev. Jno. P. Blencowe (8 by 6½ inches). Etched from the artist's drawing, 1841.

Portrait of Joseph Strutt, Esq., of Derby (15¾ by 13½ inches). From the artist's picture, in mezzotint, 1842. (Moseley, Derby.)

Portrait of 'Gen. B. Espartero' (vignette, 10 by 8 inches). Drawn on stone from the artist's portrait, 1843. (T. McLean, Haymarket.)

Portrait of William Coningham, Esq. (8¼ by 6½ inches). Etched from the artist's picture, 1843.

Four Illustrations for 'Traditional Nursery Songs of England,' by Felix Summerby (Mr., afterwards Sir H. Cole), published by J. Cundall, 12, Old Bond Street, 1843. The subjects were :

'Let's go to bed, says Sleepy Head ;'
'I've Caught a Hare Alive ;'
'The Cat sat Asleep by the Fire ;'
'There was an Old Woman,' etc.

Portrait of Lady Beauchamp (16 by 13 inches). On stone, from the artist's portrait, 1845.

Portrait of Lord Methuen. On stone, from the artist's portrait, 1846.

PORTRAITS FROM THE LIFE. OIL PAINTINGS.

Picture (small) of 'A Woman at Table Drinking' (1811). Painted from Mr. Mulready's mother, and very like her. Purchased by Mr. Ridley Colborne (1811) for 25 guineas.

A companion picture, entitled 'A Boy Reading,' was painted from William Mulready (1811).

Linnell's first (recorded) commission for a portrait was from
. Ridley Colborne, Esq. (afterwards Lord Colborne), for whom he painted (1811) a picture containing small whole-length portraits of himself, Mrs. Colborne, and child. Mr. Colborne appears as a gamekeeper bringing a hare to his wife, who stands at a cottage door. (Panel, 15 by 12 inches.)

In 1811 he commenced a portrait (head) of Francis Beckford, Esq., of Southampton.

Mr. John Martin (Baptist minister), half-length, life-size, 1812. (Engraved.) Exhibited at the 'Old Masters' in 1883. In possession of the artist's family.

In 1815 the artist painted about a dozen small portraits at Newbury and Kingsclere.

Rev. George Pritchard, Baptist preacher. Painted by the artist for himself, and exhibited at Spring Gardens.

Mr. Bryan (author of the 'Dictionary of Painters'), 1816.

Mr. Fisher (of the Exchequer Office), 1816.

Mr. Druysdale (from Russia), 1816.

Lord Strangford (for Mr. Carpenter, of Bond Street), 1816.

Miss Sophia Gwilt, 1816.

Mr. John Gage (3 portraits), 1816-17.

Mr. Shirley, Baptist minister at Sevenoaks, Kent.

Mr. Trevithike, the engineer and inventor (life-size), 1816.

Mr. Chin (Baptist minister at Walworth), 1816.

Dr. Steadman (Baptist minister), 1817.

The Dowager Countess of Errol (small), 1817.

The Right Hon. J. H. Frere (small), 1817.

Portraits in group of Philip Thomas Wykham, Esq., Mrs. Wykham, and two sons, and Mrs. Trottman (small whole-lengths), 1817. Painted at Tythrop House, near Thame, Oxon.

Portraits in group of Fiennes Trottman, Esq. (brother to Mrs. Wykham), and Mrs. Trottman (small whole-lengths), 1817. Painted at Tythrop House.

The Duke of Argyle (small), 1817.

The Duchess of Argyle (small), 1817.

Lord John Campbell (brother to the Duke of Argyle), (small), 1817.

C. Gusley, Esq. (West Indian), (small), 1818.

Dr. Jenkins (Baptist minister at Walworth), (small), 1818.

Mr. James Upton (Baptist minister at Blackfriars), (small), 1818. (Engraved.)

Colonel Dumaresque (small), 1818; again in 1819.

Mr. Ivemy (Baptist minister), (small), 1818.

John Varley (the water-colour painter), (small), 1818.

Miss Furnell (of Henley-on-Thames), (small), 1818.

Henry Hervey, Esq., 1819. Also of Edward Hervey, Esq.

Lieut -Colonel Torrens (small), 1819.

Mr. Sweatman, senr., (half-length, life-size), 1819

Mrs. Allies (of Southampton), (life-size), 1819.

Portraits in group of Lady Torrens and Family—(Miss Torrens, Miss Hannah Torrens, Henry Torrens, Esq., Masters Arthur, Frederic and Charles Torrens), 1819-21. Width, 60 inches. (Small whole-lengths.) For Sir Henry Torrens, of Fulham. R.A., 1821.

Miss Waring (afterwards Mrs. J. Brooks), as Rowena in 'Ivanhoe,' 1820. R.A.,* 1821.

Colonel Maxwell, Governor of St. Kits (R.A.), and Mrs. Maxwell, 1821.

The Earl of Denbigh, 1821. R.A., 1823.

* The letters 'R.A.' indicate that the portrait or picture was exhibited in the Royal Academy Exhibition.

E. Denny, Esq., 1821. R.A., 1822.

Sir Edward Denny, Bart. (of King's End House, near Worcester), 1821 ; also Lady Denny.

Master William Denny (youngest son of Sir E. Denny), 1821. R.A., 1822.

Miss Charlotte Fector (afterwards Mrs. Bayley), (small), 1821.

–– Bayley, Esq. (son of Judge Bayley), (small), 1822.

Mrs. George Stephen (small), 1822. R.A.

Miss Anne James, 1822. R.A., 1823.

The Right Hon. Lady Agnes Buller (twin-sister to the Duke of . Northumberland), 1822-23, (whole-length, life-size). R.A., 1823.

Colonel Buller (of Whitehall Place), (whole-length, life-size), 1822-23.

Joseph James, Esq. (of Esher), 1823. R.A.

Captain Craigie, 1824.

Mrs. William Wilberforce, 1824. R.A.

Mrs. Digby Murray (whole-length, life-size), 1824.

General Darling, of Cheltenham ; also Mrs. Darling, 1825.

Portrait group of Miss C. Darling and Master F. Darling (small whole-lengths), 1825.

Portrait group of Mrs. Darling and Children (small whole-lengths), 1825.

Colonel Kingscote (of Kingscote, Gloucestershire); also Mrs. Kingscote (both half-length, life-size), 1825.

Miss Denny (small), 1825. R.A.

Mrs. Garratt (of Hampstead), 1825.

Edward Sheppard, Esq. (of 'The Ridge,' Gloucestershire), 1825. R.A., 1826.

Miss J. Puxley (life-size), 1826. R.A.

— Kennerly, Esq. (half-length, life-size), 1826.

Miss Macdonald, 1826. R.A.

Mrs. Aders, 1827. (Engraved.)

Robert Gooch, M.D., 1827. Painted for Sir William Knighton. R.A. (Engraved.)

Miss Knighton (afterwards Mrs. Seymour), 1827. For Sir William Knighton. R.A.

Lady Lyndhurst, 1827. For the Lord Chancellor. R.A., 1830.

George Stephen, Esq., 1827. R.A., 1829.

Miss Hawkins (and her dog), small whole-length, 1829.

Portrait group of Colonel Smith's four children, 1829.

J. B. Flint, Esq. (of Canterbury); also of Mrs. Flint, 1830.

Miss Knighton (second daughter of Sir William Knighton), 1830.

Portrait group of William Garratt, Esq., and family (of Hampstead), 1830.

Mrs. Young (aged 81, mother of Mr. Young, the actor), 1831. R.A., 1832.

A. W. Callcott, Esq., R.A., 1831. R.A., 1832. (Engraved.)

William Collins, Esq., R.A., 1831. Sold to J. Gibbons, Esq., 1846.

Thomas Hill, Esq., 1831. R.A., 1832.

William Mulready, Esq., R.A., 1831. R.A., 1833. Sold to J. Gibbons, Esq., 1846.

Lady Anstruther (late Miss Torrens), (life-size, with harp), 1831. R.A., 1832.

Charles Aders, Esq., 1832. R.A., 1835.

The Rev. Edward Osborne, 1832.

Lord King; also Lady King, 1832. R.A.

Mrs. Ann Hawkins (9 by 7 inches), 1832. In the National Gallery.

William Bray, Esq. (of Shere, Surrey) in his 97th year, 1832. R.A., 1833. (Engraved.)

Miss Fowke (life-size), 1832.

Sir Frederick Fowke, Bart. (of Lowesby Hall, near Leicester, 1833. R.A.

The Rev. C. G. Boyles (of Buriton, near Petersfield, Hants), 1832.

Mrs. Osborne (of Horndean, Hants), 1832.

The Rev. T. R. Malthus, M.A., F.R.S., etc., Professor of Political Economy at the East India College, Herts; also Mrs. Malthus, 1833. R.A. (Engraved.)

The Rev. H. G. Keene, Professor of Languages at the East India College, 1833.

The Rev. Dr. Batten, Principal of the East India College, Herts, 1833. R.A. (Engraved.)

Mrs. Batten, 1833. R.A., 1834.

The Rev. J. Jeremie, Professor at East India College, 1833.

William Empson, Esq., 1833. R.A., 1834.

Samuel Rogers, Esq. (the poet), 1834. Sold to J. Gibbons, Esq., 1846.

E. Stirling, Esq., 1834.　R.A.

Mrs. Sarah Austin, 1834.　(Painted for Lord Jeffrey.)　R.A,
　1835.

Mrs. Sarah Austin (second portrait, small), 1840.

— Austin. Esq., senr., 1834.

The Rev. — Musgrave, 1834.

Charles Plastow, Esq., 1834.

— Nasmyth, Esq.; also Mrs. Nasmyth, 1834.

The Rev. E. T. Daniel, 1835.　R.A., 1836.

The Right Hon. Thomas Spring-Rice, 1835.　R.A.　(Engraved.)

— Stokes, Esq. (of Oakover Hill, Derbyshire); also Mrs. Stokes,
　1835.

Thomas Phillips, Esq., R.A., 1835.　R.A.

Major Dundas, 1835.

Pelham Warren, M.D., F.R.S., 1835.　R.A., 1837.　Second
　portrait of Dr. Warren, 1835.　(Engraved.)

E W. W. Pendarves, Esq., M.P., 1835.　R.A., 1836.　(En-
　graved).

G. W. Wood, Esq., 1835.

Professor Mylne, 1835.

The Rev. John Leifchild (half-length, life-size), 1835.　R.A., 1837.
　(Engraved.)

General the Honourable Sir Galbraith Lowry Cole, G.C.B., etc.,
　1835.　R.A., 1836.

Major-General Sir Charles Maxwell, 1836.　R.A., 1837.

Zachariah Langton, Esq., 1836.　(Engraved.)

Skinner Langton, Esq., also Mrs. Skinner Langton (life-size), 1836.

The Rev. James Stratten (half-length, life-size), 1836.

Thomas Norris, Esq., F.R.A.S., (of Preston, Lancashire), 1836.
　(Engraved.)

Second portrait (half-length, life-size), 1837.

Edmund Pattison, Esq., 1836.　R.A., 1837.

The Rev. E. Grubbe, 1836.

Mrs. Bray (of Clapham Common), 1836.

Richard Whately, D.D., Archbishop of Dublin, 1837.　R.A.,
　1838.　(Engraved.)

E. W. W. Pendarves, Esq., M.P., 1837 (second portrait, half-
　length, life-size).　R.A., 1838.

William Russell, Esq. (son of Lord William Russell), 1837.　R.A.,
　1838.

— Tremayne, Esq. (ex-member for Cornwall), 1837.

The Right Hon. Sir Robert Peel, Bart., M.P., 1837. R.A., 1838. (Engraved.)

Portrait of J. M. W. Turner, Esq., R.A. (painted 'from recollection '), June, 1838.

Writing, July, 1861, to Walter Thornbury, Esq. (who made inquiry of the artist respecting this portrait), the latter says : 'The history of my portrait of Turner the Great is a very short one. I painted it from recollection at the request of a friend of his, at whose table we frequently met. I made no memorandum at the time of meeting, but painted from memory entirely the first opportunity. [The diary notes "June 29, 1838," as the date of the painting] . . . I have a very careful outline of Turner's father, taken when attending his son's lecture at the Royal Academy about 1810, and a sketch of the eyes and brows, looking down, of the lecturer, both of which I will show you if you think it worth coming to R. H. for.'

Captain Leckey, also of Mrs. Leckey, 1838.

R. B. Lopez, Esq., 1838. R.A., 1839.

William Bagge, Esq., M.P., 1838. R.A., 1839.

Robert Peel, Esq. (half-length, life-size), 1838. R.A., 1839. (Engraved.)

Miss Peel (daughter of Sir Robert Peel), (life-size), 1838.

Mrs. Henslowe, 1838 ; Rev. E Henslowe (of Old Charlton, near Woolwich), 1839.

— Farrant, Esq., 1839. Brit. Inst., 1840 (as ' the Connoisseur ').

The Earl of Shelbourne, 1839. R.A., 1840.

Major Farrant, K.L.S. (and his Arabian horse), (small whole length), 1839. R.A., 1840.

Arthur Aston, Esq., Minister Plenipotentiary to Madrid (half-length), 1839.

Earl Talbot (of Ingestre, Stafford), (half-length, life-size), 1839.

The Marquess of Lansdowne, K.G., 1840. R.A.

John Claudius Loudon (life-size), 1840. Purchased 1877 'for the Linnean Society.'

Miss Bingham, 1840. R.A., 1841.

Dr. Otter, Bishop of Chichester, 1840. R.A., 1841. (Engraved.)

Sir Alexander Duff Gordon, also Lady Duff Gordon (both small), 1840.

Mrs. de Bertodano Lopez (whole length, small), 1840. R.A., 1841.

George Strutt, Esq. (of Belper), 1840.

Joseph Strutt, Esq. (of Derby), 1840. R.A., 1841. (Engraved.)

Sir Erskine Perry, 1841.
Portrait Group of General L. Mesurier, his Wife and Son, 1841.
Thomas Baring, Esq., 1841.
Mrs. Labouchere, 1841.
— Walker, Esq. (Surgeon at St. George's) (small), 1841.
Sir Thomas Baring, Bart. (small, whole length), 1841. R.A., 1842.
Lord Grey's three grandchildren—Miss Georgina Bulteel, Miss May Bulteel, and Miss May Barrington (daughter of Lady Caroline Barrington)—(small), 1841.
Richard Bagge, Esq. (twin brother of William Bagge, Esq., M.P. for Norfolk), 1841.
The Right Hon. Francis Baring, M.P. (half-length, life-size), 1842. R.A.
Lady Baring (small, whole-length), 1842. R.A.
William Coningham, Esq. (half-length, life-size), 1842. R.A.
Mrs. William Coningham (half-figure), 1842. R.A., 1843.
Mrs. de Bertodano Lopez and Son (small, whole-lengths), 1842. R.A., 1843.
Stewart Marjoribanks, Esq., M.P., 1842. R.A., 1843.
Portraits (in group) of the three eldest children of Robert Clutterbuck, Esq., 1842. R.A., 1843.
Thomas Carlyle, Esq., 1843-4. R.A., 1844.
John Mosely, Esq. (of Suffolk), (half-length, life-size), 1843.
The Earl of Ilchester, 1843. R.A., 1845.
Mrs. Coningham (small, whole-length), 1843. R.A., 1844.
James Pattison, Esq., M.P., 1844. R.A.
Lord Methuen, 1844. R.A., 1845. Also Lady Methuen, 1844.
R. B. Lopez, Esq. (half-length, life-size), 1844. R.A., 1845.
Lady Beauchamp, 1845. R.A.
Lord Methuen (second portrait, in peer's robes), 1845.
— Tremayne, Esq., junior, 1845.
Mrs. Pendarves (half-length, life-size), 1845. R.A., 1846.
Henry Colman, Esq. (of Boston, U S.), 1845-46. R.A., 1846.
Alexander M. Sutherland, Esq. (son of Sir James Sutherland), 1846. R.A.
Lady Sutherland, 1846.
Stewart Marjoribanks, Esq., M.P. (whole-length, life-size), 1846. Painted for the Members of the Watford Masonic Lodge.

— Fonnereau, Esq., also Mrs. Fonnereau (both half-length, life-size), 1846.

Mrs. Gibbons—'The Morning Walk'—(three-quarter figure), 1847. R.A., 1847.

Dr. Meryon, 1850 (painted for J. Gibbons, Esq.). R.A.

The Rev. — Peirson, 1850 (painted for J. Gibbons, Esq.).

— Carter, Esq. (solicitor to the Great Northern Railway), 1850 (painted for J. Gibbons, Esq.).

MINIATURES ON IVORY (IN WATER COLOURS) FROM THE LIFE.

(SELECTED LIST.)

Mrs. Linnell (wife of the artist), 1818-20. (His first miniature upon ivory.)

Lady Elizabeth Belgrave (daughter of the Marchioness of Stafford), 1820.

Second portrait of the same (in profile), 1820.

Lord Belgrave, 1820.

Lord Francis Leveson Gower, 1820.

Viscount Ebrington, also Vicountess Ebrington, 1820-21.

The Hon. Mrs. Leslie Cumming, 1820.

Lady Frederica Stanhope (daughter of Lord Mansfield), 1820.

Sir Roger Gresley, 1820.

Lady Sophia Coventry, 1820.

H.R.H. The Princess Sophia Matilda (sister of George IV.), (an oval for the pocket), 1821.

Second miniature, larger, showing another view of the face, 1821.

The Hon. H. G. Bennett, M P., 1821.

Lady Elizabeth (daughter of Lord Mansfield), 1823.

Vernon Smith, Esq. (nephew of the Countess of Warwick), also Mrs. Vernon Smith, 1823.

Miss Beresford (daughter of Lady Anna Beresford), also Lady Anna Beresford, 1823.

'The Favourite, a group, with portraits of the Artist's children,' 1823-24. R.A., 1825.

Miss Otway, and Miss Georgiana Otway, 1823.

— Inglefield, Esq. (son of Sir Harry Inglefield), 1824.

Mrs. Barclay, 1824.

George Rennie, Esq., Miss A. Rennie, and Miss E. Rennie, 1824.

Captain Boger, 1824.

Colonel Moore, 1826.

Captain Englefield, also Mrs. Englefield, 1826.

Miss Sophia Pocock (daughter of Sir George Pocock), 1826.

Portrait of William Blake (unfinished). This is the one engraved for Gilchrist's Life.

Sir George Pocock, Bart. (of Twickenham, 1827-28. R.A., 1832.

Miss Otway, 1827.

Mrs. Goring, 1827.

Miss Torrens, 1827.

Henry Torrens, Esq. (eldest son of Sir Henry Torrens), 1828.

Sir Jeremiah Dixon, 1828.

Miss Jackson (Mrs. Rennie), 1828.

George Stephen, Esq., 1829.

Mrs. (Captain) Stephen, 1829.

Frederick Torrens, Esq., 1829.

Captain Torrens, 1831.

George Pocock, Esq., also Mrs. Pocock, 1831.

Miss Laura Coventry (sister to Mrs. Pocock), 1831.

Captain Eyres, 1831.

Miss Rushbrook, 1831.

Miss Illingworth, 1832.

PORTRAITS FROM THE LIFE: DRAWINGS IN
WATER-COLOURS, CHALKS, Etc.

(SELECTED LIST.)

The Rev. J. M. Bletsoe, 1814. (Engraved.)

Mrs. Kilpin (of Kingsclere), 1815.

Thomas Chevalier, F.R.S., F.S.A., etc., 1817. (Engraved.)

The Rev. Rowland Hill, 1817. (Engraved for a new edition of the 'Village Dialogues.')

Portrait-group, Philip Thomas Wykham, Esq., and Mrs. Wykham (of Tythrop House, Thame—small, whole-lengths), 1817.

J. Cochran, senior, and Mrs. Cochran, senior (of Glasgow), 1817.

Mrs. Cochran senior's mother, aged 90 (drawn at Kilbarchin, near Paisley), October, 1817.

Portrait (sketch) of Dr. Chalmers, November, 1817.

Portrait-group of Mrs. Harris and two children (for the Hon. and Rev. A. Harris), 1818.

Dr. Jenkins (Baptist minister at Walworth), 1818.

The Rev. Thomas Allies (of Southampton), 1819.

Wilson Lowry, F.R.S., etc., 1820. (Engraved by Linnell and Blake.)

Lady Denbigh, 1822.

Mrs. Hay and child; also Captain Hay, 1823.

Captain Craigie's son (small, whole-length), 1824.

Hugh Sandeman, Esq. (in Highland garb—small, whole-length), 1824.

Second portrait (small, whole-length—in ordinary dress), 1824.

Thomas Sandeman, Esq., 1824.

— Hennessey, Esq., 1824.

Mrs. Birkbeck, — Birkbeck, Esq. (of Leyton), Miss Gurney, and Mrs. Gurney (all executed at Leyton), 1824.

Miss Kingscote, Miss C. Kingscote, Miss Fanny Sheppard, and
  Mrs. Wedgewood (all executed at Kingscote), 1825.
Mrs. Dumaresq (whole-length), 1828.
Master Charles Collins (son of William Collins, R.A.), 1830.
Miss Johnstone (for the Earl of Essex), 1831.
Miss Stephens (the singer), 1831.   Old Masters, 1883.*
Miss Flint (of Canterbury), 1832.
Thomas Flint, Esq. (of Margate) ; also Mrs. T. Flint, 1833.
Abraham Flint, Esq. (of Canterbury), 1833.
Francis Flint, Esq. (of Stroud), 1833.
Mrs. Daniel (mother of Rev. E. T. Daniel), 1835.   (Engraved.)
Chambers Hall, Esq. (four portraits), 1835.
Portrait of a child—' Sally ' (small, whole-length), 1835.   R.A.
  (Sold to C. Hall, Esq.)
Portrait of a child—' Polly ' (small, whole-length), 1835.   R.A.
Lady Frances Harley (small, whole-length), 1835.   R.A.
Rev. G. Marsh (engraved) ; also Mrs. G. Marsh (two portraits),
  1835.
Mrs. Marsh, 1835.
Alexander Bailey, Esq., 1835.
Rev. E. T. Daniel (for C. Hall, Esq.), 1835.
Miss Wildman (small, whole-length), 1836.   R.A.
Portrait-group of Mrs. Wildman and boy, 1836.   R.A.
Albin Martin, Esq. (for C. Hall, Esq.), 1836.
Miss Wilton (whole-length), 1836.
Portrait-group—Miss Grubb, with brother and sister (small, whole-
  lengths), 1836.   R.A., 1838.
Sydenham Malthus, Esq.
Mrs. Smith (late Miss Batten); also Miss Charlotte Batten, 1836.
Major Williams, 1836.
Mrs. Harry Martin (whole-length), 1837.
The Rev. W. F. Groves (of Zeals, Dorset, whole-length), 1837.
Reginald Bray, Esq., and Mrs. Bray, 1838.
Major Beamish, 1838.   (Engraved.)
Lady Mary Fitzmaurice (infant daughter of the Countess of Kerry,
  small, whole-length, with dog), 1838.   R.A., 1839.
Portrait-group of Mrs. Huddleston and children, 1838.   R.A.,
  1839.

---

* The words 'Old Masters,' or (later) 'O.M.,' mean that the portrait or
picture was exhibited in the Winter Exhibition of the Royal Academy in 1883.

The Rev. Harry Martin (whole-length), 1838.

Mrs. Alexander Trotter, 1838.

The Rev. J. P. Blencowe, 1838. (Engraved.)

The infant daughter of Le Comte de Pollon, 1838.

Dr. Crotch, 1839. R.A.

The Countess of Mount Edgecombe (whole-length, for Lord Shelborne), 1838. R.A., 1840.

Patrick Talbot, Esq. (for Lord Talbot), 1839.

The Hon. and Rev. Arthur Talbot (whole-length), 1839.

Mrs. Talbot (whole-length), 1839.

Lord Ingestre (whole-length), 1839.

Portrait-group of Mrs. W. S. Fry and children (small, whole-lengths), 1840. R.A., 1841.

The Rev. F. Fowler, 1840.

Lady Perry, 1841.

Lady Heywood, 1841.

Master Heywood (son of Sir B. Heywood, small, whole-length), 1842.

Master E. Heywood (small, whole-length), 1842.

Portraits (in group) of Lady Mary Lambton and Lady Emily Lambton (daughters of Earl Grey), 1841.

— Grundy, Esq. (of Manchester, whole-length), 1842.

Portrait-group—the two children of Jonathan Peel, Esq., 1843.

Dr. Stanley (Bishop of Norwich), 1843. R.A., 1844.

General B. Espartero, 1843. (Engraved.)

The Duchess of Victoria (wife of the above), 1843.

Lady Beauchamp, 1843.

C. Kerr, Esq., 1844.

R. B. Lopez, Esq. ; also Miss Lopez, 1844.

Lady Kerry, 1844.

Miss Methuen, 1844.

F. Tollemache, Esq., 1844.

Rev. — Bury (of the Isle of Wight), 1844.

Henry Colman, Esq. (of Boston, U.S.), 1845.

Dr. Mackenzie, 1845.

Master Ormsby (of Brighton—whole-length), 1846.

— Methuen, Esq. (eldest son of Lord Methuen), 1846.

Master Lopez (whole-length), 1846.

Miss Mitford, 1846.

Samuel Bagster, senior (drawn at Windsor), May, 1849.

OIL PAINTINGS : LANDSCAPES AND SUBJECT-PICTURES.

'A Study from Nature' (10 by 12 inches), 1807. Exhibited at the Royal Academy the same year.

'A View near Reading,' 1807. R.A.*

'Fishermen—A Scene from Nature' (panel, 14 by 20 inches), 1807. Brit. Inst., 1808.

'Fishermen' (30 by 36 inches), 1808, R.A. Painted for Mr. Ridley Colborne.

'Removing Timber—Autumn' (26 by 34½ inches), 1808. Brit. Inst., 1809, gained the prize of 50 guineas offered in 1808 by the Institution for the best landscape painted that year. The principal figure is a portrait of the father of W. Mulready, R.A. Exhibited at the Old Masters, 1883.

'Landscape—Morning,' 1809. R.A.

'A Cottage Door' (about 18 by 14 inches), 1809. Brit. Inst., 1810.

'View of the Beach, Hastings,' 1809. Brit. Inst., 1810.

'Fishermen Waiting for the Return of the Ferry-boat [Fishing-boat?], Hastings' (upright panel, 12 by 8 inches), 1810. R.A. Brit. Inst., 1811. Purchased by the Earl of Camden at the Brit. Inst.

'A Scene on the Bank of the Thames' (28 by 36 inches), 1810. Brit. Inst., 1811.

'Fishing-boats—A Scene from Nature' (panel, 20 by 24 inches), 1810. Brit. Inst., 1811.

'The Quoit Players' (panel, 32 by 41 inches), 1810. Brit. Inst., 1811. Purchased at the exhibition by Sir Thomas Baring. Bought at the sale of the latter's collection (1848) by Creswick, the dealer, for 230 guineas, and subsequently sold to George Simpson, Esq., for 1,000 guineas. Old Masters, 1883.

* When the year is not given, the picture was exhibited the same year as painted.

'The Ducking—A Scene from Nature,' 1811.   R.A.

'A Scene on the Coast near Dover' (16 by 18 inches), 1811. Brit. Inst , 1812.   Spring Gardens,* 1816.

'A View on the Thames' (16 by 18 inches), 1811.   Brit. Inst., 1812.   Spring Gardens, 1816.

'Fishing Houses' (small), 1811.

'The Dairy—Morning' (33 by 31 inches), 1811.   Brit. Inst., 1812.

'Washerwomen's Cottages, Bayswater, in 1811 '(18 by 24 inches). Retouched and worked all over, 1871, for Mr. White.

'View from Window, Edgware Road,' 1812.   Retouched, 1865.

'The Gravel-Pits' (25 by 39 inches), 1812.   Brit. Inst., 1813. Sold at the Liverpool exhibition (1813) for 45 guineas. Purchased (1847) by Creswick for £220.

Replica, with additions (25 by 39 inches), 1857.   Old Masters, 1883.   Lent by Ralph Brocklebank, Esq.

Replica, finished sketch (panel, 12 by 19 inches).

*'The Bird Catcher—A Scene from Nature.'   Also known as 'Bayswater in 1814' (37 by 51 inches), 1813.   Retouched, with additions, in 1859.   Brit. Inst., 1814.   Old Masters, 1883.   Sold at Christie's, 1891, for 750 guineas.

*'Evening-view in Wales' (24 by 36 inches), 1813.   Sold to Mr. Chance.   Retouched, 1860.

'Midday, Wales,' 1813.   Spring Gardens, 1815.

'Morning' (small), 1813.   Spring Gardens, 1815.

'Fishing-boats, Hastings' (small), 1814.   Painted for Mr. S. Woodburn.

*'Fishing-boats, Hastings' (upright panel, 9 by 6 inches), 1815.

*'Windmill' (small), 1814.

'The Fair upon the Thames when frozen over in January, 1814' (small), 1814.   Sold to General Maitland.

'Coast Subject, Fishing-boats' (small), 1814.   For Mr. S. Woodburn.

*'Barges on the Thames,' 1815.

*'Afternoon—Going to Milk' (5 by 6 inches), 1814.

'Milking,' 1814-15.   Spring Gardens, 1814.

*'Snowdon from Dolwydellan' (evening), 1814.

* The show rooms of the Society of Painters in Oil and Water Colours. After this all pictures exhibited there the year of painting will be marked thus *.

'Distant View of Snowdon,' 1816. Brit. Inst.

'Pike Pool, Derbyshire' (panel), 1815. Painted for Mr. S. Bagster to illustrate the 'Complete Angler.' Retouched, 1871.

*'A View in Dovedale, Derbyshire' (panel, 7½ by 12 inches), 1815. Old Masters, 1883. Lent by A. T. Hollingsworth, Esq.

A second picture with this title was painted in 1815.

*'Crossing the River Ford—North Wales' (morning), 1814. Retouched (1871) for Mr. Dixon of Wolverhampton.

*'A Fine Evening after Rain—A Scene in Wales' (panel, 17 by 26 inches), 1815. Bought by Mr. Tomkinson.

'Shepherds' Amusement' (40 by 50 inches), 1815. Spring Gardens, 1816. Retouched and exhibited at the Brit. Inst. in 1836 as 'Evening.' Sold to Mr. R. Thomas in 1846 ; afterwards bought by Mr. Gibbons for 250 guineas.

*'The Haymakers' Repast—A Scene in Wales,' 1815. Retouched in 1850.

*'Fishing-boats' (or 'Shipping'), 1816.

'Hanson Toot, View in Dovedale, Derbyshire' (36 by 48 inches), 1815. Spring Gardens, 1816. Retouched in 1854, also in 1870, for Mr. Dixon, of Wolverhampton. Christie's, 1873.

*'Evening,' 1816.

'View on the River Kennet' (near Newbury), 1815. Spring Gardens, 1816. Brit. Inst., 1826. Sold to Mr. Blackie, 1831. Retouched, 1868.

*'A View near Steep Hill, Isle of Wight' (small), 1816. Sold to Mr. Vines.

Replica, 1816, for Mr. Thos. Landseer, senr.

*'A Potato Field' (view in the Isle of Wight), (small), 1816. Sold to Mr. A. Robertson.

Replica (panel, 10 by 13 inches), 1829. Brit. Inst., 1830. Sold to Mr. Thomas, 1846. Old Masters, 1883. James Orrock, Esq.

'Forest Scene, with Bark Renders' (panel, 8½ by 6¼ inches), 1816. Old Masters, 1883. Hubert Martineau, Esq.

*'Near Windsor Forest' (millboard, 7 by 10 inches), 1816.

Replica, with variation (panel, 9 by 15 inches), 1834. Brit. Inst., 1835. Purchased at the exhibition by Mr. Vernon. Now in the National Gallery.

'A Fall of Timber' (or 'Falling Timber'), (40 by 50 inches), 1816. Spring Gardens, 1817. In the summer exhibition of the Brit. Inst., 1825, being 'Pictures by Living Artists of the English School.' Title in catalogue 'Woodcutters—A Scene in Windsor Forest.' Purchased in 1817 by J. Alnutt, Esq., of Clapham (for 50 guineas), who sold it through Mr. Colls to Mr. Gibbons for £250 (1846).

Replica (with variations—'sketchy'—30 by 43 inches). Sold to Mr. Thomas, 1846; Christie's, 1848, for 200 guineas, and again to Mr. Birch, of Birmingham, for 300 guineas. Old Masters, 1883, as 'Meat in the Wood.'

*'A View near Shanklin, Isle of Wight,' 1817. Bought in exhibition by Mr. Vines.

'A Study of Trees' (near Thame), (18 by 25 inches), 1817. Retouched in 1868. Old Masters, 1883. (Henry A. Brassey, Esq.)

*'A View at Niton,' 1817.

*'Mid-day'—sheep lying under tree (panel, 9 by 15 inches), 1818. (Engraved.)

Replica (enlarged). Finished 1847. Sold to Mr. Gibbons.

*'Dairy—Morning' (small upright), 1818. Spring Gardens, 1819.

*'Isle of Wight by Moonlight' (panel, 8 by 12 inches), 1818. (Companion to Steep Hill, Isle of Wight.) Painted for Mr. Vines.

*'John Preaching in the Wilderness,' 1818 (38 by 53 inches). Spring Gardens, 1818. Retouched and finished 1838, and exhibited at Brit. Inst., 1839. Purchased at the private view by Sir Thos. Baring for 150 guineas. Exchanged by Sir Thos. Baring, 1841, for the picture of 'Flight into Egypt' in Brit. Inst., 1841. International Exhibition, 1862. Old Masters, 1883. (Mrs. Grove.)

*'Evening' (small), 1818-19. Spring Gardens, 1819.

'Sheep' (small), 1818. To Mr. Holmes in exchange.

*'View near Windsor Forest,' 1819. Brit. Inst., 1826.

*'Twilight' (small, upright), 1819.

*'Windmill,' 1819. Sold to T. M. Belisario, Esq.

Replica (with variations), 1830. Brit. Inst., 1831.

*'Evening, Bayswater,' 1818. Sold to Mr. Vines.

[Replica ?]. Sold to Mr. Belisario for £16. Retouched 1856. Sold at Foster's in 1857 for 100 guineas.

'Barges' (on the Thames), (small, upright), 1819. Companion to 'Fishing-Boats,' 1815. Painted for Mr. White, engraver.

*'Evening—Storm Clearing Off,' 1819. To Mr. Hall, of Southampton, in exchange for the picture of 'Itchen Ferry' painted for him. In 1846 in the possession of Mr. Gibbons.

*'East Window of Netley Abbey,' 1819 (painted on the spot), (39 by 49 inches). Spring Gardens, 1820. Old Masters, 1883. In the possession of the family.

*'Windsor Forest—A Forest Scene,' 1818. Sold to Mr. Robson for 85 guineas.

'Windsor Forest' (Children Picking Flowers), 1819. Sold to Mr. S. Woodburn for £30.

'View of Southampton' (18 by 31 inches), 1819. Painted at Southampton.

'Fine Evening after Rain' (North Wales). See 1815.

A Replica (varied) of this subject for Mr. Tomkinson, in exchange for a 42 guinea pianoforte, 1820.

Second Replica, smaller, for Mr. J. Harman, Governor of the Bank of England, 1820. (30 guineas.)

Third Replica (14½ by 23 inches) for Mr. Pepper, 30 guineas (1820).

Fourth Replica sold at the Edinburgh Exhibition for 35 guineas (1822).

Fifth Replica, 1829, sold at the Manchester Exhibition in 1829 for 50 guineas.

Sixth Replica (panel, 15 by 23 inches), 1836. Sold to Mr. Thomas, 1846, for 50 guineas. Old Masters, 1883. Sold at the Price Sale (Christie's), April, 1892, for 1,000 guineas.

Replica (sketch in oil, 7 by 12 inches). In the possession of the Linnell family. Old Masters, 1883.

*'Woodcutters' Repast' (panel, 9 by 15 inches), 1820. In the summer exhibition of the Brit. Inst., 1825. Brit. Inst., 1827. Sold to the Hon. A. Ellis for 35 guineas.

Replica, 1826 (panel, 9 by 15 inches). Purchased by Mr. Webster, R.A., 1846, for 40 guineas. Old Masters, 1883. Now in the possession of Jas. Orrock, Esq.

Replica, 1830.

'Kingsey Village, Buckinghamshire,' 1821-2. R.A., 1822. 'A Village Scene,' Brit. Inst., 1827, when purchased by Sir Geo. Crew, of Calke Abbey, Derbyshire, for 100 guineas.

Replica (small), ' Kingsey Village ' (7 by 10 inches).

Replica (varied), 'View near Kingsey, Bucks.' Brit. Inst., 1834.

*' The Young Gleaner ' (panel, 7 by 5 inches), 1820. Brit. Inst., 1827. Sold to Mr. James Brown in 1829.

*' The Windmill ' (42 by 48 inches), 1821. R.A. (' Landscape '). Brit. Inst., 1824 (' Windmill '). Old Masters, 1883. [The description agrees exactly, but the size given is different— 35 by 42 inches.] Sold to Thomas, 1846, for £100. Sold by Foster, 1856, for 500 guineas; at Christie's in 1891 for £800.

' The Radish-Stall by Candlelight ' (small), 1822. R.A. Brit. Inst., 1827, where purchased by Lord Ellenborough.

Replica (smaller). Sold to Mr. Webster.

' Windsor Forest ' (small), 1822.

' Moonlight ' (Moonrise), (24 by 24 inches), 1822. R.A. Brit. Inst., 1823. Retouched 1868.

' The Anglers—Sunset ' (18 by 23 inches), 1822. Sold at Christie's in 1890 for 145 guineas.

' Southampton from the River near Netley Abbey ' (14 by 36 inches), 1824-5. Painted for Mr. Hall, of Southampton.

' Itchin Ferry ' (1825), (14 by 36 inches). Brit. Inst., 1828.

' Isle of Wight from Lymington Quay ' (11 by 15 inches), 1825. Sold to Mr. E. T. Daniel for 30 guineas. Sold at Christie's in 1883 for £409 10s.

Replica (panel, 15 by 18 inches), 1826. Brit. Inst., 1829. Sold to Mr. John Morris for 35 guineas.

' Mid-day ' (' Sheep Reposing '), (panel, 9 by 15 inches), 1826. Brit Inst., 1827.

' View at Southampton ' (panel, 8 by 10 inches), 1825. Brit. Inst., 1826. Sold to Sir J. Leicester for 25 guineas.

Replica, 1830.

Replica, drawing in water-colour, 1863.

' Hampstead ' (panel, 6 by 9 inches). Old Masters, 1883. Lent by Linnell family.

' A View near Hampstead ' (with donkey), 1826 (panel, 8 by 10½ inches), Brit. Inst., 1827.

' Hampstead, North End ' (panel, 7½ by 9½ inches). Old Masters. 1883. Linnell family.

' Evening, the Vicinity of a Farm,' 1827. (Hampstead.) R.A. Sold to Thomas, 1846. Afterwards sold for £70.

'A Sandy Road' (36 by 42 inches), 1828-9. R.A., 1829. Brit. Inst., 1830. Retouched all over 1839; again in 1847 for Mr. Gillott.

'A Village near a River, Showery Weather' (panel), 1828. Brit. Inst., 1829, where purchased by Mr. Turner, of Clapham, for 65 guineas.

Replica, 1830 (rather larger.)

'A Study from Nature' (millboard, 6 by 8 inches), 1828. A bank and pond on Hampstead Heath. Brit. Inst., 1829.

Replica (panel, 8 by 10 inches), 1831. Brit. Inst., 1832. Sold to Mr. Plestow.

'Mercury and Argus' (panel, 14 by 12 inches), 1828. Water-colour finished in oil. Brit. Inst., 1829. Retouched 1859, and again in 1876. At one time in the possession of the Right Hon. W. E. Gladstone, M.P.

'Interior of a Welsh Cottage' (panel, 15 by 16 inches), 1828. Brit. Inst., 1829. Sold to Lord Selsey for 30 guineas.

'Christ and the Woman of Samaria,' or 'Jacob's Well' (panel, 10 by 8 inches), 1828. Brit. Inst., 1829. Old Masters, 1883, Linnell family.

'Milking' (small upright panel), 1828. Brit. Inst., 1829. Given to Mr. Mulready.

Replica (larger—16 by 21 inches), 1830. Brit. Inst., 1831. Sold to Mr. Thomas, 1846, and by him to J. Gibbons, Esq., for 100 guineas. Sold at Christie's, 1883 ('Milking Time') for £320.

'The Dairy Farm'—a Welsh Farm-Yard (panel, 20 by 30 inches), 1828-9. Brit. Inst., 1830. Purchased, 1843, by B. Lopez, Esq. Sold at Phillips's in 1848 for £194.

Sketch (first) of this [1827] (millboard on panel, 10 by 14 inches), finished 1847, and sold for 125 guineas. Sold at Christie's (Eden collection), for 600 guineas.

'Fishermen, A View near Twickenham' (panel, 9 by 15 inches), 1829. Brit. Inst., 1830. Sold to Mr. Norris. Old Masters, 1883. Sold at Christie's, 1892, for 220 guineas.

'A Heath Scene,' North End, Hampstead (panel, 9 by 15 inches), 1829. Brit. Inst., 1830. Sold to the Earl of Essex, 35 guineas.

Replica, 1830.

'Sheepfold, Evening' (panel, 10 by 12 inches), 1829. Brit. Inst.,
   1830.
'The Farmer's Boy' (panel, 24 by 18 inches), 1829-30. R.A.,
   1830. Given to Mr. Daniel. Old Masters, 1883.
Replica (small), 1830.
'The Wild-Flower Gatherers' (8 by 10 inches), 1830. Brit. Inst.,
   1831. Purchased by J. Sheepshanks, Esq., and now at South
   Kensington.
'The Cow-Yard' (panel), 1831. Brit. Inst., 1832. In the
   Sheepshanks Collection, South Kensington.
'Landscape, Morning'—(A Boy Minding Sheep), 1831. Painted
   from a sketch made in Porchester Terrace in 1830. Brit.
   Inst., 1832. Sold to Mr. Daniel for 50 guineas; at Phillips's
   (1848) for £84.
'Unlading Boats' (small), 1832. Brit. Inst. 1833.
'Fish-Market, Hastings,' 1833 or 1834. R.A., 1834; Brit. Inst.,
   1835. Sold at Phillips's (1848) for £136 10s.
'The Sand-Pit, Hampstead Heath' (panel, 9 by 15 inches), 1834.
   Brit. Inst., 1835. Art Treasures, Manchester. Sold (1849)
   to Mr. Bayley (Yorkshire) for 90 guineas. Old Masters,
   1883.
'Christ's Appearance to the Two Disciples journeying to Emmaus'
   (panel 22 by 30½ inches), 1834-5. R.A., 1835; Brit. Inst.,
   1836. Sold in 1838 to the Art Union for 60 guineas, and
   engraved for the Society by the artist.
'Windsor Forest' (panel, 9 by 15 inches), 1834. Brit. Inst.,
   1835. Purchased then by Mr. Vernon for 30 guineas. Now
   at South Kensington.
Replica (larger), 1837, R.A. Brit. Inst., 1838. To Mr. Thomas,
   1846.
'The Fruit-Stall' (panel, 12 by 10 inches), 1834-5. Brit. Inst.,
   1835. Art Treasures, Manchester. Purchased by Sir
   Thomas Baring for 50 guineas. Old Masters.
'Fishing-Boats' (panel, 9 by 15 inches), 1835. Brit. Inst., 1836.
   To Mr. Thomas, 1846.
'The Hollow Tree' (or 'The Nest'), 1836. From an oil study
   at Bayswater, 1834. R.A., 1836. Brit. Inst., 1837.
Replica, 'Nest' (small, millboard on panel, 10 by 14 inches),
   1859. Old Masters.
Replica, 'Nest' (kitcat), 1860.

'Jeanie Deans and Madge Wildfire in the Churchyard' (small), 1836. Painted for Messrs. Fisher and Son, Caxton Press, to be engraved for a new edition of Scott's works.

'View near Thame' (panel, 12 by 15 inches), 1836. Bought from Mr. Thomas by Mr. Gillott, and retouched for him, 1847.

'View of Southampton' (by Moonlight), 1836. R.A., 1837. To Mr. Thomas, 1846.

'Noon' (29 by 38½ inches), 1839. Brit. Inst. 1840. To Mr. Thomas, 1846. Old Masters.

'Hampstead' (panel). Painted on the spot in 1827; finished at home about 1839. To Mr. Thomas (1846), and by him to Mr. Gillott. ('Gipsies' in Brit. Inst., 1840.)

'Philip baptizing the Eunuch' (39 by 54 inches), 1840. R.A. Sir Thomas Baring, 150 guineas. Subsequently bought by Mr. Rutherford for £500.

'The Watering-Place' (24 by 30 inches), 1840. Brit. Inst., 1841. To Mr. Lopez, 1843. Retouched 1857.

'The Flight into Egypt' (38 by 54 inches), 1840-41. Brit. Inst., 1841. Exchanged with Sir T. Baring for 'St. John Preaching.' Old Masters. Lent by C. W. F. Fryer, Esq.

'The Cottage Door,' or 'Winding the Skein' (33½ by 57½ inches), 1841. R.A. Brit. Inst., 1842. Mr. Thomas, 1846.
Replica (small), 1848.
Replica (panel, 10 by 14 inches), 1860. To Mr. Fallows, Manchester. In the Old Masters (1883) as 'Winding the Skein.' (George Gurney, Esq.)

'A Forest Scene from Nature' (three-quarter canvas), 1842-3. Brit. Inst, 1843. To Mr. Thomas, 1846; by him to Mr. Gibbons, 1847.

'The Supper at Emmaus' (canvas), 1842-3. R.A., 1843; Brit. Inst., 1844. To Mr. Thomas, 1846. Purchased by Mr. Gillott for £500. Retouched for him.

'Windmill'—A Landscape with Cows in Water (17 by 21 inches), 1844. Brit. Inst., 1845. Bought then by R. Vernon, Esq., for 50 guineas. Now in the Vernon Collection at the National Gallery.
Replica (varied), being the sketch for the above, finished for Mr. Wethered in 1848 for 150 guineas (canvas, 17 by 21 inches.)

'River Scene—Boy Fishing' (panel, 12 by 15 inches), 1846. Old Masters.

'A Wood Scene'—Woodcutters and children gathering chips (canvas, kitcat), 1844. Brit. Inst., 1845. Sold to Mr. Brown, of Chester, for 125 guineas (he having a prize of £80 in the Art Union).

'A Spring Wood Scene' (26 by 38 inches), 1845-6. Brit. Inst., 1846. Retouched 1848. To Mr. Birch, of Birmingham (1850), with the sketch of 'Philip,' for 350 guineas. At the Old Masters as 'The Fallen Monarch.' (J. B. Dugdale, Esq.)

'Abraham entertaineth Three Angels' (panel, 11 by 17½ inches), · 1845-6. Brit. Inst., 1846. To Mr. Cocksholt, holder of Art Union prize of £80. Old Masters. (The late David Price, Esq.)

'The Young Brood'—Chickens (panel, 21½ by 27½ inches), 1846. Sold (1846) to J. Hogarth, to be engraved in the Finden Gallery (200 guineas).

'A Mountain Road, N. Wales' (canvas, 17 by 25 inches), 1846. An early picture, 'Travellers in Wales,' 1814. Repainted all over, and altered 1846, and named 'A Mountain Road.' Brit. Inst., 1847. Sold to Mr. Gillott.

'A Dell' (panel, 10½ by 12 inches), 1846-7. Brit. Inst., 1847. Mr. Dillon, of Croydon, 1854.

'The Mill' (panel, 18 by 21 inches), 1846-7. R.A., 1847. Finished for Mr. Gibbons.

'Mid-day—"While nature lies around deep-lulled in noon"' (Thomson), 1847. R.A. To Mr. Gibbons.

'A Hillside Farm' (16 by 23½ inches), 1847. Finished for Mr. Gillott. Brit. Inst., 1848. Sold at Christie's in 1881 for £950. Old Masters as 'Harvesting.' (D. Thwaites, Esq.)

'The Last Gleam before the Storm' (canvas, 35 by 50 inches), 1847-8. Brit. Inst., 1848. To Mr. Gillott, 1848; subsequently to Mr. Eden, of Lytham. Retouched 1863. Sold at Mr. Eden's sale (1874) for 2,500 guineas. Old Masters. (Henry Mason, Esq.)
Replica (sketch, varied), 1848.

'The Eve of the Deluge' (canvas, 59 by 88 inches), 1847-8. R.A., 1848. To Mr. Gillott. Sold at his sale (1872) for £1,099. Old Masters. (Angus Holden, Esq., M.P.)

Sketch of this subject (1850) for Mr. Gillott. Retouched 1858.

Replica (second sketch, varied), showing the disc of the sun (panel, 25 by 34 inches), 1858. Sold at Christie's in 1881 for £399.

Replica (sketch, panel, 11½ by 15½ inches). Old Masters. (The Linnell Family.)

' The Return of Ulysses ' (canvas, 48 by 72 inches), 1848. R.A., 1849 ; Manchester Art Treasure Exhibition, 1857. Painted for Mr. Gillott. Sold at Christie's, 1887, for £1,470. Old Masters. (John Graham, Esq.)

' Fishermen—Evening ' (kitcat), 1848. Also known as the ' Fishing Party.' Painted for Mr. Gillott.

Replica. ' Sketch of Fishing Party,' 1848.

' A Summer Evening : Regent's Park ' (canvas, 15 by 23¼ inches), 1848. Brit. Inst., 1849. Old Masters. (Richard Newsham, Esq.)

' The Flight into Egypt ' (38 by 53 inches), 1848. Brit. Inst., 1849. Bought by Gillott, the same year, for 300 guineas. Retouched and in part altered, 1867. Sold at Christie's, 1890, for 1,079 guineas.

' Watering Cows ' (small), 1848. Painted for Mr. Wethered.

' Sleeping Disciples ' (Gethsemane), 1848-9 (canvas, kitcat). Sold to Mr. Gillott for £210, 1849 ; afterwards bought by Mr. Naylor, of Liverpool, for £700.

' A Country Road ' (canvas, kitcat), 1849. Painted for Mr. Gillott for £210.

Replica. Sketch, 1849.

' Sand-Pits ' (canvas, 38 by 50 inches), 1849. R.A. ; International Exhibition, 1862. Painted for Mr. Gillott for 300 guineas.

' Hoppers—Evening ' (small), 1849. To Mr. Gillott.

' Evening ' (Farm), 1849 (small). To Mr. Gillott.

' Clearing Up.' Also known as ' The Clear-up Shower ' (small), 1849. To Mr. Gillott.

' The Hillside Farm ' (Upland Farm), Isle of Wight, 1849 (canvas, half length). Painted for Mr. Gillott for 300 guineas. Retouched for Messrs. Agnew and Son in 1859. Sold with the Mendell Collection for £2,300 ; again (1891), with the Bolckow Collection, for 2,000 guineas. Samuel Montagu, Esq., M.P., is its present possessor.

Sketch of this Subject, varied.

'L'Allegro'—Dancing in the chequered shade (panel, 17 by 24 inches), 1849. Old Masters. (Richard Newsham, Esq.)

'Gravel Diggers'—Gravel-Pits (canvas, kitcat), 1849. Painted for Mr. Gillott.

Sketch (small) of a similar subject.

'Crossing the Brook' (canvas, half length), 1849. Sold to Mr. Gillott for 2co guineas. R.A., 1850; Art Treasures Exhibition, Manchester, 1857.

Replica. Sketch, varied.

Also Replica (kitcat). Sold to Mr. Huth.

'Hampstead Heath,' a Sunset with fir trees (panel, 18 by 24 inches), 1849.

'The Purchased Flock' (panel, 18 by 24 inches), 1849. Painted for Mr. Miller. Brit. Inst., 1850.

'Opening the Gate: Hampstead Heath' (canvas, 27 by 35½ inches), 1850. Brit. Inst. Sold to Mr. Fordham. Purchased at Christie's in 1874, by the late Mr. David Price, for £1,000. Old Masters. Sold at Christie's (Price Col.), April, 1892, for £798.

Replica, the study for this subject, finished 1858 (panel, 16 by 29 inches).

'Woodcutters' (kitcat), 1849-50. Sold to Mr. Gillott. Same as 'Chips.' Brit. Inst., 1851.

'Harvest' (canvas, kitcat), 1850. Sold to Mr. Gillott for 200 guineas. Retouched in 1854.

'Christ and the Woman of Samaria' at Jacob's Well (canvas, 38 by 56 inches), 1850. R.A. Painted for Mr. Holmes, of Birmingham, as a companion to 'Philip Baptizing the Eunuch.'

Replica (first study, in water-colour, about 1840, 40 by 50 inches; finished in oil, 1866). Sold to Mr. Bowring, 1866, for £1,000. Sold at Christie's, in 1887, for £598.

'Heath Scene, Evening' (canvas, 48 by 72 inches), 1850. For Mr. Gillott (300 guineas). This was the 'Hampstead Heath' of Mr. Gillott's Collection sold at Christie's, in 1872, for 1,660 guineas; again, in 1888, for £1,585.

'Woodlands' (canvas, 40 by 50 inches), 1850. Painted for Mr. Pennell for £500. R.A., 1851. Sold at Mr. Gillott's sale, 1872, for 2,500 guineas. Old Masters, 'Moving Timber.' (Ralph Brocklebank, Esq.)

'David and the Lion' (canvas, 54 by 84 inches), 1850. Finished for Mr. Gillott and sold by him to Mr. Holmes. Retouched 1859, and again 1873, for Mr. White, who sold it for £1,700.

'Ulysses and the Boar'—Hunting the Boar on Mount Parnassus (panel, 14 by 21 inches), 1850. For Mr. Gillott. Retouched in 1859.

'Woodcutter' (14 by 20 inches), 1850.

'The Farm, Evening,' being a View at North End, Hampstead (panel, 10 by 16 inches), 1850. Brit. Inst., 1851.

'Morning'—Sheep (canvas, 27½ by 35½ inches), 1851. R.A. Old Masters, 'Landscape with Sheep.' (S. Asheton Critchley, Esq.)

Collins's Farm, North End, Hampstead' (panel, 6¼ by 10, inches), 1851. Old Masters. (Charles Neck, Esq.)

'Sand Cart' (panel, 26 by 36 inches), 1851. Retouched 1866. Old Masters. (Holbrook Gaskell, Esq.)

'Death of the Boar' (canvas, 34 by 58 inches), 1851. Brit. Inst., 1852. Retouched 1874.

'Boys Fishing' (canvas, kitcat), 1852. Sold to W. A. Joyce, Esq.

'Sheepfold, Evening' (canvas, kitcat), 1852. Sold to Mr. Todd (400 guineas). Art Treasures Exhibition, Manchester, 1857. Replica (half length, 40 by 50 inches), 1858. Replica, Drawing.

'David mocking Abner,' 1 Sam. xxvi. (canvas, 40 by 50 inches), 1853. Sold to E. Gambart for 300 guineas.

'The Timber Waggon' (canvas, 34 by 56 inches), 1852. R.A. Painted for Mr. Oxenham, who had the Paris gold medal for it. Subsequently bought by the late Mr. David Price for 1,000 guineas. Retouched for Mr. Price in 1860. Old Masters. Sold at the Price Sale (Christie's, April, 1892), for 3,100 guineas. Study for this Picture, finished 1855.

'The Sear Leaf' (canvas, 28 by 36 inches), 1852-3. Sold to Mr. Oxenham. R.A., 1852. Retouched in 1859 and again later. Old Masters. (Wakefield Christy, Esq.)

'Barley Harvest, Evening' (canvas, 35½ by 44 inches), 1852. Sold to Mr. Gambart for 300 guineas. R.A.; Paris Exhibition, 1855. Sold in 1872 (Gillott sale) for 1,630 guineas. Old Masters. (Thomas Jessop, Esq.) Replica (drawing). For Mr. D. White.

'Fishermen, Evening' (canvas, 25 by 29½ inches), 1847. Painted
for Mr. Gambart. Retouched 1853. Old Masters, 'Landscape, Evening.' (C. F. Huth, Esq.)

'Travellers' (canvas, 28 by 36 inches), 1852. Finished for Mr.
Gambart. Sold, in 1857, at Foster's, for 280 guineas. Old
Masters, 'Inquiring the Way.' (Mrs. A. J. Brunton.)

'Redstone Wood' (canvas, 26 by 37 inches), 1852. For Gambart.

'The Wold of Kent' (canvas, 26 by 37 inches), 1852. Brit. Inst.,
1853.

'Shallow Rivers' (panel, 13 by 18 inches), 1852. Brit. Inst., 1853.
Replica (drawing), 1852. For L. Colls.

'View in Surrey' (canvas, 28 by 35 inches), 1852-3. Old
Masters. (Chas. Butler, Esq.)

'A Forest Road' (canvas, 35 by 56 inches), 1853. R.A.; in
Paris Exhibition, 1855. Sold to Agnew, 1859, for £600.

'Under the Hawthorn' (canvas, 36 by 54 inches), 1853. For Gambart. R.A. International Exhibition, 1862. Sold at Christie's
in 1887 for £1071. Old Masters. (James Taylor, Esq.)

'The Village Spring' (canvas, 28 by 36 inches), 1853. For
Gambart. R.A.

'Sand-Pits'—Hampstead (kitcat), 1853. Sold to Gambart. Old
Masters, 'Hampstead Gravel-Pits.' (Charles Butler, Esq.)

'Harvest Home—Sunset' (canvas, 35 by 57 inches), 1853. Brit.
Inst., 1854. To Gambart.
Replica (varied) 'Load of Wheat' (kitcat).

'The Refuge'—Storm (35 by 57 inches), 1853. Brit. Inst., 1854.
Replica (kitcat), 1853. Retouched, 1859.
Second Replica (kitcat), 1853. Retouched, 1859.
Replica (small drawing).

'On Summer Eve by haunted stream' (canvas, 27½ by 35 inches),
1853. Old Masters. (W. Cuthbert Quilter, Esq.)
Replica (drawing).

'The Covenant with Abraham' (kitcat), 1853. Sold to Gambart.
Replica (varied, 35½ by 47½ inches). In possession of the family.
Sketch of this (small). In possession of the family.

'The Disobedient Prophet' (canvas, 102 by 80 inches), 1851-54.
R.A., 1854; Paris Ex. Universal, 1855. Sold to Agnew,
1860. Old Masters. (Mrs. John Elder.)
Replica (drawing), Agnew.

'The Invitation' (Emmaus, kitcat), 1853. Retouched, 1860.

Replica, in possession of the family (27½ by 35½ inches), 1860.

'The Gleaners' (kitcat), 1854.   For Gambart.   Sold in 1857 at Foster's for 240 guineas.

Replica (small), to Wethered.

'Road through the Wood'— Redstone Lane (canvas, 35½ by 44 inches), 1854.   For Gambart, 300 guineas.   Sold April, 1890, at Christie's, for £1,102 10s.

'The Donkey' (canvas, kitcat), 1854.   For Hooper and Wass.

'The Brook' (panel, 10 by 7 inches), 1854.   Old Masters. (B. W. Leader, Esq.)

'Heath Scene, Sunset'—Hampstead Heath (canvas, kitcat), 1854.   For Hooper and Wass.

'Wheat Harvest' (canvas, 35 by 56½ inches), 1854.   For Gambart.   Old Masters.   (T. D. Pritchard, Esq.)

'Sunset'—Harvest (kitcat), 1854.   For Gambart.

'Sheep Reposing' (26 by 37 inches). 1854.   For Hooper and Wass.   Old Masters.   (James Wilson, Esq.)

'Carrying'—Wheat (canvas, 27 by 39 inches; 26 by 38½ inches), 1854.   Painted for Mr. Wethered.

Replica, with variations, 1854-55 (36½ by 55 inches).   For Mr. Hooper.   Sold, April, 1890, at Christie's as 'The Harvest Field,' for £1,701.

Replica (small sketch).   Sold to Mr. L. Huth.

'Harvest Moon' (26 by 39 inches), 1855.   Painted for Mr. Wethered.   Sold by Rought to Mr. Louis Huth for 400 guineas.

Replica (original sketch).   Finished in 1858 for Mr. Wethered.

'Reaping' (canvas, 26 by 39 inches), 1855.   Painted for Mr. Wethered.   Afterwards bought by C. F. Huth, Esq.

Replica (small).   First sketch, finished in 1858 for Wethered.

Replica (drawing), without the figure on the right hand, 1863 (10 by 14 inches).

'Harvest Field' (canvas, 37 by 56 inches), 1855.   Painted for Mr. Hooper for 400 guineas.

'Timber Waggon' (small study of 'The Timber Waggon' of 1852, finished in 1855; 17 by 24 inches).   Sold to Wethered.   Old Masters.   (A. T. Hollingsworth, Esq.)

'Leith Hill from Redhill' (canvas, 18 by 24 inches), 1855.   Sold to Mr. Wethered.

Replica (24 by 30 inches).   Painted for Mr. Stokes.

'The Woodcutters' (canvas, 21 by 28 inches), 1855.   Old Masters.   (J. A. Gardiner, Esq.)

'Hampstead Heath' (panel, 18 by 24 inches), 1855.   Old Masters.   (George Gurney, Esq.)

'The Harvest Cradle' (36 by 56 inches), 1855.   For Hooper and Wass.

'The Dusty Road'—Sheep passing a cart in the road, (canvas, 28 by 36 inches), 1855.   Sold to Mr. L. Huth for £300. Sold, May, 1868, at Mr. Fallow's sale, for 1,000 guineas.

'The Stirrup Cup' (panel, 10 by 12 inches), 1855.   For Wethered

'Gleaners' (panel, 14½ by 18 inches), 1855 or 1856.

'Harvest Sunset' (canvas, 37 by 52 inches), 1856.   R.A.   Painted for L. Huth, Esq.   Sold by Mr. L. Huth to Mr. Vokins, and by the latter to Mr. Bigg.   Sold at Mr. Bigg's sale, 1868, for 1,050 guineas.   Old Masters.   (Sir T. Fowell Buxton, Bart.)

Replica (first sketch), finished 1859 (19½ by 28 inches).

'Storm in Harvest' (canvas, 37 by 53 inches), 1855-56.   Finished for Mr. Hooper.   Sold at Christie's (1860) for 630 guineas, and subsequently to Sir William G. Armstrong.   Old Masters.

Replica (with variations, 49 by 72½ inches), 1873.   Sold to Mr. White.   Old Masters.   Now in the possession of Samuel Montagu, Esq., M.P.

Replica.   Sketch finished for Wethered (canvas, 18 by 24 inches).

'Sand-Pits'—Heath, Sandhill (canvas, 36 by 48 inches), 1856. Old Masters.   (J. Broughton Dugdale, Esq.)

Replica.   Original sketch for the above, finished 1856 for Mr. Colls (panel, 18 by 24 inches).

'Return from Market' (canvas, 37 by 55 inches), 1856.   Retouched, 1857.   Painted for Hooper and Wass.

'Timber Waggon' (canvas, 36 by 48 inches), 1856.   For Hooper and Wass.

'Heath' (canvas, 18 by 24 inches), 1856.   Painted for Mr. Smart. Closs was tried at the Old Bailey in 1857 for fraud in selling a copy of this picture, with a forged signature, as the original.

'The White Cow' (canvas, 18 by 24 inches), 1856.   Mr. L. Huth.

'Sunny Gleams' (canvas, 36 by 52 inches), 1856-57.   Hooper and Wass.   Old Masters, 'The White Cloud.'   (John Graham, Esq.)

'Labour' (panel, 26 by 39 inches), 1857.   Engraved in the *Art Journal*.   Painted for Mr. Wethered for £300.   Sold at Mr. Fallow's sale (1868) for 1,000 guineas.

'Rest' (panel, 26 by 39 inches), 1857.   Engraved in *Art Journal*. Painted for Mr. Wethered for £300.   Sold at Mr. Fallow's sale for 1,000 guineas.   Old Masters.   (C. F. H. Bolckow, Esq.)

'A Clear-up Shower' (canvas, 19½ by 28 inches), 1857.

'The Rise of the River' (canvas, 37 by 52 inches), 1857.

'The Farm' (canvas, 17 by 26 inches), 1857.

Replica (36½ by 56 inches), 1858.

'Shepherds' (canvas, 37 by 55 inches), 1858.   Painted for L. Huth, Esq.   R.A.   International Exhibition, 1862.

'The Brow of the Hill' (canvas, 21 by 30 inches), 1858. Exhibited at the French Gallery, 1858.   Engraved in the *Art Journal* in 1859, and called 'Sunshine.'

'Evening in the Cornfield' (canvas, 26½ by 38 inches), 1858. Brit. Inst., 1859.   Old Masters.   (F. Pennington, Esq., M.P.)

'Clearing Up' (canvas, 19 by 31 inches), 1858.

'The Ford' (26 by 37 inches), 1858.

'Under the Beech' (canvas, 19½ by 28 inches), 1858.   Old Masters, 'The Old Oak.'   (H. J. Turner, Esq.)

'The Farm' (canvas, 35 by 56 inches), 1858-59.

'Evening' —Sheepfold (canvas, 40 by 50 inches), 1859.   R.A. International Exhibition, 1862.   Sold at Mr. Unwin's sale, Sheffield, 1866, for 1,300 guineas.   Old Masters.   (Mrs. Beaumont.)

'The Paddock' (panel, 8 by 11 inches), 1859.

'Spring Wood Scene' (kitcat), 1859.

'My Garden'—Lady Reading, and Children with a Dog (canvas, 24 by 30 inches), 1859.

'Barley'—Sunset (canvas, 28 by 39 inches), 1859.

'The Thunder Cloud' (canvas, 21 by 29 inches), 1859.

'Balaam' (canvas, 20 by 26 inches), 1859.

'Disobedient Prophet' (canvas, 20 by 26 inches), 1859.

'River Country' (canvas, 28 by 39½ inches), 1859.

'Cornfield Cradle' (panel, 27 by 39 inches), 1859.   Not a replica of a former picture.

'The Keg,' companion to the above (canvas, 27 by 39 inches), 1859.

'The Green Lane' (canvas, 28 by 36 inches), 1860. Old Masters,
    'The Tramps.' (David Jardine, Esq.)
'Harvest Dinner' (canvas, 39½ by 54½ inches), 1859. Inter-
    national Exhibition, 1862. Sold to Captain Fenton. Bought
    by Agnew, at Christie's in 1879, for £1,690.
'Sunset and River' (8 by 10 inches), 1860. (Huth.)
'Road by a River' (8 by 6 inches), 1860.
'Isaac and Rebecca' (panel, 10 by 15 inches), 1860.
'Shepherd' (kitcat, canvas, 26 by 36 inches), 1860. Old
    Masters. (Louis Huth, Esq.)
Replica drawing for Agnew.
'Barley' (panel, 18 by 24 inches), 1860. For Agnew.
'Setting Up'—Wheat (canvas, 37 by 55 inches), 1860. R.A.
    Paris Exhibition, 1867.
Replica (28 by 39 inches), 1869. For R. Brooks. Sold at
    Christie's, 1871, for 890 guineas.
'Meadow' (canvas, 13 by 17 inches), 1860. Sketch by his
    daughter Elizabeth, finished and painted all over by J. L.
'The Mill' (canvas, kitcat), 1860.
'Dairy Farm' (panel, 28 by 39 inches), 1860.
'Leith Hill, Surrey' (panel, 13½ by 18 inches), 1861. Old
    Masters. (J. A. Baumbach, Esq.)
'Woodcutter' (20 by 24 inches), 1861. (Agnew.)
'Barley Cart' (28 by 36 inches), 1861.
'Homeward Bound'—Sunset (27 by 36 inches), 1861. Sold at
    Christie's, 1873, for 740 guineas.
'The Brook' (panel, 20 by 24 inches), 1861.
'The Brow of the Hill,' Sunset (21 by 27 inches), 1861. R.A. in
    1866.
'Folding Sheep'—Sunset (canvas, 20 by 30 inches), 1861. Re-
    touched in 1871.
'Paddock'—Cow (panel, 8 by 10 inches), 1861. Old Masters,
    'The White Cow.' (David Price, Esq.)
'Sheep' (8 by 10 inches), 1861.
'Travellers' (canvas, 14 by 18 inches), 1862.
'Gleaner' (panel, 8 by 10 inches), 1862.
'Carrying Wheat' (canvas, 39 by 54 inches), 1861-62. R.A. in
    1862. Sold at Christie's in 1867 for 1,650 guineas. Damaged
    by fire in 1874, and repaired for E. F. White (lined and
    restored), August, 1874. Old Masters. (S. G. Holland, Esq.)

Replica (first study) finished 1862 (18 by 24 inches) for Agnew.
Bought by Mr. Somes, of Roehampton, 1866, for £500.

'Sheep' (canvas, 28 by 38 inches), 1862.

'Sheep' (canvas, 28 by 38 inches), 1862. A different subject
from the last.

Replica (sketch), 1862. Sold at Christie's, 1873, for 125 guineas,
to J. W. Adamson, Esq., for whom it was retouched in consequence of illusage.

'Reapers'—Noon (canvas, 39 by 54 inches), 1862. Sold to Mr.
Brooks under promise of exhibition, but not fulfilled; hence
a duplicate, improved, was painted in 1865. Old Masters,
'Noonday Rest.' (Jas. Hall Renton, Esq.)

Replica—'Mid-day Rest' (38 by 54 inches), 1865. R.A. Retouched, 1875. Replica of 'Noon.' Sold at Christie's, in
1883, for £1,585.

Replica (kitcat, 28 by 39 inches), 1871.

Replica—drawing (10 by 16½ inches), 1867. In possession of
the family.

'Sunset—Cornfield' (canvas, 40 by 50 inches), 1862. International Exhibition. R.A., 1863. Sold to Mr. Agnew, and
by him to Captain Fenton as companion to the 'Harvest
Dinner.'

Replica, varied in the figures, etc. (28 by 39 inches), 1873-74.

Replica (drawing, 10 by 14 inches).

'Heath and Common' (canvas, 28 by 39 inches), 1863.

Replica (small study, 10 by 12 inches).

'Sunset'—Feeding Sheep (panel, 28 by 39 inches), 1863. R.A.
Old Masters. (H. J. Turner, Esq.)

Replica study (9 by 12 inches).

Replica study (drawing in water-colour, 9 by 12 inches).

'Sheep in Lane' (canvas, 20 by 28 inches), 1863.

'The Milking Pail' (canvas, 20 by 30 inches), 1863. Sold at
Christie's, 1892, for 405 guineas.

Replica (canvas, 35½ by 55½ inches), 1866-68. Sold at Christie's,
1874, for 1,105 guineas. Old Masters, 'Milking Time.'
(J. W. Adamson, Esq.)

Replica (drawing).

'The Cloud' (panel, 18 by 24 inches), 1863. Sold to Agnew for
£275.

Replica (39 by 54 inches), 1863. Sold to Agnew for £700.

Replica (drawing in water-colour, 10 by 12 inches).

'Cornfield' (canvas, 28 by 39 inches), 1863.

Replica (drawing in water-colour).

'Windsor Forest' (drawing, 20 by 28 inches).

'Windsor Forest' (canvas, 28 by 39 inches), 1863 (?).

Replica (drawing, 10 by 14 inches).

'Pastoral'—Companion to Windsor Forest (28 by 39 inches), 1863. In 1866 in possession of Mr. Northcote, Forest Hill.

'Sheep' (drawing in water-colour, 10 by 14 inches). Sold to Mr. Colls for Mr. Birket Foster.

'Barley' (drawing in water-colour). Sold to Mr. Colls for Mr. Birket Foster.

'A Country Road' (panel, 28 by 39 inches), 1864. R.A. Sold to Agnew for £350.

Replica (drawing, 10 by 14 inches), 1863.

Drawing, as companion, 'Cows in a Road.'

'Haymakers' (28 by 39 inches), 1864. R.A. Old Masters, 'The Hayfield.' (C. P. Matthews, Esq.) Sold at the Matthews' sale, 1891.

Replica (drawing, 9½ by 15 inches).

'Harvest Dinner' (panel, 10½ by 15 inches), 1864. Old Masters. (The Linnell family.)

'Sunset' (28 by 39 inches), 1864.

Replica (first study) finished 1864 (panel, 14 by 18 inches). Sold to G. Simpson, Esq., Reigate, 1865, for £300.

'Traveller' (canvas, 28 by 39 inches), 1864.

'Windsor Forest' (canvas, 28 by 39 inches), 1864.

'Wales' (canvas, 39 by 54 inches), 1863. Sold to Agnew for £700. Retouched, 1870.

'Over some Wide Watered Shore' (canvas, 28 by 39 inches), 1864.

'Sunset—Gleaners' (canvas, 28 by 39 inches), 1864. Sold at Christie's, 1874, for 810 guineas.

'Rainbow' (canvas, 20 by 30 inches), 1864.

'Contemplation' 28 by 39 inches), 1865.

'Thunderstorm and Sheep' (20 by 30 inches), 1865.

'Moorlands—Sunset'—Horses and Cows Watering (28 by 39 inches), 1865.

'Barley-cart' (panel, 19 by 24 inches), 1865. Sold at Christie's, 1879, for 500 guineas.

'The Woodlands' (panel, 28 by 39 inches), 1865. R.A., 1866.
Sold at Christie's, 1874, for 800 guineas. Old Masters.
(George Gurney, Esq.)

'Gee-Up'—Sunset (28 by 39 inches), 1865.

'Southampton Water' (canvas, 28 by 39 inches), 1865-66.
Sold at Mr. A. Tooth's, 1865, for 600 guineas. Old Masters.
(H. J. Turner, Esq.)

'The Bridge Tree' (panel, 18 by 21 inches), 1866.

'Harvest Showers' (canvas, 28 by 39 inches), 1866. R.A., 1867.
Sold at Christie's, 1873, for 1,000 guineas.

'Sheep' (28 by 39 inches), 1866. R.A., 1867. Old Masters.
(Frederick A. Tidd, Esq.)

'Chalk' (canvas, 28 by 39 inches), 1866. R.A., 1867.

'Sunset' (canvas, 28 by 39 inches), 1866. Sent to R.A. 1867,
but not hung. Retouched and sold to Mr. E. F. White,
1872, for £700.

'Surrey Woodlands' (canvas, 38 by 54 inches), 1867-68. R.A.,
1868. Old Masters. (Mrs. W. Muir.)

'Woodland — Timber Waggon' (canvas, 28 by 39 inches),
1867-68.

'Tramps' (canvas, 28 by 39 inches), 1867-68. Sky retouched in
1869 for Agnew.

'Wood' (28 by 39 inches), 1867-68.

'Thirsty Shepherd' (28 by 39 inches), 1867-68.

'Forest' (28 by 39 inches), 1867-68.

'Emigrants' (35 by 56 inches), 1867 68. From a study from
nature made in 1817 at Keswick.

'Good Samaritan' (paper on panel, 13 by 16 inches),
1867.

'Sheep' (panel, 7½ by 10 inches), 1868.

'Hawthorn' (panel, 11¾ by 16¼ inches), 1868.

'The Woodcutters' (panel, 18 by 24 inches), 1868. Old Masters.
(H. M. Steinthall, Esq.)

'Clearing Off' (canvas, 13½ by 23½ inches), 1868.

'The Thunder Cloud' (28 by 39 inches), 1868. Retouched in
1871.

'Travellers' (30 by 39 inches), 1868-72. Sold to Thos. Taylor,
Esq., for £800.

Replica (sketch, 28 by 39 inches), 'The Cloud.' Finished in
1874 for Mr. White.

'Moving the Punt' (canvas, 28 by 39 inches), 1868. Sold in 1872 to Mr. Thomas Taylor. Sold at Christie's, 1890, as 'The Fishermen,' for 700 guineas.

'Tree and Faggots' (7½ by 10 inches), 1868.

'Mountain Track' (canvas, 28 by 39 inches), 1868. Sold at Christie's, 1871, for 800 guineas.

'Woodcutters' (canvas, 28 by 39 inches), 1869. Christie's, 1871, 750 guineas.

'Mountain Shepherds' (canvas, 28 by 39 inches), 1870. Christie's, 1871, 850 guineas. There are forged copies of this picture.

'The Lost Sheep' (canvas, 39 by 54 inches), 1869. R.A.

'Travellers' (canvas, 28 by 39 inches), 1869. Agnew, £700.

'Redstone Wood' (18 by 24 inches), 1869.

'Dust' (kitcat, 28 by 39 inches), 1869. Sold to White for £700. Old Masters, 'Dusty Road.' (Jas. R. Hoare, Esq.)

'The Baptism of Christ' (canvas, 28 by 36 inches), 1867-69. Old Masters. (Charles L. Collard, Esq.) Sold at Christie's 1892.

'Sunset' (canvas, 28 by 39 inches), 1869-70. Sold at Christie's, in 1890 for 870 guineas.

Replica (15 by 20 inches), 1869.

'Redstone Wood' (18 by 24 inches), 1870. A companion to the 'Redstone Wood,' 1869. Sold to Brooks for £300. Sold at Gillott's sale, 1872, for £600.

'Asses' Bridge' (canvas, 28 by 39 inches), 1870. Sold to White for £700.

'Sleeping for Sorrow'—Gethsemane (canvas, 38 by 54 inches), 1870. R.A.

Replica (sketch for picture, first).

'Shelter'—Storm Cloud (28 by 39 inches), 1871. R.A. Sold to Mr. Worrall for £800.

'Woodcutters' (canvas, 28 by 39 inches), 1871.

'David and the Lion' (28 by 39 inches), 1871.

'Timber Waggon' (28 by 39 inches), 1871.

Replica (considerable variation, canvas, 28 by 39 inches), 1872. Old Masters. (Charles Gassiot, Esq.)

'The Pull' (28 by 39 inches), 1871.

'Emigrants' (canvas, 28 by 39 inches), 1872.

'The Ford—Sunset' (canvas, 45½ by 59½ inches), 1871-72. R.A. Sold to Mr. White for 1,400 guineas.

Replica (varied, 28 by 39 inches), 1872.   Sold to Mr. White for £700.

Replica (varied, 15 by 18 inches), 1875.   Sold at the Neck Sale at Christie's.

'Wood Scene'—Three studies (of different subjects) on the spot in 1852; finished into pictures 1872 (18 by 24 inches), for Mr. White.

'Up Rays'—Gleaners (28 by 39 inches), 1872.   Mr. White, £700.

'Down Rays'—Cows (28 by 39 inches), 1872.   Mr. White, £700.

Replica, with sheep and variations (28 by 39 inches), 1872.

'The Piper' (28 by 39 inches), 1872.   Mr. White, £700.

Replica (smaller), variations; shepherd in smock-frock.

'Cornfield' (16 by 25 inches), begun 1850; finished 1873. Painted from a cornfield at Redstone Wood.

'Lambeth in 1806' (15 by 22 inches), 1873.   In possession of the family.

'Cows' (28 by 39 inches), 1873.

'A Coming Storm' (canvas, 51 by 65 inches), 1873.   R.A.   Mr. White for £1,400.

Replica, 'Storm,' with variation (28 by 39 inches), 1873.   Mr. White, £750.

'The Valley' (28 by 39 inches), 1873.

'A Bye-Road' (28 by 39 inches), 1873.

'The Happy Valley' (28 by 39 inches), 1873.   For Mr. White, 750 guineas.   Retouched in 1874.   Sold at Christie's, in 1890, for £940.

'Good-bye' (28 by 39 inches), 1873.   Mr. White, £750.

'The Woodcutters' (49 by 73 inches), 1873.   R.A., 1874.   Sold to Mr. Grove, by Mr. White, for £3,000.   Old Masters. (Mrs. Grove.)

'The Haystack' (28 by 39 inches), 1873.   Sold to Mr. Price for £1,000; at Christie's, 1892, for £630.

'Sand-Pits' (28 by 39 inches), 1874.

'Cattle Pond' (28 by 39 inches), 1874.

'Morning—Sunrise' (28 by 39 inches), 1874.   Sold to Mr. White, as 'Misty Morning,' for £750.   Sold at Christie's, in 1890, for 720 guineas.

'Cricket' (28 by 39 inches), 1874.   Mr. White, £750.

'Crossing the Ford—Sunset' (15 by 18 inches), 1875. Sold at the Neck sale.

'A Sultry Day' (canvas, 28 by 39 inches), 1874-75. Mr. White. Sold at Christie's, in 1890, for 700 guineas. Old Masters. (Chas. Neck, Esq.)

'Tramps,' or 'Pointing the Way' (canvas, 31 by 43 inches), 1874. Sold at Christie's, in 1890, for 1,140 guineas. Old Masters. (Chas. Neck, Esq.)

'Barley,' or 'The Barley Harvest' (31 by 43 inches), 1874. Sold at Christie's, in 1890, for 1,150 guineas.

'Asses' Bridge' (31 by 43 inches), 1874-75. Sold at Christie's, in 1890, for 900 guineas. A different subject from the 'Asses' Bridge,' 1870.

'Hay and Haste' (28 by 39 inches), 1874-75. In possession of the family.

Replica (31 by 43 inches), 1874-75. Mr. White.

'Last Load' (50 by 66 inches), 1874-75.

'Woods and Forests' (canvas, 41 by 57 inches), 1875. R.A. Sold at Christie's, 1890, for 1,900 guineas.

'Sunset, with Rooks' (panel, 15 by 17 inches), 1875.

'Cornfield—Sunset' (panel, 15 by 18 inches), 1875. In possession of the family.

'Windsor Forest' (panel, 11 by 19 inches), 1875.

'Wood' (31 by 43 inches), 1876. Mr. White.

'The Creek' (31 by 43 inches), 1876. Mr. White.

'Woodcutter' (panel, 17½ by 20½ inches), 1876. R.A., 1881. The last picture the artist exhibited. In the possession of the family.

'Rooks' (30 by 40 inches), 1877. In possession of the family.

'Crossing the Bridge' (canvas, 31 by 43 inches), 1877. Mr. White, £1,000. Sold at Christie's, in 1890, for 1,120 guineas. Old Masters. (Chas. Neck, Esq.)

'Autumn'—Cows in Water (canvas, 28 by 39 inches), 1877. R.A. In the possession of the family.

'Red Sunset' (canvas, 31 by 43 inches), 1878. Unfinished. In the possession of the family.

'The Heath' (canvas, 31 by 43 inches), 1878. R.A.

'Sweet fa's the Eve'—Sunset on Redhill Common (canvas, 31 by 43 inches), 1878. R.A., 1879. In the possession of the family.

'Fat Pasture' (28 by 39 inches), 1878-79. R.A., 1879. This was the last picture of which J. L. made a sketch in his *Liber Veritatis*.* In possession of the family.

'The Hollow Tree,' 1875-76. R.A., 1876. Sold by the family to Mr. McLean for £1,600.

---

* This *Liber Veritatis* was a pen-illustrated list of the major part of the pictures the artist executed. It is still extant, and has been drawn upon very largely for the identification of works in this catalogue. Doubtless there are other pictures in existence of smaller size, and of less importance, of which the artist did not keep a record. Certain of these (before unrecorded) works were collected for the Old Masters in 1883, and these have been added to the list from the catalogue of the exhibition; those amongst them which were undated being placed by themselves at the end.

UNDATED WORKS.—OIL PAINTINGS.

'Near Windsor Forest' (panel, 18¾ by 23½ inches). Signed, 'J. Linnell fecit.' Old Masters. (Jas. Reiss, Esq.)

'On Hampstead Heath' (canvas, 20½ by 25½ inches). Signed, 'J. Linnell.' Sold at the Santurce sale, 1891. Old Masters. (Marquis de Santurce.)

'View near Hampstead' (panel, 8 by 11 inches). Signed, J. Linnell f. Old Masters. (George Gurney, Esq.)

'Landscape, with a Haystack' (panel, 18 by 23 inches). Old Masters. (Jane, Countess of Caledon.)

'The Farmyard' (panel, 12 by 15 inches). Signed, 'J. Linnell.' Old Masters. (David Price, Esq.)

'Gathering in the Corn' (panel, 8 by 12 inches). Old Masters. (Louis Huth, Esq.)

'Shepherds' (panel, 6¼ by 8¾ inches). Old Masters. (Jas. Orrock, Esq.)

'Landscape' (panel, 7¼ by 11 inches). Old Masters. (Thos. Webster, Esq., R.A.)

'Sheep at Rest—Minding the Flock' (panel, 6 by 9 inches). Sold at the Santurce sale, 1891. Old Masters. (Marquis de Santurce.)

THE END.

BILLING AND SONS, PRINTERS, GUILDFORD.
J. D. & Co.

www.ingramcontent.com/pod-product-compliance
Lightning Source LLC
Chambersburg PA
CBHW020855020726
47497CB00005B/1413